THE CHEAT KILLERS

GORDON WARDEN

PROLOGUE

They'd had such a wonderful time, so he couldn't understand why he was suddenly being looked at in such a sorrowful, almost apologetic manner. By the time he realised, it was already too late.

Paul Hamilton slid sideways from his seat and fell onto the tiled floor, his body joining forces with the remnants of the smashed plate. He lay amongst the fragments like a surreal jigsaw.

The almost empty champagne glass still stood on the table where he had been sitting, almost proudly, as if defying the surrounding mayhem.

His blurring vision directed itself towards the unfamiliar figure that stood over him and he strained to speak, his mouth moving, but no words were forthcoming.

1

Harry Black stared ahead, willing the passengers to hurry and sit down. He scowled at a couple who were standing in the centre aisle of the plane arguing, blocking others from taking their seats.

He peered out through the cabin window, rubbing ineffectually at the glass with his sleeve. The flickering lights of the various service vehicles were pixilated against the driving rain that swept across JFK Airport. Terminal staff rushed around, pulling their yellow hoods tightly.

Finally, the last of the passengers were on, the cabin doors shut, and it was nearly time for the stewards to perform their usual mime of what action to take should the plane crash.

Harry contemplated the empty seat next to him, with an anticipation of leaning across and getting some sleep.

A few rows ahead, the argumentative couple, who were finally sitting in their places, continued their exchange in not-so-restrained, hissy tones while fellow passengers watched with interest. A free cabaret was always welcome on a boring flight.

He closed his eyes, his thoughts drifting back to recent events.

It had worked out well; Vincent Dempsey was now behind bars, and Harry had received plenty of well-deserved praise.

When he had first arrived in New York, the reception had been cool. Whilst there had been welcoming handshakes on his first day working with the NYPD, he could detect an underlying air, which he could understand. Who the hell likes someone coming into their territory from another country and interfering in an investigation?

But he had done just that. He knew that he had earned the respect of his American colleagues by catching Dempsey. The thought made him smile.

A waft of perfume interrupted his thoughts.

'Excuse me, do you mind if I take this seat?'

'No, not at all,' he said, attempting to conceal his sudden irritation.

Harry looked up to see the source of the enquiry. An attractive lady smiled down at him. She seemed to be in her late thirties and had long, blonde-streaked brown hair. She was wearing a crop-top and jeans.

'Are you sure you don't mind?' she asked, as she slid next to him.

'No, not at all,' Harry said, now being almost over-effusive, 'it's great to have a flight companion.'

Her face relaxed into a smile. 'Jane Cooper,' she said in a soft British accent, offering her hand. 'I found myself wedged in between two men who were going on about some Boston football team, who apparently have red socks, so I wanted to find a more peaceful place to sit.'

'No problem,' he said. 'Pleased to meet you. I'm Harry Black.'

Her grip was cool and firm, and as she shook Harry's

hand, an oversized bracelet nearly slid off the end of her wrist and onto his own.

'Sorry,' she laughed, pushing the jewellery back up her arm. 'I bought this at the airport and now wish I hadn't!'

'No problem. Incidentally, that Boston football team is actually known as "Boston Red Sox."'

'Really? You'd think they'd find a better name.'

They laughed and, with the ice broken, settled back in their seats ready for take-off.

After half-an-hour of dozing, Harry woke up feeling a sharp nudge on his elbow. Some turbulence had caused her shoulder bag to overturn, and it was now resting against Harry's arm.

'Sorry,' she said, leaning over to rescue the spilt contents. 'And I was just thinking how peaceful you looked.'

'Doesn't anyone when they are asleep?' Harry asked with a grin, enjoying a further waft of perfume.

'No,' she said. 'Some people twitch in their sleep, some frown, some fidget...'

'Have you had a lot of experience watching people sleep then?' Harry asked, immediately wishing he hadn't.

She grinned at his discomfort. 'I'm not exactly new to life, you know!'

They laughed and Harry put up a hand to stop a passing steward.

'Could I have a beer, please? And can I offer you anything?' he asked his companion.

'That would be lovely. I'll just have a coffee, thanks.'

'Actually, could you change my order to a coffee, please?' Harry said. 'I think I've over-done it on the booze recently.'

They fell into a comfortable silence as they sipped their drinks.

'So, what do you do?' he asked, eventually. 'For a living, I mean.'

'Me? I work for a travel company. My job is to ensure that our customers have the best possible experience, so I frequently fly to the USA and back again. It's a dream job, the only thing is...' She paused and ran a hand through her hair. 'It would sometimes be nice to settle in just one place for a while and make some proper friends.'

'I can understand that.' Harry nodded. 'Although my job doesn't take me all over the place like yours, the hours are antisocial, and it's a relationship-killer.'

'What do you do?' she asked.

'Ah, when I tell people what my job is, they normally move to other seats. Even if there are passengers with red socks,' he said with a grin.

'Go on then.'

'I'm a police officer.'

'Really? You don't look like one,' she said, looking surprised.

'What does a police officer look like? Did you expect me to have a magnifying glass and a deerstalker hat?'

'No,' she said, 'but your hair seems too long for a policeman, and you seem sort of refined.'

'Refined? Thank you, you're very kind. I'll take that,' Harry replied, with a mimed doff of a hat. 'It's good to know that I don't look like a policeman, otherwise I might be in trouble if I went undercover. I'm a detective.'

Ordinarily, Harry was reluctant to talk about his work to the outside world, but this woman seemed to be having a magnetic influence on him.

'Do detectives go undercover in real life?' she asked.

'Oh yes, we may have a modern police force, but we still use many of the older methods.'

'So, are you married? Have you any children? Or have you managed to remain free and single?'

'I am totally free. I'm divorced and have no children, no ties, not even a dog.'

'Oh dear,' she said, with a mock sad-face. 'Poor you!'

'Yes, poor me. Listen, how do you fancy upgrading your coffee to something stronger?'

'That's a good idea, but it's my shout – no arguments.'

'I won't argue.'

When their drinks arrived, Harry raised his glass. 'Here's to meeting strangers on planes.'

'Strangers on planes.'

They clinked glasses, just as the captain's voice resonated through the cabin, advising passengers that they would arrive at Heathrow in thirty minutes.

Damn, thought Harry, disappointed. He wanted to chat to Jane more – a lot more. He wanted to see her again but didn't want to look too keen. Taking the bull by the horns, Harry took a gulp of his drink to give himself some Dutch courage. As he did so, the plane hit an air pocket causing beer to dribble down his chin.

She laughed at him, which had the effect of easing his schoolboy nervousness.

'I hoped that we could get to know each other better,' he said. 'So would you like to meet up sometime soon? I'm not one for rushing things. How about at the airport terminal after we've landed?'

She looked serious for a minute and then grinned. 'Yes, okay.' She pointed back towards the rear of the plane. 'I have to retrieve my luggage from where I was sitting before, so we'll be leaving from different exits when we get off the plane. I'll meet you, let's say, at the Costa Coffee just after customs?'

Harry grinned back. 'Sounds perfect.'

As the exit doors opened, he pushed past the other passengers to be among the first to leave. As he walked down the steps onto the tarmac, he noticed that the rear exit doors of the plane were only just being opened, so he knew he was in front of her.

Out on the main concourse, Harry wandered into the Costa, ordered a coffee, and sat down. He carefully scanned the new arrivals who were pouring out of the customs area, keeping watch for Jane's streaky blonde hair.

As a large group of people suddenly funnelled through the gate, Harry stood up to make sure he had an unobstructed view.

Some arrivals were being met by taxi drivers and chauffeurs, who were holding placards. Walking in Harry's direction, was a formal-looking man with sunglasses pushed onto the top of his head. He was holding up a large, white card on which was daubed, in large, red letters, "Jane Cooper."

Harry immediately felt an anticipatory tightening in his gut, followed by confusion. Why had Jane agreed to a coffee date at an airport terminal if she was being collected?

The man with the placard nodded at him pleasantly. 'All right, mate?'

'Yes, thanks,' Harry replied. 'Are you waiting for family or a wife?'

The man pointed to his placard. 'Miss Cooper is my boss, and I wish she'd bloody well hurry. I've been here for ages.'

'Are you her chauffeur?' Harry asked.

'Yes, for my sins, of which there are many.'

Harry laughed, and the pair engaged in casual conversation while they waited.

'Ah, here she is!' the chauffeur said, looking up suddenly.

Harry spun round expectantly, only to see an elderly lady approaching, wearing a light blue two-piece. She walked up to the chauffeur and greeted him warmly. He took her case and vanity bag, nodded to Harry, and the pair walked off towards the exit.

Harry stared at them, trying to work out the probabilities of there being two people called Jane Cooper on the same flight.

For nearly an hour, Harry waited, almost mechanically watching the last of the passengers drift through the arrivals gate. When he saw the group of flight attendants and the pilots from his flight exit the gates with their cabin bags, he decided to call it a day.

2

Harry drove straight to work from the airport. Although he was still disappointed at Jane Cooper's no-show, he was already thinking ahead to what might await him at Farrow Road. He had missed the comfortable familiarity of his UK colleagues, and was even looking forward to the police canteen with its daily offerings of dodgy pies and stale doughnuts, and the best apple crumble and custard he had ever tasted.

He parked at the rear of the police station, and hurried through the rain into the familiar doors of Farrow Road, leaving drips on the tiled floor in his wake.

'Lovely weather we're having, sir. Nice to see you back,' called the desk sergeant from behind his screen.

'Thank you, Frank,' Harry replied.

Frank was the station gossip. Even if there was no scandal, Harry was convinced Frank would either find or invent something.

He slotted his identity card into the reader, and with a buzz, the door to the inner sanctum unlocked and he was now officially back.

As Harry walked up the stairs towards his office, a familiar voice exclaimed, 'Bugger me, the hero's returned!'

Detective Inspector Will Kidman was as close to Harry as anyone could be. They had shared quite a few interesting – and dodgy – times together. Will was middle-aged and stocky. He had a shaved head and a goatee beard, which he stroked frequently, particularly when he was thinking.

After a quick man-hug, Harry followed Will along the corridor to the offices. The air smelled musty, and he noticed that the office doors badly needed painting. *It's strange, the things you observe after being away for such a length of time*, he thought.

'So, how's it going? Anything new and exciting been happening while I've been away?' he asked.

'Nothing much,' Will replied, stroking his beard. 'However, you might have heard, whilst you were on the other side of the pond, that our old boss has gone? Well, we now have a newly appointed Führer.'

'A newly appointed what? I knew that John Pickard was thinking about going for early retirement.'

'He ended up taking it. You missed a great event, the place was awash with wine and champagne and John made this lengthy speech during which he said that he would spend a lot more time with his wife and on the golf course, but not necessarily in that order.'

Harry laughed. 'I missed out by the sound of it. Tell me about the new boss. What's his name and what's he like?'

'Sexist or what? It's a *she* actually... Liz Mainwaring. Do you know her?'

'I remember Liz from when she first started in the force. She's done well in a short time.'

'Yes, but be careful with Little Miss Fast-Track. Watch what you say and how you say it. She's the sort that latches onto anything. Her world is all about the paperwork, efficiency, all that stuff. It's enough to drive you bloody bonkers.'

'You called her The Führer – surely she's not that bad?'

'Well maybe, maybe not. You'll be able to judge for yourself. She wants to see you as soon as you arrive.'

'Does she know I'm here?'

'I don't know for certain, but I'd bet that our friendly desk sergeant downstairs picked up the phone the minute he saw you.'

Harry nodded. 'Frank can be a little weasel sometimes.'

'Absolutely. Good luck with Mainwaring. I'll say one for you.' Will made the sign of the cross on his chest.

Before going to see his new boss, Harry went to his own office to dump his case and see how full his in-tray was. On the way, he received a warm welcome back from passing colleagues.

In his office, he sat and stretched out his legs, enjoying the familiar feel of his comfy, worn office chair, and looked out of the window. The North London traffic was almost stationary, thanks to malfunctioning traffic lights that were causing mayhem. A hairy youth with a squeegee and a bucket was offering his windscreen-cleaning services to the waiting drivers, most of whom waved him away impatiently.

Harry was thankful that he didn't have to live here anymore. For the past few years, he'd lived a few miles north of the Farrow Road station.

He enjoyed a few more moments of quiet reflection before making his way to the offices on the next floor. Harry knocked on the door marked "Detective Chief Inspector."

There was still the outline of a previous sign on the door. A while ago, it would probably have had the occupant's actual name, but these days, promotions seemed to happen much more quickly, so the rank on the door was the only clue of the inhabitant of the office.

The woman behind the desk stared up at Harry. She appeared younger than him – in her late thirties, Harry thought. She had reddish brown hair that swept away from her face, leaving a fringe almost in line with her eyebrows, which made her look hard-faced and bad-tempered.

'Good morning, Inspector,' she said, putting down her pen, removing her glasses, and folding her arms, seemingly in one fluid motion.

'Good morning, ma'am. Congratulations on your recent promotion.'

'Sit down, Inspector.'

A manila folder was placed to her right. Harry could see his name on the cover. You become an expert at reading upside down in this job. Pens, a calculator, and various documents were all positioned on her desk neatly. Very neatly.

Harry Black sighed inwardly as he took a seat. He had a feeling that he wasn't going to enjoy this. Word had it that Liz Mainwaring had worked her way up the ranks with a quiet, ruthless efficiency, always ensuring she was in the right place at the right time.

She had a reputation for being over politically correct. There wasn't even a trace of a speck of dirt as far as her own performance record was concerned. She ensured that everything was signed for and authorised before she took any action, keeping herself well protected from criticism or comebacks.

Part of Harry was envious of people who could work in that way. He could never be like that, even if he tried. It just wasn't in his DNA. Many a time, he had gone out on a limb and had loosely strayed from the official straight and narrow, but had many times felt the biting consequences of his actions.

On this occasion, he was expecting praise for a job that had gone well. In fact, very well. But, as Mainwaring's comments continued, it became apparent that his expectations were misjudged.

'And to top it all,' she went on, 'you didn't even come straight back to the UK as soon as the job was complete. I suppose you hung around enjoying the praise and the socialising with your American colleagues before deciding to grace us with your presence.'

To be fair, there was a grain of truth in this.

'There were cheaper flights available by waiting for a few more days...' Harry started to explain, but she cut him short.

'Yes, yes, I'm sure,' she said curtly, 'but I'd rather you had got back here sooner. Never mind the American dream, it's time to wake up and get back to work.'

She stood up and poured some water from a jug into a glass. She didn't offer Harry any.

'I demand professionalism, loyalty, and hard work from all officers under my command. I do not expect my officers to waste taxpayers' money.'

Harry tried to keep his voice level. 'I disagree. Surely I've helped the economy by putting away someone who was a prolific drug trafficker. Someone who, had he not been nicked, would have enticed kids into a life of crime, who would have got more and more people hooked on drugs, resulting in thousands more of taxpayers' money being spent on rehabilitation, not to mention the effects of those crimes.'

Mainwaring looked at him as if seeing him for the first time. She sat back in her chair, picked up her glasses, and inspected the lenses.

'Yes, I'm sure that you've helped the economy, particularly the American economy, but we need help here right now. Knife crime, gun crime, muggings, and internet fraud are rife here in the UK and deserve more attention than we can give them with our monetary constraints.'

Harry suspected that this was a rehearsed spiel that she'd given to the top brass or media recently.

She continued, 'I will not be recommending that my officers go on any more trips to help out other forces when we need focussed attention on our own patch.'

'All right, ma'am, I'm getting the picture. Did you call me in here just to give me a dressing down, or was there something important?'

She ignored his sarcasm. 'I assume that you've heard about our Northolt Strangler?'

'No, I've only just got back.'

'Really? Weren't any newspapers available on your flight?' She pulled a folder towards her and opened the cover. 'A man was found dead three days ago outside a property near Northolt. Apart from being strangled, early indications suggest that he was also given some sort of knock-out drug.'

'That's unusual,' Harry said. 'Drugged and then strangled.'

'Yes, precisely. That's why I want you on this case, showing off those wonderful talents that you displayed so successfully in New York.'

Harry studied her face. There wasn't the slightest trace of a smile to accompany the apparent sarcasm. 'Do we have anything at all that will give us a start?'

'I've asked Inspector Kidman to brief you.'

'Any motives, suspects... anything?'

But Detective Chief Inspector Mainwaring's glasses were back on, and she seemed to have moved onto her next task. 'Inspector Kidman will brief you. That'll be all, thank you,' she said in a distant voice.

Harry shut the door to her office, feeling like a schoolboy leaving the head teacher's study.

3

'So, what did you think of her?'

Harry looked across the desk at Will and made a face. 'To be honest, I'm buggered if I know. I think it's more of a case of what did she think of me. It felt like she hated me already. It certainly didn't go very well. I reckon she will either be brilliantly efficient or frighteningly bad. One thing's for sure, she terrified me.'

'I'm sure she'll eventually succumb to your natural charm, Harry, like all the girls. She'll get taken in by that mass of wavy hair and those come-to-bed eyes.'

'I'm getting worried. Are you starting to fancy me or something?'

Will laughed. 'No, seriously, she'll calm down when she's been in the job a bit longer – they always do. Fancy a catch-up beer later this evening?'

Harry shook his head. 'It's a nice thought, but no, at least not tonight. I haven't even been home yet and my luggage is still in the boot of the car. You'd better give me anything you've got on this Northolt murder that Mainwaring was on about.'

'Okay, the murder victim was a Mr Paul Hamilton, who was in his early fifties. It's looking like he was drugged with a substance yet-to-be-confirmed and then strangled to death with a rope.'

'Strange,' Harry said. 'Why drug someone before strangling them? Have we any motive for the murder?'

'It would be pointless to drug them *after* they were strangled, wouldn't it?' Will said with a smile. 'But no. There don't appear to be any indications of why he was killed. He was discovered in the back garden of an empty house lying on the patio.'

'Who found him?'

'Some estate agent.' Will pushed a folder across the desk. 'It's all there for you.'

'What about witnesses?'

'None that we've found yet.'

'Were there any unusual circumstances?'

'Ah,' Will said, 'indeed there were!' He paused for dramatic effect. 'The murderer left a clue for us to find. We very nearly missed it.'

'Go on.'

'The loose end of the rope that was used to strangle Mr Hamilton was formed into a word.'

'A word? How?'

'Apparently the rope was flexible enough to form letters.'

'That's a new one on me,' Harry said. 'What word?'

'Herg.'

'Herg? What the hell's that?'

Will held up his hands. 'Absolutely no idea, but the team are on it. We've tried to research it. There's nothing on Google or anywhere.'

'What about forensics, do we have anything? Where the rope came from? Fingerprints?'

'Nothing so far, but it's still early days.'

'Any suspects, persons of interest, leads?'

'No. All we've got is this bloody Herg thing.'

Harry looked at Will in mild disbelief. 'Okay, so apart from a rope-wielding maniac, and a new boss who seems to hate me already, is there anything else?'

'Not really,' Will said. 'It looks like you had most of the fun across the pond. Oh yes, I almost forgot. We're looking for a missing man...'

'To go with my missing lady,' muttered Harry, thinking about earlier.

'Sorry?'

Harry grinned. 'I'll tell you all about it later, maybe. Go on.'

Will cleared his throat. 'So, this woman was upstairs doing the ironing and her husband was sitting in the lounge in his pyjamas watching telly. When she eventually came downstairs, he'd disappeared. The TV was still on and there was a half-empty mug of cold tea on the side.'

'Let me get this straight. This man disappeared from his house wearing his pyjamas?'

'Correct.' Will's laughter lines deepened with amusement as he stroked his wispy goatee. 'We checked with the landlord of his local pub, and with the neighbours, but no one saw him that evening. There are no CCTV cameras for the immediate area. His coat and a cloth cap were missing, but his outdoor shoes were still there. So I guess we're searching for a man wearing pyjamas, slippers, and a hat and coat.'

'Well, that should make him easy to find. Was there anything else unusual? Did he have any mental health issues that could have prompted him to wander off?'

'Not that we're aware of, but we haven't spoken to Patricia Evans yet, the missing man's wife. The husband's name is George.'

'Okay, so why the hell are *we* dealing with this? This is just routine stuff that can be dealt with by any junior officer.'

Will looked embarrassed. 'Normally, yes, but there is a special interest in this case.'

'Go on.'

'George Evans's wife, Patricia, is related to our new boss, DCI Mainwaring. She's a very close aunt, apparently, so we should be seen to be making it a priority.'

Harry wasn't convinced. 'I suppose.'

Harry spent the rest of the morning going over paperwork and reports about the strangling. He was exhausted after his flight, but forced himself to concentrate.

Paul Hamilton's body had been discovered at an empty house in Northolt by the local estate agent, Don Fox, who had been measuring the property to put it on the agency books.

He had apparently let himself in through the front door and had immediately noticed a strong smell of bleach.

The police report stated that Fox didn't want potential buyers to be put off by the smell, so he had opened the back door to let in fresh air and dispel the odour.

While outside, Fox had loosened his tie, lit a cigarette, and looked around the garden. He had then seen what looked like a man lying asleep on the patio wearing a scarf. After taking a closer look, he discovered that the scarf was actually a rope, and had called the police.

The victim was a married man with two daughters, both at university. Thanks to the wallet inside his jacket pocket, it had been easy to track down his details.

Harry put down the report and sat back in his chair. It had been a deliberate killing and pre-planned. The murderer was announcing something – or trying to put people off the scent – with his twisted rope message. *Twisted rope message.* That was funny, somehow. Herg. Who or what the hell was Herg?

After negotiating the rush-hour traffic, Harry arrived at his flat. He had to push the front door hard to sweep aside a few weeks of letters and junk mail.

A growl in his tummy reminded him he had nothing edible in the fridge. He picked up a pizza menu from the pile on the floor and wandered into the lounge, leaving his bags in the hallway, promising mentally that he wouldn't leave the unpacking for the next day.

The flat felt unfriendly, cold, and damp. He thumbed the wall thermostat and there was a satisfying roar as the heating came on.

Two hours later, with an empty Domino's box on the coffee table together with three squished cans, Harry stared at his lounge wall blankly. He had barely slept in recent days and was exhausted and jet-lagged.

He closed his eyes. In his mind's eye, he could see a skeleton dressed in a suit, a rope around its neck. The end of the rope was dancing and bobbing and twisting around forming unfamiliar shapes until finally, with a flourish, the word "Jane" appeared, with an image of her face.

Jane Cooper, where the hell did you go?

Harry stumbled off to bed, unable to think anymore. His sleep was interrupted by weird, unsettling dreams until eventually the jangle of alarms woke him. His mobile phone was ringing at exactly the same time as the digital alarm clock.

For a few seconds, he stared at the bedside cabinet, his eyes bleary and his head thumping, not knowing what to do first. He pressed the stop button on the alarm, then picked up the phone.

Will's tone sounded almost formal. 'Good morning, Harry. I didn't wake you, did I?'

'No, not at all,' Harry fibbed, switching on his brain and swinging his legs onto the floor as if to give the lie credibility.

'Good. The Führer said I should give you a hand for a

couple of days. Are you up for a visit to the murder victim's wife, Laura Hamilton?'

'Definitely,' Harry said, rubbing his head with his free hand. He still felt groggy, but he was keen to get going.

'I'll pick you up in half an hour. That should give you time to wake up properly.'

After standing under a hot shower for ten minutes and shaving away his three-day stubble, Harry was feeling better. He examined his face in the mirror and smoothed back his dark, wavy hair. Harry Black thought he looked okay, all things considered.

Will arrived with two polystyrene cups of coffee and a bag of pastries.

'You look bloody dreadful,' he said.

'Thanks, mate, you're a charmer.'

Will grinned. 'No worries. Eat up, then let's get going.'

Harry climbed into the passenger seat of Will's Range Rover. He had to be careful where he put his feet. The interior was like an enormous toy box with plastic figures and playthings everywhere. The footwell was about an inch deep in sweet and chocolate wrappers.

'How are the family, Will?'

'Well, as you can see by the mess, they haven't reached the age of responsibility yet.' He grinned.

Will had had his family late in life. For many years, he had enjoyed the single lifestyle, staying out late, clubbing, and enjoying the company of lots of women. Although he and Harry were close, Harry had never been into the nightclub scene, preferring to amble off to the nearest quiet pub.

Everything had changed on Will's fiftieth birthday, when his sister had introduced him to her friend Angela from work.

It hadn't gone very well.

Angela didn't like what she called "players." Men who would smile into your eyes, say all the right things, go to bed with you, then disappear, leaving you feeling grubby and used. It wasn't the fact that she was a prude, she just hated dishonesty.

'If you just want sex, tell me, then at least we both know where we are,' was her attitude. When she had met Will, he had looked deeply into her eyes and had said all the right things. She responded coldly and made it apparent to Will that she wasn't keen on him.

The trouble was, Will *had* meant everything he'd said to her. He thought Angela was the most beautiful and interesting woman he'd ever met and had pulled everything out of his armoury to entice her into his life. But she was having none of it.

Reluctantly, he had given up the chase, deciding that it wasn't meant to be. Or maybe it was the fact that she was a few years younger than him.

Angela was secretly disappointed and cursed herself for not giving him more of a chance.

A year later, the pair met again when Will's sister got married. They found themselves sitting next to each other at the reception, which wasn't entirely by coincidence; his sister had put together the seating plan.

This time, they hit it off perfectly, and a few months later, they married. They were more than ready for children, so their two boys came along quickly to complete their family.

'Do you think you'll have any more?' asked Harry, picking up a plastic action figure and moving its arms around.

'No. I think we're now too old and too tired,' Will grunted. 'You wait until you have a young family. It knackers you. Anyway, what about you? Did you meet anyone in the States?'

'No, but I met a woman on the plane coming home.'

'Ah, tell me more!'

'Unfortunately, she stood me up.'

Harry told Will about his disappearing travel companion.

'I'm glad to see that you haven't lost your touch with women,' Will said, laughing. 'With your track record, she probably had a lucky escape! Have you thought about online dating?'

But Harry didn't answer. They had turned into the cul-de-sac where the Hamiltons lived, and Harry was suddenly aware of thick, black smoke pouring from one of the properties.

'Shit. That's the Hamiltons' house,' said Will. 'I'll phone the fire brigade.'

A crowd of onlookers had gathered outside. The officers drew up and leapt from the vehicle.

'Does anyone know if there's anyone in there?' Harry asked.

'Don't know,' one of them said. 'It's only just happened. We heard a noise and came out to see wha–'

A deafening bang followed by a high-pitched scream came from inside the house. Harry and Will hared across lawns and driveways towards the burning building, where an elderly gentleman was ineffectually kicking at the front door.

'There's someone inside!' He gestured frantically to them to hurry.

'Is there no way to get around to the back?' Will shouted.

'No, not with these houses, you'd have to go around the whole estate.'

The terraced houses all had fenced gardens at the rear, adjoining each other.

'Mind out of the way, please, sir,' Will said.

The officers kicked down the front door, but when they tried to rush inside, a blast of choking smoke sent them tumbling back into the garden.

They picked themselves up, coughing and spluttering. There was a small fish pond on the lawn. Harry tore off his jacket, soaked it in the pond, then placed it over his head. He ran back into the house, keeping low. As he entered, a load of flaming ceiling tiles fell down by the front door, trapping Harry inside the building and preventing Will from following him.

Will stepped back, shielding himself from the heat. 'I'll find another way in,' he shouted, running back towards his vehicle.

Inside the house, Harry had started up the stairs. He could see that it was already too late. The fire had taken hold, blocking his way.

'Anyone up there?' he shouted.

He jumped back down the stairs and looked around wildly. Flames and smoke stopped him from going down the hallway towards what looked like the kitchen area at the rear of the house.

'Hello?' he shouted. 'Anyone in here? Hello?'

There was no reply, although it was hard to hear anything above the crackle of the flames.

Harry kept his head down and tried to peer through the dense haze. He ran into the living room and immediately fell over something soft, which sent him stumbling across the room and smashing onto a glass coffee table.

The shock of the fall made him inhale sharply; he choked, then heaved on the acrid smoke. Tears streamed down his face as he lay on the carpet, trying to breathe.

Fragments of the coffee table had ripped open the sleeve of his white, cotton shirt and blood streamed down his arm. He looked across to see what he had tripped over. A body lay face-down on the carpet. He tried to shout, but only a croak came out of his mouth. He coughed again. There was a deep pain in his chest. Visibility was quickly diminishing as more and more of the thick, black smoke took over. It astounded him how quickly the smoke had spread in the short time he'd been inside the house.

He crawled over to the body, elbowing himself across the floor. He could see that it was a woman with long hair. He felt for a pulse and was amazed to find that she was alive.

Harry grabbed her under the armpits and attempted to drag her towards the door, coughing and retching. He got her into the hallway, hoping to see signs of help – the fire brigade – anybody. But the searing heat of flames made everybody stagger back away from the building.

Realising that there was no escape to any other part of the house, he heaved her back into the lounge and closed the door. That would at least block some heat for the time being. However, he knew it wouldn't be too long before the door itself would be ablaze.

The smoke was getting steadily thicker in the lounge. Harry put his still-damp jacket around the woman and grabbed a cushion from the settee. He held it to his face in a vain attempt to block the smoke and crawled around the floor, trying the window at the front of the room and the patio doors at the rear. To his frustration, both were locked, with no sign of a key anywhere.

Harry kicked at the patio door forcefully. There was no sign of it giving – these were high-grade doors. Looking around for anything he could use to smash the glass, he grabbed a standard lamp from the corner of the room and tried to use it like a battering ram, but it snapped in two. He threw the pieces to one side in frustration and picked up an earthenware jug which he used to bash the side of one of the patio doors.

Over the years, he had instructed his team that whenever they attended the aftermath of a burglary or were asked to discuss security matters, they should advise that additional locks be installed to windows and patio doors. The occupants of this house must have heeded that advice because there were about half a dozen bolts protecting the glass doors.

When he realised that he had no chance of breaking the locks, Harry hurled the earthenware jug at the window in frustration. It bounced off the strengthened glass and fell onto the floor, where it shattered.

He sat back on his haunches, staring at the pieces of earthenware. He felt that the seriousness of their situation had gone up by a few notches and he was running out of ideas.

Harry crawled back to the recumbent woman. At first, he couldn't make out whether she was still breathing, but then he felt a weak pulse in her neck. He stripped the cover off one of the cushions and put the fabric over her nose and mouth to try to lessen the inhalation of the smoke, but he knew that this was a temporary fix.

Time was against them.

Harry was starting to feel slightly dizzy. He put his head next to the woman's, face-down on the floor, and breathed through the pile of the carpet. He could smell cigarettes and an animal – a dog, perhaps? And smoke. More and more smoke. *Where's the fucking fire brigade?*

He heaved into the carpet, his tears mixing with the fumes, blinding him. He rubbed at his eyes and looked up. Through the haze, he could make out the flames licking around the door frame. His heart sank. They were trapped, and about to be burnt alive.

Harry felt that he had misjudged things somehow, but what else could he have done? If he hadn't closed the lounge door, she would have been charcoal by now. They both might still be.

Perhaps I should start praying, he thought, screwing his eyes shut to give some relief to the stinging that was blinding him. He could barely breathe and there was a thumping in his ears.

Then he heard a screech.

The woman had returned to consciousness and pushed off the material covering her face. She was sitting bolt upright, looking terrified. Her face streamed with tears and black residue. As the smoke entered her mouth, her scream cut off, and she emitted a strangled gasp.

She was jabbing her finger urgently to somewhere behind Harry. He looked around to see a chunk of ceiling falling into the room, bringing with it a burning bed which immediately set the lounge furnishings ablaze.

Suddenly she was looking directly at him, her eyes filling with terror. He suddenly felt an intense heat coming from the top of his head. Harry automatically put his hands up to stop the burning sensation and felt pain sear through his palms as the flames found a new target. He could hear the woman's strangled scream once more and could smell something horrible. It was his own hair burning.

Fuck, he thought, *this is it, this is the end of the line for us.*

He threw himself headlong into an armchair and frantically rubbed his head on the cushions to try to snuff out the flames. He had never known such intense pain; he felt as though his scalp was being skewered. But, for now, he seemed to have stopped his hair burning.

He crawled back to the woman. He could see her staring up at him, her eyes desperate. Maybe he was imagining it, but somewhere, through the noise of the flames, he could hear an engine being over-revved. The sound got louder and then stopped. Was it the fire brigade at last?

Suddenly there was a deafening crash as splinters of glass rained into the room, followed by lumps of masonry.

Harry threw his body over the woman's protectively. The patio window and the wall at the end of the lounge had completely disappeared, replaced with the front end of a vehicle, headlights on, horn blasting. There was a blinding flash, followed by more searing heat. The wall being smashed down had caused a back-draft that had blown down the lounge door, sucking the inferno into the room.

Harry, working on pure adrenaline, sprang up and heaved the woman towards the vehicle, which was reversing into the back garden, allowing them to stumble over the steaming rubble. Exhausted, Harry and the woman collapsed onto the patio outside.

Harry felt a pair of powerful arms take the woman from his grasp, then seconds later felt those same arms envelop his chest, as it was his turn to be dragged backwards towards the vehicle.

'I can't leave you for a bloody second, can I?' he heard a familiar voice say.

After that, Harry wasn't truly aware of what was going on. It was as if he was in a state of intense drowsiness, where dream-like events were taking place around him, but he had no control over these events, or even over himself.

A series of faces from his past floated into his consciousness – his ex-wife, school friends, his parents, looking as they had when he was a little boy. Then there was his mother, looking as she did now, slightly stooped and smiling.

She was trying to say something to him. He could see her lips move, but could only hear the surreal sounds of movement around him. He desperately tried to answer her, but she disappeared into a blinding light that overwhelmed him. He tried to open his eyes, but the feeling of brightness beyond his eyelids made it difficult. An intense stabbing pain in his scalp brought recent events floating back into his consciousness.

Harry could hear unfamiliar noises and the hum of quiet conversation. Footsteps echoed somewhere, and a phone rang in the distance. He could sense a presence next to him. Slowly, he forced open his eyes, blinking in the harsh light.

'It's about time you woke up, you lazy bastard.'

Harry looked in the direction of the voice and gave a weak smile. He tried to say something, but started to cough instead.

A nurse came running over. 'Mr Black, please try not to speak.'

She looked disapprovingly at Will.

'Sir, can I ask you not to talk to my patient? In fact, it would be better if you came back later.'

Struggling to speak, Harry waved an arm to attract her attention. That his arm was bandaged came as a surprise to him.

'It's okay, nurse,' Harry said hoarsely. 'He saved my life, so he can stay. He can even sing to me if he wants.'

The nurse gave them a "boys will be boys" look and went on her way.

Harry looked down at himself. As well as his bandaged hands and arms, he was on a drip. The pain from his head was still excruciating and coming in waves.

He focused on Will. 'How is the woman? I presume it was Laura Hamilton?'

'Yes, it was. Talking of saving lives, you did some of that yourself. She's not in a good way, but she's lucky to be around. Just like you.'

The nurse came back to Harry's bed, holding a bottle.

'What's that?' Harry asked.

'These will help with the pain,' she said.

'Thank God, I need some relief.'

The nurse looked sympathetic. 'These are quite serious burns. You will feel discomfort for a while yet, I'm afraid.'

'Do you have a mirror?' Harry asked her as he knocked back the tablets.

'This is no time to be thinking about your looks,' Will said.

The nurse came back with a mirror and held it while Harry examined the bandaged head that stared back.

He looked up at the nurse. 'How bad am I?'

She smiled at him reassuringly. 'You were fortunate,' she said. 'You've burnt off a lot of your hair and eyebrows, but your scalp isn't as bad as it might have been.'

'Then why does it hurt so bloody much?'

'Because burns can create the worst pain imaginable. Just think about being scalded with boiling water...it's going to hurt a lot. Those tablets should help, but just let me know if you need anything else.'

As she left, Will leaned towards Harry. 'You know what, mate? She's right. You were fortunate. As I was approaching the house, I feared the worst, because the fire looked so bad, but here you are, alive and kicking.'

'And sore,' Harry added.

'Listen,' Will said, 'I've been googling information to do with burns, and I read that because your nerve endings are close to the skin, superficial burns hurt a lot more. If you can't feel your burns, that's when they are really serious.'

Harry looked at Will with amusement. 'Ladies and gentlemen, may I present Doctor Kidman!'

'Er, Doctor Bennett, actually,' said a new voice.

They looked up at the doctor, who had seemingly appeared from nowhere. He reached down at the foot of the bed and picked up the board containing Harry's notes.

'Mr Black, it looks like you are lucky to be alive. You were fortunate to be rescued from the fire just in time and it seems that you haven't any serious injuries, apart from the fact that...' He looked at Harry's bandaged head. 'You will lose some hair, temporarily.'

'That's all right, mate, you'll look like me,' Will said, rubbing the top of his bald head.

'Great,' Harry said, unimpressed.

'You will need rest,' the doctor went on, 'lots of it, and you must keep well hydrated.'

'Thanks, doctor.' Harry reached over for the plastic beaker on the side table, but couldn't hold it in his bandaged hand.

'Let me,' said Will, taking the beaker and holding it to Harry's lips.

Harry gulped down the cool water, not caring that most of it had spilled down the sides of his face and neck.

'More, please.'

Will fetched another jug from the nurses' station.

'So, what happened?' Harry finally asked. 'One minute I was about to meet my maker, and then, instead of Saint Peter, bloody Rambo appears.'

Will told Harry that he had no way of getting into the front of the burning building to help him, so he'd looked for another point of entry. He had driven the Range Rover around the back of the estate, using the plume of smoke as a guide.

To get to the rear of the burning property, he had driven the Range Rover over a series of wooden garden fences, flattening washing lines, vegetable patches and flimsy wooden garden sheds in the process. He could see Harry inside the house attempting to break open the patio doors, so decided he had to take immediate action. Will had used the Range Rover as a battering ram, taking out the French doors and most of the wall at the back of the house.

'It's lucky the children weren't at home,' Will concluded.

Harry nodded. 'Absolutely. Where's Laura now?'

'She's in the women's ward, just down the corridor. If you

weren't so ill, you could have gone down and seen her. But don't go visiting her hospital bed looking like that.'

Harry looked down at himself. He was wearing a white, cotton gown that covered his front, but exposed his rear end.

'Do me a big favour, Will.'

'What's that?'

'Get me some clothes.'

4

In the days that followed, the bandages were removed from Harry's hands and his throat began to feel much better. The gash on his arm had required stitches and was healing nicely, but he still had the bandages around his head.

Harry had many visitors and messages from well-wishers. Even the DCI sent a card; it was curt and to the point, but it indicated that she might be human after all.

Will was a constant and welcome source of company. He spent plenty of time with Harry, reminiscing about past events, and their laughter echoed throughout the ward.

On at least a couple of occasions, one of the nurses would gently admonish the pair. 'Please keep it down, there are other patients here.'

Eventually, Harry was allowed to go home, but the bandages remained around his head. At first, he lay on his settee watching television, but after a while, he grew bored and couldn't take any more. He wandered across to the Saracen's Head where he found himself being stared at by other customers as he walked up to the bar.

'What happened to you then, Harry? Had an accident?' the landlord asked.

Other customers fell silent as they listened for his answer. 'Just a routine transplant,' Harry said.

'Okay,' the landlord said, none the wiser. 'Pint of Fullers?'

After that, no one took any more notice of him, and he felt he could relax. He quickly realised that, while he wanted company, it couldn't just be *any* company; it had to be people he related to. He phoned DCI Mainwaring. If he'd been expecting a warm response from her, he would have been sorely mistaken.

'If you want to come back to work, fine, but remember you'll be treated just like anyone else. You won't get any special dispensations from me.'

'Thank you, ma'am. I wasn't expecting any.'

Harry was welcomed back by his colleagues and praised for his part in rescuing Laura Hamilton from the fire, which he deflected, saying with sincerity, 'All I did was shut a lounge door. Will's the hero.' There was also gentle banter about his bandaged head and lack of eyebrows, which he took in good part.

On his second day back at work, he was called in to Mainwaring's office.

'Sit down.'

He sat.

Mainwaring looked at him with her cold, grey eyes. Her glasses were off and an open folder lay in front of her, together with the usual array of pens and a calculator. 'They are saying that you did an impressive job in rescuing Laura Hamilton from the fire.'

'Thank you, ma'am,' Harry said, bracing himself for what was to follow.

'However, while your bravery is not in question, I'm not convinced that it was such a great performance.'

'Ma'am?'

She looked down at the report. 'The fire brigade were there fourteen minutes after the first call. Was there any necessity for such dramatic heroics? Couldn't you just have waited for the fire services?'

'I'm sorry?'

'I'll put it another way, Inspector. I could see this as a gross misuse of police resources. You unnecessarily put lives at stake – your own and Inspector Kidman's. In addition, because of your actions, we now need to pay compensation to the angry neighbours whose sheds and fences were knocked down by Inspector Kidman's vehicle. We'll probably have to pay for the vehicle itself, and Health and Safety are all over the fact that the house could have collapsed when Inspector Kidman drove into the French windows.'

Harry leaned forward. He was unflustered and not particularly surprised by this turn of events. Mainwaring was part of a modern breed of police officer who had a very different idea to Harry of how the job should be done.

'Really?' he said, keeping his voice low and calm. 'All I can tell you is if I hadn't gone into the building straight away, the fire would have entered the lounge and Laura Hamilton would definitely now be dead. She was lying on the floor unconscious when I entered the building.'

He sat back. There was nothing else to add.

She looked directly at him. 'But we just have your word for that.'

'What do you mean? Are you suggesting that I'm lying?'

'No. I'm just saying that I have to have all the answers for when I'm questioned by *my* superiors.'

'Look,' said Harry, feeling a prickle of anger, 'how about the next time a fire starts somewhere, we just stand around and watch people burn? Perhaps we could hand around sandwiches and drinks and enjoy the spectacle until someone else comes along to save the day. Maybe we could all take bets on what time the fire brigade will arrive.'

He stood up, feeling that he had let himself down with what he would ordinarily consider an immature outburst, but he couldn't stop himself from continuing.

'Unless there is anything else, ma'am, I have work to do, which, in my role of Detective Inspector, for some reason, includes finding your beloved aunt's missing husband, George Evans. Is that not a misuse of police resources and public funds?'

Harry walked out, leaving the DCI staring after him. There were a couple of constables hanging around in the corridor who must have overheard part of the conversation, judging by the looks on their faces.

Harry pushed past them angrily and then stopped off at Will's office.

'You all right, mate?' Will asked. 'You look ready to go to war.'

'No, it's okay, Will. I've already been.' Harry flopped into the seat opposite.

'What happened?'

'Nothing really. I was called in to see Mainwaring, who was quite scathing about the way we handled our rescue attempt.'

'I know, she gave me a hard time too. I wouldn't worry, mate. It's probably just the way she's made.'

Harry examined his hands, which still had residual pink burn marks. At least they were no longer swollen and blistered.

'You're right, Will. No matter what she says, I know that we did the right thing. Most importantly, Laura Hamilton is still alive and not a pile of ashes.'

'Do we know how she's doing?'

'She suffered from burns from the initial explosion and

smoke inhalation, but she's apparently fine. In fact, I wanted to pay her a visit today and ask her some questions.'

Will looked at his watch. 'If we can go now, I'll come with you.'

They drove across North London in the fleet vehicle. Will's Range Rover was being kept in the police garage until the final investigations were complete, not that it was drivable after its demolition duties.

Harry picked up a tiny football boot and a toy car. 'I see old habits die hard.'

'Well, I've still got to run my lovely family around.'

They pulled up at the house belonging to Laura Hamilton's parents. Laura came running out of the front door and hugged them both.

'Thank you,' she said emotionally.

She looked very different from the corpse-like figure Harry had first encountered in the burning house. She had blonde hair scooped into a ponytail and was wearing dark glasses.

They were shown into a large sitting room in which there was a striped, blue-and-grey, three-piece suite, and an illuminated fish tank. A huge flat screen television took centre stage.

'Have a seat,' invited Laura. 'Tea, coffee, anything?'

They refused the offer and settled into seats that faced her.

'I can't thank you both enough for saving my life,' she said. 'I am so grateful.' She looked at Harry's head. 'And so sorry.'

'You're welcome,' Harry said, rubbing self-consciously at the bandage. 'I know you've already spoken to my colleagues and given a statement, but could you take us through it once more? From the very beginning, if you don't mind.'

Laura perched on the edge of the settee. She placed her

head in her hands and was still for a while. The officers kept quiet and waited. Eventually, she looked up, smoothing back the sides of her hair.

'I decided that my children, my family, and the world would be better off without me.'

'Really? Why?' Harry asked.

'I blame myself for my husband's death. I could have worked harder to be a better wife to him. I could have tried to be a more forgiving, more reasonable person.' She took off the dark glasses, revealing eyes that were red and sore looking, and looked straight at the officers. A tear rolled down her cheek.

'Paul had an affair. He admitted it straight away when I found out. I wanted to kill him. I felt worthless, a failure, and when he was found murdered, I thought that I couldn't go on living.' Laura Hamilton put her head back into her hands and sobbed gently. 'I couldn't even kill myself properly, I even fucked that up.'

'Take us through what happened,' Harry said in a soft voice.

Laura told them that she had decided to end her life with a mixture of sleeping pills and vodka. After downing plenty of both, she had decided that she would enjoy a final cigarette. She had tried to light it using the gas cooker, which refused to ignite. Frustrated, she had searched the kitchen for matches but, in her disoriented state, left the gas on. She had then vomited some drink and pills into the sink, and then found the matches to light her cigarette, which also ignited the gas.

The force of the consequential explosion had blown her across the kitchen and into the hallway.

Miraculously alive, but in a woozy state, she had lain for what seemed like ages, staring at a photo on the wall of her and her children. They were at a theme park, riding in a log flume, waving at the camera, their faces happy and smiling.

Her wooziness and mindset had made her indifferent to the fire that had taken hold in the kitchen, and was now growing rapidly.

There had been another smaller bang as an aerosol can near the cooker exploded. This had jolted her into action. The picture of her and her children had made her want to live, so she had weakly crawled into the lounge away from the flames. She had screamed for help and passed out, which was how Harry had found her.

'Do you still want to kill yourself?' Harry asked.

Laura looked down at the floor. 'Good God, no,' she whispered.

'Good,' said Harry. 'Then perhaps you can help us find your husband's murderer.'

'How?'

'Let's start off by looking at anyone who had a reason to murder your husband. Any ideas? What sort of man was he? Did he have any enemies? Do *you* know of any reason anyone would want to murder him?'

Laura looked up at Harry. Her red-rimmed eyes seemed to reflect a mixture of anger and sadness. 'He sold plastic sandwich wrappers. That's all he did. He went around the country talking to caterers and other people and sold plastic wrappers. No enemies. He didn't upset anyone. He'd drive to wherever he had to go, stay overnight, get back here. He was always tired. He normally watched some TV and then went to bed. That's it. There's nothing else to add.'

'Had he been acting differently to normal in recent times?'

Laura thought for a minute. 'No, I wouldn't say so.'

'Did he say anything that you thought was unusual? For example, did he mention any names of anyone he was meeting in the last couple of weeks? Anyone new? Anything different to his usual routine?'

'I don't think so. I can't really think.'

'All right. What about the affair?'

'What about it? It was only a quick fling.'

They waited patiently while Laura started to sob again.

Harry handed her a tissue from a box on the armrest of his chair. She blew her nose and faced them.

'The girl he was seeing, she was just a casual shag in the car park of some pub. She was the barmaid, a young girl called Tiffany. Stupid name. Anyway, it's finished now. I made sure of that.'

'How?' asked Will.

'When Paul told me about the affair, I went straight round to the pub and smacked her one. I felt sorry afterwards. She was only about nineteen. God knows what she saw in him.' As if only just realising what she was saying – and who she was saying it to – Laura once more put her head into her hands.

'Laura, just one more thing, if you don't mind,' Harry said, wanting to move on. 'Does the name Herg mean anything to you?'

'Herg?' She looked up confused. 'No, what's Herg?'

'Oh, just something that came up,' Harry said vaguely, standing. 'Okay, we'll leave you in peace. If you think of anything else that might be relevant, please ring me.' He handed her his card.

Will Kidman was studying the photos on the sideboard. 'Are these your children?'

'Yes.' She smiled proudly. 'They're out with their grandma just now. Obviously they're very upset.'

'Yes, of course. They look like lovely kids. You must be very proud.'

'Oh, I am,' said Laura. 'They are my life.'

'Thank you for your time,' Harry said. 'We'll be in touch. Don't worry, we'll see ourselves out.'

They got back into the car and drove towards Farrow Road in silence, each locked in their own thoughts.

Finally, Will said, 'Those photos on the sideboard...'

'What about them?'

'There was no wedding photo.'

'What are you getting at?'

'Just saying. You'd expect Laura's parents to have some pictures on show of their daughter's joyous day.'

'Well, that might be odd, but it doesn't make Laura guilty of anything, does it?'

Harry's mind flashed back to his own failed marriage. He didn't have many photos to show from that either. In fact, he only had vague memories about that time in his life.

'Everyone's life can seem strange to other people. Perhaps Laura's parents know about his affair and haven't forgiven him yet. Perhaps they will, now he's dead.'

Will nodded. 'Perhaps.'

'I think what's more concerning to me is that Laura even thought about committing suicide in the first place,' Harry said.

'How do you mean?'

'Think about it. Your husband has an affair. Surely, you get upset, angry, violent even. But would you get suicidal?'

'You might,' Will said. 'Particularly if other negative things are affecting your life, and your mind.'

Harry nodded. 'I suppose so. No-one truly knows anyone else and what they're going through.'

Will slowed the car down. 'Aren't we near to where that missing man lives?'

'George Evans?'

'Yes, him. Instead of going back to Farrow Road, how about we pop in and see Mainwaring's aunt? See if we can score a few brownie points with the Führer at the same time?'

Harry smiled. 'I'm not sure that's possible, but let's pay her a visit anyway.'

'Great. A tenner says she's buried him under the patio.'

5

He moved his bulk from behind the wheel of his freshly washed Volvo and looked eagerly at the smart, detached house across the road. Pulling down the back of his collar and straightening his jacket, he walked purposefully across the street.

Warm sunshine had replaced the rain and there was an enticing smell of barbecue in the air as people squeezed out the last drops of summer, getting a final wear out of flip-flops and shorts. Kevin Stock didn't have that luxury; he was a successful financial adviser, and his work demanded that he always wore a suit.

Closing the wrought-iron gate after him, he walked down the gravel path to the front door. He adjusted his jacket and smoothed back his hair. He rang the doorbell, the sound of which echoed throughout the house. The place sounded empty, and Kevin Stock had a fleeting thought that this might be the wrong place.

He took out his mobile phone and studied the notes he had made. No, he was definitely at the right house at the right time on the right date.

He knocked loudly, waited for a few seconds, then made his way to the side of the house where the gravel path took him to the rear of the property. Behind the house was a patio that edged a lawn that clearly hadn't seen a mower for weeks. An upturned wheelbarrow and a rusty barbecue sat next to each other, drowning in nettles and weeds.

He peered through the kitchen window. Whoever was living here was very neat and tidy, he thought. It was as if the house had been deserted.

After knocking on the back door, he then tried the handle, with no success.

Two sun loungers lay on their sides. He turned one up the right way and sat down, feeling weary from his journey and the warmth of the sun. He took off his tie and carefully folded it up, placing it in his pocket. Again, he looked at his watch. How long should he wait before it was an official no-show?

Then he heard the metal gate at the front of the house clang shut. He stood up in anticipation. He could hear footsteps coming from the side of the house and automatically composed his face into a welcoming smile.

6

Patricia Evans had grey eyes and grey hair. She wore a grey two-piece. Even her face seemed grey. A string of green pearls around her neck gave some relief.

As the officers introduced themselves, she looked at Harry's bandaged head.

'Looks like someone got the better of you,' she said. 'Come in, the pair of you, I've just made a fresh pot.'

Harry wondered for the umpteenth time what it was about police officers and tea. Everywhere he went, people offered tea, or maybe on the odd occasion, 'Something stronger, perhaps?'

Not that he wasn't grateful.

'We're very sorry to learn of your husband's disappearance, Mrs Evans,' Will started, but she seemed much more angry than worried.

'Call me Pat,' she cut in. 'Everyone else does.' She pursed her lips as she poured the tea. 'I don't know why I bother with him. All he thinks about is the pub, the bookies, and the telly. Oh yes, and himself.'

Harry waved away an offer of sugar. 'You're not worried about him then, Pat?'

'Me, worried about George? No. Not at all. After forty years of marriage, you get to know a person. He'll be up to something or other.'

'Has he ever done anything like this before?' Harry asked.

She took a sip of tea and grimaced. 'I don't know why I drink tea. I don't even like it. I only make it because he likes it. Yes, he has disappeared a couple of times. It's normally to do with booze and him wanting to surround himself with drinking buddies.'

'When was the last time?' asked Will.

'Oh, probably about five years ago. It was just after he had a big win at the bookies. They found him wandering around the pubs in Brighton, making a nuisance of himself. A nice policeman brought him home. I didn't speak to him for days after that, but he charmed me round, like he always does.'

'Did he disappear in his pyjamas and slippers on that occasion?' asked Will, amusement in his eyes.

'No, he didn't, but he did end up wearing tights and a tutu.'

'Tights and a tutu?' spluttered Will, holding his cup away from him, his tea nearly spilling.

Pat smiled for the first time. 'Yes, you heard right. There was this stag party, and the guy who was getting married was dressed as a ballerina, for reasons best known to himself. Anyway, there was so much drink involved that my old man and this groom-to-be swapped clothes, then George continued his pub crawl dressed like one of the cast of Swan Lake. The police saw the funny side, though.'

'I should think they did!' Will exclaimed, smiling at the thought.

Harry put his cup down. 'Did George have any concerns, anything that would make him want to run away, or...'

'George, concerns? No. I look after everything. I feed him, I buy all his clothes... No, he has no worries. His biggest concern in life is getting to the pub or the bookies on time.'

'What about his friends?'

'He doesn't have friends... more like drinking acquaintances. You'll find that the more money he has on him, the more acquaintances he seems to have, especially if he's had a win on the horses.'

'There's no chance that he's just round a mate's house, perhaps having had a few too many?'

She wrinkled her nose. 'Hard to say, but I doubt it. He's never disappeared quite as dramatically as this before.'

Harry stood up. 'We'll be off. Thanks for the tea. If we hear anything, we'll let you know.'

'Before you go,' said Pat, her face serious, 'yes, I'm angry with my husband, and I'll probably throttle him when he turns up, but he's not a bad old stick and I am actually quite worried about him. Please try to find him.'

When they returned to Farrow Road, Harry sat behind his desk still grinning at the image of a middle-aged man prancing through Brighton dressed in a frilly tutu. Will had gone to his office to catch up on his administration, which prompted Harry to do the same. The time he'd spent in hospital had created a backlog of paperwork which was peeping at him accusingly from his in-tray. There was a knock at his door. He barked out an impatient, 'Yes?'

A constable poked his head nervously into the office. 'Good afternoon, sir. Very sorry to trouble you, but I've been told to tell you that there's been another one.'

7

Blue lights flashed, lighting up the sides of buildings, as Harry arrived on the scene. He ignored the members of the press and the small groups of onlookers who were being kept at bay by local uniformed officers.

'Who's the SOCO?' Harry asked.

'Rosko, sir.'

'Where is he?'

'He's around the back, sir, but he said not to let–'

'That's all right, Constable.' Harry pushed through the taped area and went to the rear of the house where a tall, thin man wearing a ponytail and Lennon-style glasses was on his knees peering at a patio slab.

'Rosko, how's it going?'

'I wondered how quickly you'd get here. Don't step over that, please. Be careful, we haven't finished that bit yet.'

'Don't worry,' Harry said.

After working with Rosko for some time, he had got used to the man's ways. Rosko was fastidious in his approach to the job and could appear rude on occasions. His nickname had come from a famous 1970s music presenter, Emperor Rosko, because they shared the same birth name, Michael Pasternak.

'Mind if I look over the victim?' Harry asked politely.

'Help yourself. You can look but don't touch.'

'Rosko, you sound like a striptease performer.'

'Very funny. Just don't get in the way.'

The victim was splayed out on a sun lounger. He was wearing a grey suit with a pale, yellow shirt, open at the collar. The rope around his neck looked as if it was trying to separate his head from his torso. It was so tight, flesh bulged out on either side of the cord.

'Was there a word of any kind formed at the end of the rope?' Harry asked.

'A word? What are you talking about?' Rosko asked brusquely. Then his face showed an understanding. 'Oh, sorry, this Herg thing. No, there wasn't. I suppose there's a possibility that, if there was a word, whoever was first on the scene may have accidentally moved the rope out of place.'

'Do we have a name for the victim?'

'According to the information found on his person, his name was Kevin Stock. He has a wife and children.'

'Who discovered the body?'

Rosko shrugged. 'I believe it was called in by a neighbour. You'd better check with Control.'

'What about the owners of the property?'

'Apparently they live in the Caribbean three months of the year. Lucky bastards!'

Harry nodded in agreement. 'I need to see inside the house. The killer could have entered the property. It's doubtful, but I need to look anyway.'

Breaking into the house through the back was easy, just a shoulder to the door and the inside bolt gave way instantly.

Harry could justify breaking into the property by the fact

that a killer was on the loose and there could be an important clue within the house. Or even another victim.

He was half-expecting an alarm to go off, but there was nothing, the silence only disturbed by the ticking of a clock. He noticed that the carpet looked as though it had been vacuumed within an inch of its life, judging by the tramlines in the thick pile. The zealous cleaning was belied by the fact that there was a bowl of crockery in the kitchen – probably the residue of a last-minute meal before they'd left for their holiday home in the Caribbean.

At the front door, Harry picked up a business card that had been pushed through the letterbox. *Foxes. The same estate agency that discovered the body of Paul Hamilton*, he mused.

He left the property and re-joined Rosko.

'No luck?' Rosko asked.

Harry shook his head. 'Is it possible that the body was moved here from another location?'

'I've still got plenty of tests to do, but I'd say it was unlikely. I'd put money on the fact that the victim died right here.'

Harry got onto Control and found that it was the next-door neighbour who had discovered the body.

He strolled around to the property, taking time to admire the neat lawn and well-stocked borders as he walked up the garden path.

The door opened almost before he had started to knock. 'How may I help you?'

The booming voice belonged to a bald, elderly man who sported a magnificent handlebar moustache that wouldn't have looked out of place in the Wild West.

'Are you the gentleman who reported the incident that occurred next door?'

'Yes, I am,' the man said, drawing himself up to his full

height. 'I am the chairman of the local Neighbourhood Watch.'

Brilliant, thought Harry. 'Can I ask a few questions, Mr...'

'Carling,' the man replied. 'Amos Carling. Like the beer, you know.' He opened the door wider. 'Come in.'

Harry walked into a hallway that hosted a variety of framed sepia pictures of war-time aircraft and portrait photos of people, who, Harry guessed, were family.

'Thank you, Mr Carling. So what exactly did you see?'

'Well, I was confused because I thought my neighbours had gone away for quite a while, and then I saw this man lying on the sun lounger, so I thought to myself that perhaps he was looking after the place. I wasn't spying on him, you understand, I was just upstairs looking out of the window in that direction.'

'Yes, of course.'

'Anyway, there he is, sitting in the sun, and then the phone rang, so I had to go downstairs to answer it. Good job I did too – it was Mrs Brampton from the council telling me that I can have a stairlift installed for my wife. I was delighted because–'

'How long were you on the phone for?' Harry cut in.

'About half an hour, or maybe more. It was an important call because the local authority is paying for–'

'What happened then? Did you go back upstairs to the window?'

'I did, but when I looked out, the man was lying down asleep, or so I thought. I kept looking and then realised that the man hadn't moved an inch. I didn't know what to do, at first, but then I thought, well I'm the damn chairman of the Neighbourhood Watch so I've got a perfect right to go around to that house and make sure that everything is okay.'

'Go on,' Harry said, wishing that there were more Amos Carlings around – from a policeman's point of view, anyway.

'I went around to the house and found him lying there, dead.'

'Would you show me the window that you were looking out of?'

They went upstairs and into what looked like the spare room. Harry looked out of the window, but there was a conifer blocking his view of the patio next door.

'I can't see a thing,' he said. 'How did you manage?'

'Oh right,' said Carling, looking embarrassed. 'You have to pull this stool over and stand on it if you want to see anything – not that I wanted to see anything, of course. The family who live there have gone away for a long holiday, so they would probably want me to keep an eye on the place.'

Harry stood on the stool. Beyond the trees, he could see the patio, but it would have been impossible to distinguish the features of any person.

'That's great,' Harry said. 'Now, thinking about when you went to the house, what happened?'

'Well, I just arrived and there he was, lying there. There was no sign of anyone else.'

'What did you do then?'

'I wasn't sure if the man was actually dead, so I tried to get the rope off.'

'You touched the rope?'

'I had to! I might have saved him.'

'All right, no problem,' Harry said calmly, mentally cursing the man. 'So, when you first saw the rope, before you touched it, did you notice anything strange? Did the loose end of the rope form a pattern, or a word, or anything?'

Carling looked blank. 'I don't know. I don't think so.'

Harry sighed. 'Does the word Herg mean anything to you?'

'No. Should it?'

'No, that's okay, Mr Carling, you've been a big help.'

'Will you need me to come to court and testify or anything?'

'There probably won't be a need.'

'Oh,' Amos said, disappointment clear on his face. 'In that case, what shall I do about the card?'

'What card?'

'The card that was under the lounger where the body was. I've got it here.'

Carling fished in his trouser pocket and handed what looked like a business card to Harry.

Harry carefully took the card by the edges. The card was blank except for the word "Sam" and a telephone number.

Harry fixed Carling with a stare. 'Let me get this straight. You've tampered with a crime scene by moving the rope around the victim's neck and then, to make things worse, you removed what could be further evidence? This card could have helped us catch the murderer, but now any fingerprints will probably be obliterated.'

Carling shifted uncomfortably. 'I'm sorry, I didn't realise. When I saw the card on the ground, all I could think was, what if it rained?'

'Mr Carling, was there anything else that you picked up at the scene, or is there anything else that you can add?'

'No, that's everything.'

'Are you sure?'

'I'm positive.'

'In the light of you discovering this card, there may now be a need for you to testify in court.'

Carling brightened up. 'Excellent. I'll look forward to it.'

'Mr Carling, you are damn lucky that you're not being summoned to court on a charge of tampering with police evidence.'

Harry drove back to Farrow Road frustrated. When he got into his office, he put his face in his hands, as if trying to block everything in the world out – except for his own thoughts.

So far, they had absolutely nothing. Zero. Zilch. Amos Carling had seen a dead man on a sun lounger. That was it.

There was no actual evidence that the card had come from the victim, although it would have to be examined for fingerprints. Had it fallen from Kevin Stock's pocket, or had he placed it there? Who was Sam?

Harry leaned back in his chair and clasped his hands behind his neck. What else did they know at this stage? Both men were murdered. One – or possibly both – had been given some knock-out drug before being strangled.

The men's bodies were found at properties that were ostensibly empty. Both men were married with a family.

As for the location, the murders were within forty miles of each other. Did that point to anything? What about the rope? Who the bloody hell was this Herg? Was it some sort of ritual killing? What else did the two men have in common?

The door to the office opened with a polite knock. It was Will, clutching some papers. 'We've got a little update on our latest victim, Kevin Stock.'

'If you have information, please feel free to throw something – in fact, anything – into the pot.'

'I'm afraid it's not much,' Will said, pulling up a chair. 'Like the first victim, he was married with a family. He was in his mid-forties and worked as a financial advisor.' Will tapped the paper. 'It's confirmed that there are indications that there are knock-out drugs in his system, although it's too early to state which ones.'

'We thought that would be the case. Do we know of any other similarities to the first victim?'

'Only that they both travelled around the UK with their respective lines of work.'

'Yes, the first victim sold sandwich wrappers around the

UK. The second was a financial advisor. Perhaps they knew each other, somehow, or had some kind of connection.'

Harry paused, rubbing gently at an itch underneath his bandages.

'Also, both the properties where they were discovered were empty. But we know that the first house had been entered by a person, or persons, unknown, then cleaned to within an inch of its life. This points to the first murder taking place inside the property, after which the body was taken outside.'

Harry stood up and put on his jacket.

'The only thing that connects the two properties is the fact that there was a Fox's business card found at the property where the second victim was discovered. They're the estate agents who were commissioned to sell the first house where Hamilton's body was found.'

'The first property was on the market, wasn't it?' asked Will. 'So maybe we should check out any viewings. You never know.'

'I agree,' said Harry. 'I'll pay the estate agent a visit and take a look at their records. In the meantime, it's been a long, frustrating, draining day. Let's transfer this meeting to a pub. I didn't have any decent beer while I was in the States. Some real ale might do wonders for my brain cells.'

8

The Moon public house in the high street had a reputation for being slightly boisterous, but it was cheap and it was near to the Farrow Road station

After ordering their pints, Harry and Will looked for somewhere to sit and saw that two of their colleagues, Dawn Koorus and Adam "Sandy" Sanders, were already at a table.

Dawn Koorus was a thirty-one-year-old sergeant. She was from Ghana. When she had joined the division two years earlier, her colleagues had teased her. 'Tweet-tweet! Good morning, here comes Dawn Koorus!' She had taken it all in good spirits and had quickly become an effective, popular member of the unit.

Her colleague Adam Sanders, known as "Sandy" because of his mop of blond hair, was a sergeant in his thirties. He came from Bolton and was proud of his northern roots. It was an open secret that Dawn and Sandy were more than just colleagues but, because of their budding careers, they had decided to keep their relationship discreet.

'We heard that you went to see the missing man's wife,' Dawn said, sipping her wine.

'Ah yes,' Harry said. 'Patricia Evans. She's an interesting person. Her husband George, by her account, is a bit of a character.'

Will related the story of George running around in a ballet costume in Brighton.

'My God, he does sound a bit odd,' Sandy said. 'And she's apparently the DCI's auntie!'

'Yes, that's right. I suppose that's why *we're* dealing with this missing person and not you.'

Dawn smiled. 'Sandy and I took her original statements. She was furious with him.'

'She hadn't exactly calmed down when we saw her,' said Will. 'Nice enough lady, though.'

'Do you think her husband just cracked and left, or did he plan it?' asked Sanders.

'You wouldn't leave home in your pyjamas and slippers if you'd planned it,' said Dawn. 'Not unless you'd left a change of clothes somewhere else.'

Harry enjoyed these informal pub chats. It didn't matter who was there or what rank they were. Sometimes a difficult case would get "new legs" thanks to a stray comment or observation.

He stood up and scanned the nearly empty glasses on the table. 'Same again for everyone?'

There was enthusiastic agreement all round.

It was now about half past six in the evening. There was a steady flow of people coming in and out of the pub, running the gauntlet of smokers who stood outside, flagrantly ignoring the signs that said, "Keep entrance clear."

As Harry made his way to the crowded bar, a couple swept past him, the man obviously intent on grabbing the last remaining table at the far end of the pub. Harry carried on towards the bar and then stopped abruptly. It might have been his imagination, or had he smelled a familiar waft of perfume? He turned and saw the woman sit down. Her companion walked back towards the bar, feeling inside the breast pocket of his jacket for his wallet.

Good luck, Harry thought. *You'll be lucky to get served in the next half hour*. His eyes flitted back to the woman, who was holding a compact mirror and smoothing make-up on her face. It wasn't just the perfume that was familiar. He felt hairs stand up on the back of his neck as he made his way cautiously around the pub to get a better look at her.

It's her.

He slid into the seat opposite the woman and said, 'Hello, Jane Cooper, or whatever your name is.'

She looked at him, aghast. 'Who? What do you want? I'm with someone.' She looked frantically in the direction of her companion at the bar.

Harry suddenly realised that, with the bandages around his head, she had no chance of recognising him, and was probably freaked out.

'The last time you saw me, I had thick, black, curly hair, and we were sitting next to each other on a plane. I was in the window seat, and you came and sat next to me.'

The look on her face changed to a mixture of recognition, horror, then embarrassment. 'Harry the policeman! What happened to you?'

Harry couldn't be sure – was there was a touch of concern in her voice?

'Oh, I tried to put out a fire with my head,' he replied in what he hoped was a nonchalant voice. 'More to the point, what happened to you? We were supposed to meet at the airport.'

'Yes, I'm sorry about that. I did see you looking for me, but I was wearing a hat and sunglasses and ducked out of the gates behind a group of people. Besides, you were chatting to some guy anyway.'

'Oh, you mean the chauffeur holding a big placard with "Jane Cooper" on it? The same chauffeur that another Jane Cooper went off with? I'm sorry, whatever your name is, but I thought we were getting on really well. All you had to do was tell me that you didn't want to meet me.'

Her eyes flickered back to the bar. Harry guessed she was estimating how long he would be with the drinks.

'We did get on well. That was sort of the problem.'

'The problem?'

She looked directly at him. 'Harry, decent men like you aren't really for the likes of me.'

'What do you mean? I thought you were attractive, humorous, and intelligent. Any man would be honoured to have you by their side.'

She smiled, but her eyes seemed to mist over. 'Look, Harry, trust me when I say I'm no good. And now I need you to go. Please.' Her eyes flitted to the bar again.

'Just answer me one question. Why did you lie about your name? Jane Cooper obviously isn't your real name, unless coincidentally there were two on that flight.'

She shook her head. 'No, Jane Cooper isn't my real name. I borrowed the name from the tag on the old lady's hand luggage. Sorry about that.'

'Why didn't you use your real name?'

'I never do when I meet men.' She looked at him with sad eyes. 'Harry, I could never have a relationship with you – or any decent man, for that matter. I'm also sorry that I lied to you on the plane about what I did for a living.'

'You lied about that as well? So what is it you do?'

'Let's just say that my actual job is very...male-focussed.'

'What? Are you saying you are some sort of a...'

Suddenly she was looking up at her companion. He was back from the bar holding two glasses of wine, and in an instant, her face had become smiley and flirty. 'Hello, darling,

I was wondering when my drink would arrive. My friend here was just leaving, weren't you?'

As she looked back towards Harry, her eyes were anxious and pleading.

'Yes.' Harry stood up and politely extended his hand. 'Well, it's been nice to see you again. Goodbye.' He nodded affably to the man and walked back to his friends. He still didn't know what her real name was, but he realised that he didn't care anymore.

It had been a shock to see her again, and a double-shock to learn that she was...what? An escort of some sort? That was what she had intimated. It was hard to take in. The woman he had got to know on the plane hadn't seemed the type. But what *was* the type?

Anyway, it didn't matter. Harry had a string of failed relationships behind him, so what would have been the point anyway?

When he got back to the table, his colleagues were looking up at him expectantly.

'You went to get some drinks?' Will reminded him.

'Oh yes, sorry. I bumped into somebody I thought I knew.'

Harry went back to the bar, which now wasn't as busy as the early evening rush had died down. A few men leaned against the bar chatting. There was a hard-faced, older man with grey hair and stubble signalling for attention from the bar staff. Harry stood near him and waited for his turn.

There was a younger man on Harry's right, clutching the front of the bar with both hands, swaying unsteadily, staring across the bar area. Harry looked at him and the man looked back, his eyes unfocused.

Pissed out of his head, and drugged up. *Probably coke*, Harry thought, looking away. The last thing he wanted was to be drawn into conversation. He was still reeling from the shock of seeing the woman from the plane again – and discovering her apparent profession.

Bloody typical, he thought. *First woman I've fancied for ages and she turns out to be a–*

'What happened to you, then?' the man on Harry's right roared, pointing to Harry's head. 'Did you get beaten up?'

'No, I had an accident.'

'I'll bet you did!' The man gave Harry a hearty thump on the arm. 'Do ya wanna drink?'

'No thanks, I'm buying for my friends,' Harry said, indicating his table.

'Where?' The man peered across the bar. 'You don't mean that table with the black tart sitting at it, do you?'

Harry went still.

The man went on. 'Brexit was supposed to sort out the whole fucking lot of them, yet there they are, stealing into our country, taking our jobs–'

'That's enough, now shut it.' Harry's face was red with anger. He realised that he was in danger of losing it, and a voice in the back of his head was telling him to calm down. He also knew that some of his anger had a lot to do with meeting that woman from the plane again.

'Do what, mate?' The man spun towards him aggressively. 'What the fuck did you just say to me?'

Harry could smell the booze on the man's breath and decided on a calmer approach. He held both arms in the air apologetically. 'I'm sorry, mate, I didn't mean to be offensive. I'm just going back to my table. You carry on and enjoy your evening.'

He turned to go, but a beefy hand on his shoulder spun him round.

'You said something to me, I want to know what the fuck it was.' The man's drunkenness seemed to have been replaced with an animal awareness. His eyes had changed from being unfocussed to malevolent.

'I would take your hand off me now, if I was you,' Harry said quietly.

'Or what?' the man sneered.

'Take a look at me,' Harry said. 'You're seeing some guy with a bandage around his head who you think you can bully. Now take a closer look. Do I look worried?'

As Harry said this, he removed the man's hand from his shoulder and twisted it in such a way that the man was leaning back, grimacing in pain, unable to move.

'Do I look the slightest bit concerned?' Harry said, twisting the man's hand even more.

'Get off me,' the man moaned.

'Oy, you! What's going on? Leave my fuckin' son alone.'

Harry turned to face the new threat. The voice belonged to the older guy with the grey hair and stubble who had been waiting at the bar.

'Ah, so you're the person responsible for creating this racist piece of shit,' Harry said, letting go of the man who slumped to the floor.

'I'm Ron Grafton.'

Harry's face didn't move. He had heard of the Graftons – they were well known throughout the area – and he knew that the family, like many of its kind, traded on its reputation.

'You move quickly for someone who looks like he's been in a bad accident,' Grafton said.

His son was now back up and rubbing his arm whilst glaring at Harry.

'A sore head doesn't affect the rest of your body,' Harry said calmly.

'Everything okay?' Will had appeared.

'Yes, thank you,' Harry said, 'but I think we'll move onto another pub. I don't like the clientele in here.'

'Just because you've got one over on my son doesn't mean anything,' Ron Grafton said. 'In fact, I'd keep looking over my shoulder if I were you.'

'You're not me,' Harry said, 'so I won't be.'

The next nearest bar was The Blue Orchid, which was further down the street. It wasn't a pub as such, more of a bar-restaurant, but it had a good reputation for food and drink.

They sat around a polished table near the entrance. Other people were eating at a more intimate seating area to one side of the restaurant.

'What was all that about?' Will asked.

'Oh, a bit of a fuss over nothing, really,' Harry replied, not wanting to go into details. 'I think Grafton junior just had too much booze, and I also reckon he'd put some stuff up his nose.'

The waitress came over and took their order.

After a few minutes, the drinks arrived, and as the waitress put the tray down in the middle of the table, Grafton senior and his son walked past the window of the restaurant. Harry hoped that the Graftons hadn't spotted them. It had been a strange evening so far, and all he wanted to do now was have a relaxing evening.

The food arrived. As they tucked in, the restaurant door opened and Grafton junior stood there, swaying. He glared at them, holding onto the door frame for support.

Harry groaned and put down his fork.

Grafton junior stumbled forward. 'You...you lot there,' he shouted, pointing a finger at the four officers.

The restaurant went quiet.

'Can we help you?' asked Harry politely, wondering where this was going.

'You called me a piece of shit.'

Grafton junior took an involuntary step forward and had to hold onto the back of a chair for support.

'I didn't call you a piece of shit. I called you a *racist* piece of shit,' Harry said, aware that he probably wasn't helping matters.

Grafton aggressively lurched towards Harry.

Will got up and stood in front of Grafton junior, his arms folded passively in front of him. He looked at Grafton calmly and said in a low voice, 'Why don't you simmer down? You've obviously had a good time. Go home and sleep it off.'

Will didn't particularly want the man to know that they were police officers. It wasn't always helpful.

The man squared up to him. 'Who are you? Get out of my fucking way before I–'

He stopped.

Grafton junior was still glaring at Will without moving a muscle. It was as if he had turned into a statue. Life seemed to drain away from his face. He slumped to his knees, clutching his chest, his eyes wild and terrified. He fell onto his side, grabbing at the tablecloth as he fell, bringing dishes down onto the floor.

One of the other diners, a buxom lady, rushed across the restaurant shouting, 'Heart attack!' which panicked others to their feet to see what was going on. Within seconds, there was a crowd of customers, pushing and shoving to have a better look and offering medical advice.

Harry and his team identified themselves as police officers and quickly took control. They sent the diners back to their seats. An ambulance was called while Will tried to resuscitate Grafton.

Their efforts were in vain. Well before the ambulance arrived, Grafton junior was dead.

9

Phillip Greening kissed his wife on the cheek and walked down the steps to his Audi. 'I'll give you a ring later,' he called, blowing another kiss.

Sarah Greening waved back and carried on waving until his car had disappeared from sight.

She shut the front door and sighed. She had always hated him going on these damn conferences. She walked into the lounge and plumped up the cushions on the settee before going into the kitchen, where she loaded the dishwasher and wiped the surfaces.

She dried her hands on a tea towel and went back into the lounge, picked up a magazine, and sat on the couch.

When the phone rang, she nearly jumped out of her skin.

'Is that Sarah?' asked an electronic voice.

'Yes, it's me.'

'Has he gone yet?'

'Yes, just a while ago.'

'Are we still on?'

'Yes, I think so,' Sarah said.

The voice hardened. 'You think so?'

'I mean, yes, definitely.'

'Okay. Cool.'

There was a click as the line disconnected. Sarah looked at the phone in her hand and shivered.

10

Detective Chief Inspector Elizabeth Mainwaring seemed concerned.

'So that's cast-iron,' she said. 'Inspector Kidman didn't touch Edward Grafton just before he had his heart attack.'

Mainwaring had been interviewing the four officers individually, having already received their reports.

'No, he didn't,' confirmed Harry. 'Will stood in front of Grafton and tried to calm him down. He had his arms folded. In fact, he even tried to save Grafton's life when he was on the ground dying.'

'Well, that's something, I suppose. So why was Mr Grafton trying to attack you?'

'We'd had a minor disagreement in the pub we'd been in prior to the restaurant. Grafton was drunk and as high as a kite. Going by the tablets we found on his person, it seems he already had a heart condition.'

Mainwaring gave Harry a look. 'I suppose you were heavily involved in this situation?'

'Not really, ma'am. I more or less ignored all the racist and threatening comments he made.'

Harry could tell that his boss considered this situation a priority. Her desk was clear of anything except for the four folders containing his and his colleagues' reports.

'I don't mind telling you I could really do without this,' Mainwaring said. 'There's so much else to concentrate on right now.'

For a moment, Harry thought she seemed vulnerable. 'Look,' he said, 'it was just one of those things. There's really nothing for you to worry about.'

Mainwaring arched her eyebrow and looked at him as if he had just placed a lump of excrement on her desk. 'Well, thank you, *Inspector*, for kindly explaining what I can and cannot worry about. I'll be sure to contact you to seek assurance about every aspect of my job in the future.'

'I was only trying to say that–'

'That'll be all.'

Harry left her office feeling as though he had made half a step forward with the Chief Inspector and perhaps fifty steps back.

Famished, he went to the canteen to grab a sandwich and joined Dawn and Sandy, who were sitting in silence, staring at their drinks.

'Are you two all right?' Harry asked, wondering if they'd had a row.

They nodded.

'We got a hell of a grilling off the Führer,' Dawn said, looking downbeat.

I wasn't the only one then, thought Harry.

'I'm sure that you meant to say that you got a hell of a grilling off the *Chief Inspector*.'

The two were immediately contrite. 'Sorry. Yes, guv.'

Harry knew that in their comparatively brief careers they

probably hadn't seen that many dead bodies. Perhaps Eddie Grafton had been the first?

'Do yourselves a favour, don't dwell too much on this. Bosses come and go, but you need to concentrate on your own careers and the task in front of you.'

'You're right, sir. I was just having a quick wallow in self-pity,' Dawn said, forcing a smile.

'We all do that sometimes,' Harry said gently.

'Come on,' Sandy said, putting his hand on Dawn's shoulder, 'we need to get back to work.'

After they had gone, Harry sat down and stared almost unseeingly at the two vacated chairs, thinking back to his own career. It wasn't easy to impart your knowledge and experience to others in this game. You could give them advice until you were blue in the face, but until they had the same experiences for themselves...

Harry shook his head. He was getting fatherly in his outlook, and the realisation made him feel suddenly older. They said that in this game you felt ancient at forty.

Harry got in his car and looked up the Stocks' address on the satnav. He wasn't particularly looking forward to this visit. The officers who had interviewed Lisa Stock had already pre-warned him that she could be awkward.

He knew it was going to be a tough afternoon when the car satnav tried to take him the wrong way down a one-way street, then through a brick wall. After switching it off and radioing Control for directions, he eventually found a parking space outside Lisa Stock's house.

The houses in the tree-lined avenue looked as though they had all come out of the same mould – red brick, grey roofs, each with a token porch that had the same black and cream design.

For some reason, Harry hated this style of property. He had often thought that, if he *ever* settled down, he would love to live in an old, rustic cottage, perhaps somewhere rural, away from the noise and bustle.

The woman who opened the door was tiny. Harry was just over six feet, and Lisa Stock barely came up to his chest.

'Can I help you?' she asked.

'I'm DI Harry Black. I'm here because–'

'Yes, yes, it's obvious why you're here. You'd better come in.'

She looked up at his head and Harry waited for the usual comment, but none came. Harry was relieved. He was starting to get fed up explaining why he was bandaged.

'I'm very sorry for your loss,' Harry said. 'This must have been a terrible shock for you.'

She said nothing, but nodded him into the lounge. In it was opulence and good taste mixed with cheap and tacky, almost as if there had been a war between two interior designers. On the side sat a pile of empty glasses and an overfull ashtray.

'Which of you did the interior design?' Harry asked, trying to establish some common ground.

'I did,' said Lisa. 'Kevin is out – *was* out – working most of the time.'

'It's been done very nicely.'

'Thanks.'

'Mrs Stock, would you tell me about your husband? What sort of man was he?'

She undid her hair, which was pinned up, and pink tresses cascaded down. A kind of punky look, Harry thought, noticing the rings through her nose and ears.

'When we met, he was a bit of a lad, but after we got together properly and married, he seemed to mature, especially when the kids came along. We've got three, and they can be a handful.'

'I'll bet,' said Harry.

'He was a bit controlling, I suppose, but then again, so many men are.' She examined her fingernails, which were chipped and bitten.

'Did your husband ever mention any enemies? Or are you aware of anyone who'd want to hurt him or kill him?'

'No,' said Lisa. 'At least, no one I can think of. He was a financial consultant, so his work took him all over the UK. Sometimes he wouldn't be home for days, and he didn't talk much about his job. I suppose if he did have enemies, I wouldn't really know.'

She walked over to a cabinet and pulled out a bottle of Glenlivet – one of Harry's favourites.

'Want one?' she asked, as if reading his mind.

Harry Black eyed the bottle appreciatively. 'No thanks, I'm on duty, but please go ahead.'

She poured a generous measure of whisky into a crystal tumbler. Harry noticed that her hand was shaking, which seemed at odds with her calm, almost dispassionate face.

'How was your relationship with your husband?' he asked.

'Oh, you know.' She shrugged. 'We had our difficulties, just like everyone else, I suppose.'

She took a sip of whisky, paused, and then knocked back the rest of the glass. She poured another generous helping, again offering one to Harry.

Harry shook his head. 'No thanks. Much too early for me.'

'What are you saying Inspector? That I shouldn't be having one?'

Harry noticed that Lisa Stock was looking glassy-eyed. Harry guessed she might have had a few drinks earlier. He was keen to get her back on track before she lost the plot altogether.

'Mrs Stock, this is a murder enquiry. I am not interested in your drinking habits, although I would be grateful if you would slow down until you've answered my questions.'

Lisa banged the whisky tumbler down on the coffee table and turned to face Harry, arms folded, a defiant look in her eyes. 'All right, Inspector, what else would you like to know?'

'Mrs Stock, according to your husband's employers, he was supposed to be at an appointment in Northampton the day he died, about seventy miles from where his body was found. We contacted the people he was supposed to be meeting, and they told us he had phoned them, saying that his wife was ill and he couldn't attend.'

Lisa Stock's face paled.

'Mrs Stock, were you ill on that day?'

She shook her head.

'After he had left for work that morning, did you see your husband later that day?'

She shook her head again. Harry noticed that a muscle under her left eye was twitching.

'You see my problem, Mrs Stock. Your husband tells his boss in Northampton that he must get back to his ill wife, but then he's found miles away.'

Lisa Stock retrieved her whisky glass from the coffee table and took a huge gulp.

'Mrs Stock, I'm sorry to ask you, but is it possible that your husband was having an affair? We have to look at all lines of enquiry.'

Lisa Stock put her hands on her hips. She opened her mouth as if she were about to say something, then closed it again.

Harry went on, 'For example, was he getting or making suspicious phone calls? Did he sometimes come home later than expected? Were there any discrepancies in your bank account – payments being made that you were unaware of? Did he act strangely or differently in any way?'

Lisa Stock's face was getting pinker by the second. She jabbed a finger in Harry's direction.

'My husband was murdered and yet here you are, in my own house, trying to make him out to be the bad guy! You lot are a bloody joke. I'd like you to leave.'

She turned her back on Harry and looked out of the window with her arms folded.

'Mrs Stock, I need to ask you a few more–'

'Get out. Now!'

Harry now appreciated what his colleagues had meant when they had said that Lisa Stock could be "difficult."

'I think we'll leave it there, Mrs Stock. Thank you for your time.' He felt like adding, 'If nothing else.'

Harry left the house and drove back towards the station.

Something bothered him about Lisa Stock. He seemed to have touched a nerve. Maybe it was just the alcohol, but he didn't think so. Her anger had seemed too over the top. Perhaps it was just the way she was made?

He gave Sandy a call.

'I need you to find out anything you can find on Lisa Stock.'

'Why's that, guv?' asked Sandy. 'Is she a suspect?'

'I'm not sure,' Harry said, 'but something's not right.'

'Okay, I'll get onto it. Incidentally, we've had some reports back for the Paul Hamilton murder.'

'Is there anything that helps us?'

'Not really, but I'll give you the headlines. Forensics found traces of blood and micro-fragments of human skin on pieces of a smashed plate. The blood matched up to Paul Hamilton, so it's likely that the sequence of events leading up to the murder started in the house, possibly the kitchen, given the amount of bleach that was used to obliterate any evidence. Forensics also discovered black rubber marks on the patio. They matched up to the victim's heels, indicating that Paul

Hamilton was killed or rendered unconscious in the kitchen, and then dragged outside.'

'Thanks, Sandy.'

As Harry replaced the phone in his pocket, he found the estate agent's business card he had picked up from the doormat at the house where Kevin Stock's body had been found. He looked at it thoughtfully, turning it over and over in his hand, then pulled out his phone again and made a call.

A few hours later, Harry was sitting across a glass table from the owner of the estate agency, Don Fox. His secretary had laid out tea and biscuits.

'I've told you people everything I saw. I never want to look at anything like that ever again,' Fox said, munching on a custard cream. 'To find that rope around his neck, all squeezed in...' Fox shuddered. 'And there was a word spelt out with the rope.'

'Yes, that's right. Herg. Have you heard of that before?'

'Herg? No, never. What is it?'

'We've no idea yet, but the murderer seems to want us to know about it.'

Don Fox boasted a head of silver hair to be proud of, and his jet-black eyebrows made him look distinguished. Harry bet that Fox had been a bit of a ladies' man in his time. He also felt a faint sense of envy. What would his own hair look like – if he had any left – after his bandages were removed?

'It was the most dreadful experience of my life,' Fox was saying.

'I'll bet it was,' said Harry with genuine sympathy. 'Don't worry, I'm not going to make you tell me again how you found the body. I've already read the report.' He took a sip of tea. 'The victim Mr Hamilton was murdered inside the house then taken outside. The murderer scrubbed the kitchen and then took great pains to clean the house thoroughly.'

He picked up a biscuit and studied it, as if it held valuable information.

'Why not kill the victim outside, saving the hassle of cleaning the house? By committing the murder inside the house, the killer may have given us a helping hand.'

'What do you mean?' asked Fox.

'Well, it's possible that the murderer visited the property beforehand pretending to be a potential purchaser, and then stolen a key to the backdoor, or unbolted the French doors at the rear when no one was looking.'

'It could be a previous occupier. Or the existing owner,' Fox said.

'It could be,' Harry acknowledged, 'but it's unlikely. The murderer would know that it would be one of the first things that we checked. No, I think it's possibly someone that you've shown around the property.'

'What? I could have been in the house with the murderer?' Fox spluttered.

'It's certainly possible,' said Harry, 'or it could be someone connected to the murderer, like an accomplice. I assume that you keep records of everyone who's shown an interest in the property?'

'Yes, we do,' said Fox, 'but how far back do you want to go? The property has been on the market for nearly two years.'

'We need everything you've got, Mr Fox.'

After an hour, another two cups of tea and a handful of custard creams, Harry was back in his car, heading towards Farrow Road. His phone rang. It was Sanders.

'Sandy, about time. What's the news?'

'Guv, I've got that update on Lisa Stock.'

'Go on.'

'Her record is pretty clean – if you exclude speeding fines.'

'Oh well, never mind, I'll–'

'However, there was one occasion when the police were called to their home in the middle of the night by their neighbours, who were concerned because they'd heard a fight, shouting and screaming. It turned out that it was Lisa making most of the noise. She'd caught her old man doing the dirty on her.'

'Really? Now that is interesting,' Harry said.

'By all accounts, it was the classic case of the babysitter falling in lust with Mr Stock, then him trying to break it off before it went too far, then the babysitter telling the wife.'

'Christ, what happened then?'

'That was it, really. Lisa kicked out the babysitter *and* her husband. Soon after that, there was a fracas between the husband and the parents of the babysitter, to which the police were called again. Next thing, Lisa's taken her husband back and everything is rosy once more.'

So there was a motive, thought Harry.

That meant Paula Hamilton and Lisa Stock *both* had a motive to murder their husbands, who had both had an affair. It also meant that Lisa Stock had lied to him. Why? She must have known that she would be found out.

'Well done. Good work.'

'There's something else that might interest you, guv.'

'What's that?'

'We've found the pyjamas!'

'What pyjamas? What are you on about?'

It turned out that an off-duty Constable Stephens had been out walking his Yorkshire Terrier, when he saw a striped leg flapping at him from a public waste bin on the side of the pavement. His dog had pulled at the cloth with his teeth, revealing the pyjama bottoms.

After a rummage in the smelly bin, Stephens had found the matching jacket and decided to call it in, because he had vaguely remembered something being said in a briefing about striped pyjamas. As it turned out, they fitted the description of the ones worn by the missing George Evans.

Harry and Will decided to check it out and pay another visit to Pat Evans.

She answered the door and immediately spotted her husband's pyjamas through the clear plastic of the evidence bag.

'Oh my God, no!' she exclaimed. 'Not my George, no!' She started to step back into her hallway, her hand covering her mouth.

'Hold on, Mrs Evans,' Harry said. 'It's not what you think. These pyjamas were found in a dustbin. As far as we know, your husband is still alive...somewhere.'

They followed her through to the kitchen where she automatically switched on the kettle, her hands shaky.

'I'm sorry,' she said. 'I just thought...'

'No, it's okay. We just brought these around for you to identify. They weren't found next to a lake or on a beach, like Reginald Perrin.'

Patricia Evans smiled. 'I remember seeing that series on the telly years ago. Good, it was. Have a seat. Tea will be ready in a couple of minutes, and I've got chocolate biscuits.'

More biscuits, thought Harry. *My poor waistline*.

They sat down around the kitchen table, on which was draped a gingham tablecloth. A collection of condiments had been pushed to one side. At one side of the table was an open book, face down next to a folded pair of spectacles.

Harry picked up the book. 'The Legend of Zeus, this looks like unusual reading material, Mrs Evans,' he said conversationally.

'I've told you before, call me Pat. What's unusual about a book about Greek mythology?' She placed the teapot on the table and laid out cups. 'Some of the stories are fascinating.'

'Really?'

'Yes, there are murders, affairs, intrigue, romance... It's got it all!'

'The Greek gods had affairs?' Will asked, taking a chocolate digestive from the plate. 'I thought they'd be beyond all that, you know, being actual gods.'

'Oh yes, even the gods had affairs. Sometimes with us ordinary human beings. For example, this character Zeus, well, he was actually a bit of a dirty old man and he had affairs left, right, and centre. His wife was a right cow, mind you, I suppose it would make you that way with a husband like him.'

She poured out the tea.

'This stuff is so much better than any soap on telly. Each time Zeus's wife found out that her husband was being unfaithful, she tried to get her revenge – in ways that are far worse than you'd ever see on EastEnders.'

Pat dashed milk into the cups and offered sugar.

'No thanks. What sort of revenge?' asked Harry, intrigued.

'Strangulation, poisoning, all sorts. You see, Zeus had children with other women. Zeus's wife was so jealous that she sent two serpents to strangle one of the sons, Heracles. Even though he was a baby, Heracles was half-human, half-god, so he was able to kill the serpents.'

'Fascinating,' Will said, gulping his tea and glancing at his watch.

'So, Zeus's wife was a right vindictive, jealous type?' Harry said, scanning the pages.

'I've known some women like that,' Will said.

'I've known some men like that.'

Pat's statement brought curious looks from the officers.

'Before I met George, obviously,' Pat blurted. 'I haven't always been this old, you know!'

As they drove back towards Farrow Road, Will said, 'You

showed a lot of interest in that book. Surely you're not starting to develop an interest in the ancient gods?'

'No, Will, I just love interesting books. You should try reading some time.'

Will caught Harry's mischievous glance. 'I haven't got time to read anything more than the daily paper. I've got a family – you should try *that* sometime.'

11

Phillip Greening was in a buoyant mood as he walked into the reception area. He felt even better as he stared down at the receptionist's cleavage as she filled in his details on her computer screen.

She looked up at him, and he quickly averted his gaze. 'Do you need someone to take your bags to your room?'

'No, thank you.'

She handed over a key card. 'Room 212. Take the lift to the second floor, then your room is along on the left.'

Greening smiled his thanks and walked across the lobby. On an opulent looking settee next to the lifts sat a woman in a knee-length, black dress, dark stockings, and black heels. She had shoulder-length, auburn hair and looked to be in her late thirties.

She looked up at Greening and smiled as he passed.

He responded with his best dazzling smile, then carried on walking. He wanted to sit next to her and chat her up, but that would have been too obvious an approach, and Phillip Greening considered himself to be a subtle man.

He wasn't staying at the hotel in preparation for a conference. There was no conference. Greening had lied to his wife, Sarah, about that, just as he had lied to her about all the other "conferences" over the years.

Greening was a womanising philanderer and had been unfaithful to his wife Sarah on multiple occasions over the years. Often he used prostitutes, but sometimes he had full-blown affairs. He rationalised his behaviour with the fact that he would always return home to Sarah and treat her well. She could never find out about this secret part of his life. He was careful. He always used an alias in any place he wasn't supposed to be, destroyed all receipts, and was careful about how he paid for anything, normally using cash when possible.

He had two mobile phones, one of which was legitimate and could be left around for Sarah to find – and inspect if she so wished. The other phone, he kept well hidden.

Once inside his hotel room, he threw his travel case onto the bed and quickly got changed into smart jeans and an expensive shirt. He rubbed cologne on his face and studied himself in the mirror.

A fifty-two-year-old, clean-shaven face with back-combed, dark hair stared back. He frowned at the flecks of grey that were appearing at his sideburns, but was otherwise pleased with his reflection. He gave the mirror his best smile and muttered, 'You've still got it, my son!'

He drew the curtains, put on one of the bedside lamps, and nodded, pleased with himself. It looked intimate and inviting – in case he got lucky. He left the room to go back to the lobby, in search of the woman in black, hopefully to become *his* woman in black – for a night, anyway.

The lift was stuck on another floor so he ran down the stairs, not feeling as cool as he would have liked, and entered the hotel foyer.

There was no sign of the woman.

He went over to the concierge who sat behind a small desk.

'May I be of assistance, sir?' The concierge pressed his white gloved fingertips together and looked expectantly up at Greening.

'You didn't happen to notice a lady wearing a black dress?' He pointed to the sofa. 'She was sitting over there just a few minutes ago.'

The concierge smiled thinly. 'Ah yes. Excuse me, sir, I believe I have something for you.'

He went across to the main reception desk and came back with an envelope.

'Thanks,' Greening said.

The concierge coughed politely.

'Oh right, yes...' Greening handed over a five-pound note and went to sit on the settee.

In the envelope was a folded sheet of hotel stationery on which there was a handwritten message: *Meet me at Manning's bar – if you like!*

Unconsciously, he licked his lips. *I do like*, he thought.

He went back across to the concierge. 'Where's Manning's bar?'

The concierge smirked and pointed towards the hotel entrance. 'Out of this door, turn left, turn left, and then turn left again. It's actually behind the hotel, sir.'

He seemed to utter the word "sir" with contempt. Greening didn't give a damn. He left the hotel, almost trotting, and soon saw the lights of Manning's bar.

When he entered, he saw her sitting at one of the tables, drinking from a champagne flute. There was an opened bottle of beer next to a glass on the table.

She looked as lovely as she had earlier, classy and stylish. Her legs were crossed, revealing an enticing expanse of black nylon.

'You *did* want a beer, didn't you?' she asked, looking up at Greening with amused eyes.

'Yes, thank you,' he said, thinking that he must be in heaven.

She patted the seat next to her. 'Come and sit. You must tell me all about yourself.'

The combination of a beautiful woman, alcohol, and the invitation to talk about himself was almost too much for Greening. He couldn't have been more content.

He gave her an enhanced account of his life, barely pausing for breath. She looked at him with those seductive eyes, seeming to hang onto his every word.

Eventually, she said, 'My hotel is nearby. Would you like to walk me back?'

For a second, he considered inviting her to his hotel and the room he had so lovingly set up for an eventuality such as this. Then he thought of the concierge's sneering face.

'Yes,' he said, 'it would be my pleasure to accompany you.'

'Lovely,' she said. 'Perhaps we could take in another bar or two on the way.'

Greening was almost bursting with contentment. 'What a great idea,' he said.

12

Ron Grafton faced his family angrily, hands on his hips, his big, ruddy face even redder than usual. 'You know what this means? That pig was responsible for our Eddie's death.'

'Calm down, Dad, or you'll go in the same direction.'

Ron looked at his two remaining sons. James was the elder. Unlike his brothers Barry and Eddie, who had inherited the family's dark looks, James had reddish hair and startlingly blue eyes. He was also perceptive and intelligent. Rumour had it that he was the result of an affair between his mum and a local farmer.

The fact that James didn't share the family's looks fanned the flames of the rumours, which quietened down when the farmer in question was found dead in his field, having apparently been mown down by one of his own farm vehicles.

After that, Hilda had played the part of the dutiful wife, giving Ron two more sons, both of whom looked more like the rest of the family, with dark eyes and curly, black hair.

But it wasn't just in the looks department that James was

different. He was substantially brighter than his brothers and had become the brains of the family.

When the family had been told of Eddie's death, James had wanted to know more about the events that had led up to his brother's heart attack. He had gone to The Blue Orchid, bought the girl behind the bar a drink, *and* tipped her.

He had sat on the stool and smiled at her. 'Tell me more about the other night.'

The girl had told him more. She had told him she had been watching as his brother Eddie had come into the restaurant. She'd seen him speaking to some people at a table. She said that she couldn't hear what they were saying, but a sturdy man with a bald head and a goatee had stood up and faced his brother. The next thing, Eddie was on the ground.

'Did you see this bloke hit him or anything?' asked James.

'No, but something must have happened because one minute he was standing up and the next he was down.'

In fact, she'd been off-duty that evening, and had been standing drinking shots with her boyfriend, so her perception of events was sketchy.

But James Grafton thought he had heard enough. In his mind, this bloke was responsible for his brother's death.

'You don't know the name of this bald bloke with the beard, do you?' he asked.

'No,' she replied, 'but I'm sure he'll be easy to find. Someone told me they were all coppers on that table.'

'Really? They were the filth?'

James downed his drink and made his way to the police station at Farrow Road.

'Hello,' he said to the desk sergeant. 'I'm a witness to an event that happened at The Blue Orchid the other night, where some guy had a heart attack and died.'

'Oh yes?' said the desk sergeant, hiding his crossword under the counter.

'Thing is, I'm supposed to report to an officer as a witness. I can't remember his name, but he had a bald head and a goatee.'

'Ah, yes,' said the desk sergeant, 'that would be Detective Inspector Kidman.'

'That sounds familiar,' said James. 'What's his first name?'

'Will.'

'Yes, I think that's him. And he was definitely at The Blue Orchid on the night when that man died?'

'Yes, that's right,' said the desk sergeant, picking up the phone. 'I'll let him know that you are here.'

'No, no, it's okay,' said James. 'I have to do something first. I'll contact him later on.'

It had been that easy.

He had gone back to his family with the news. Now Ron Grafton and his boys were discussing what they would do next.

13

The War Office was a disused canteen in the bowels of the Farrow Road police station. The addition of a trestle table, chairs, and a flip chart at least added some credibility to the word "office."

Harry and Will were poring over the reports.

'So,' Harry said, 'both the murders were more or less identical in that both victims were drugged before being strangled. Both murders took place in properties that are empty. We now know that the drug used was Rohypnol, the date rape drug, which is widespread and easy to get hold of.'

Harry loosened his tie.

'Rohypnol is pretty much undetectable and renders the recipient unconscious. The question is, why give the victim the Rohypnol then strangle them? I think the answer is obvious. The victims didn't know about their impending fate, and the murderer may not have had the strength or capability to strangle them without drugging them first.'

'Which could point towards the wives,' Will said.

'But that wouldn't make sense. Are you saying that the

two wives got together and concocted a plan to kill each other's husbands?'

Will shrugged. 'We've got nothing else.'

'Look, Will, I'm not saying that the two women aren't involved somehow. I'm saying that there is another factor, maybe something connected to this Herg thing.'

'We've also got a potential lead with the estate agency.'

'That's right,' agreed Harry. 'We've now got the list of people who viewed the property before Paul Hamilton was found murdered.' He opened a folder in front of him. 'Here we are. There were twenty-one couples, two men, and fourteen women who looked over the property in the last two months.'

'Why so many more women than men?' Will asked.

'I suppose because many women like to view properties on their own before dragging their husbands along.'

Harry unscrewed a bottle of water and took a mouthful.

'The boss of the estate agency, Don Fox, remembers one bloke he showed around who wanted to go back into the house as they were leaving – said he'd had forgotten something. Sunglasses, I think. Anyway, it would have been easy for him to unlatch a window or door before coming back out.'

'Fox doesn't happen to remember what this man looked like?' asked Will.

'Sadly, no.' Harry stood up and stretched wearily. 'We still have nothing to go on, so we'll get our team to trawl through any CCTV we can get near the properties where the murders took place. But I'm not holding my breath for a result.'

14

Lucy Hayes had worked at the Gaumont Hotel for six months. She had got the job by accident one day, when she had popped into the hotel to meet her mum for lunch. The big Italian man behind the bar had smiled and winked at her. He'd told her that she had the right personality and looks to work with him, and that they were short-staffed and needed someone that evening.

She had turned up later, wearing a crisply ironed blouse and black skirt to find a harassed manager of the hotel working behind the bar instead.

'Where's the Italian barman who was here earlier?' she had asked.

'He's gone,' he had replied curtly. 'And who are you?'

'I'm Lucy Hayes, and this is supposed to be my first shift,' she had replied nervously.

The manager had taken Lucy to one side and explained that he had just sacked the barman for fiddling the till, and he was very pleased that Lucy was starting there that evening, as they were short-staffed. That she had no references or qualifications didn't seem to matter.

Lucy loved the job and discovered that she was a natural all-rounder. One minute she was behind the bar, the next she was waitressing in the restaurant, and then she was upstairs cleaning the hotel bedrooms. It was hard work, but she loved it, and had a permanent smile on her face.

She was working behind the reception desk late one evening when a couple came in, giggling, wet through from the torrential rain. The man was clearly drunk, but seemed friendly enough. The woman wore a floppy hat, coat, and dark glasses, which seemed at odds with the weather outside.

'I have a reservation,' she said, shaking droplets from a dainty umbrella.

'Under what name?' Lucy asked.

'Smith, of course,' the man said, and guffawed loudly. 'Can we get a drink from the bar?'

'Yes,' Lucy replied. 'Please follow me.' She showed them to a lounge area in which an open fire was burning.

'This is nice and cosy,' the man said, rubbing his hands together. 'Could we have two large brandies, please?'

'Could I have ice in mine?' asked the lady.

Lucy went behind the bar, poured the drinks, then discovered that the ice bucket was empty. She took the bucket to the ice machine, which was in the cellar. On her return, she could hear raised voices. When she entered the bar, she was shocked to see the man standing over the woman, looking intimidating. His finger was outstretched as if he was making a point, and his face looked angry.

Lucy coughed politely.

The man immediately moved away from the woman and gave Lucy a dazzling smile. 'Thank you so much,' he almost purred, as she set the drinks down in front of them. 'This is for you.' He pressed a fiver into her hand. His fingers seemed to caress her flesh at the same time.

'You're very welcome,' she replied politely, and almost ran out of the bar area. 'What a horrible man,' she remarked to the manager when she returned to reception.

'Who is?'

'That Mr Smith. He's evil, I can just feel it.'

15

The missing George Evans wasn't missing as far as he was concerned. He was having a great time. He had ended up in Brighton, the town he had loved so much some years before, and was ensconced in a comfy, leather armchair in the Hop Poles public house, holding court to his fellow drinkers, who were hanging onto his every word. He regaled them with tales of his life and pontifications about the politics of the day.

George had money, lots of it, and he was spending it on beer and companionship. Word had already got out that there was this bloke in the Hop Poles who was buying everyone drinks. All one had to do was put up with him talking at you.

The more drinks you had, the easier it was to listen to him.

There were a growing number of drinkers in the pub who were taking advantage of George's generosity. Instead of politely accepting just one drink, they were ordering triple whiskies and brandies as if they were going out of fashion.

The pub landlord and the bar staff couldn't believe the

sudden upturn in trade. They treated George like royalty, and of course, he lapped this up. Any thoughts about his wife, Pat, his family, friends, and his previous existence were a million miles away.

George was having fun.

It had all started on the previous Saturday evening. He had been sitting in his comfy chair in his pyjamas, the television on in the background, when the lottery results had come on.

He had been concentrating on the racing form guide in the newspaper on his lap when something told him to look up at the television. There, displayed at the bottom of the screen, were the first three balls out of the machine.

'Thirty-eight, twenty-four, and thirty-two,' he had said. 'Bloody Nora, I've actually won something!'

He watched, wide-eyed with astonishment, as his other numbers, seven and three, followed. He had five of his numbers. How much would that be worth? He hardly dared to breathe. He just needed number forty-seven to win the jackpot. It wasn't really going to happen to him. Only other people had that kind of luck. Hold on, no way... but there it was. Forty-seven was there! No... Way!

He stared at the screen, his heart thudding, trying to take in the enormity of what was happening.

Thoughts came flooding into his brain – a new car, holidays abroad, a new house, definitely. Pat had always been quite snooty about where she'd prefer to live.

He did the same numbers every week and knew them by heart, but he got his lottery ticket from the drawer and compared the numbers anyway, forcing himself to concentrate. Yes, it was a match!

He looked up in the direction of where his wife was ironing upstairs. He wouldn't tell her yet. She would have all the money spent in her head within two minutes. In fact, he wouldn't see a penny. No, he would figure this out first. When he had it all planned out, he would tell her.

Better than that, he would make some expensive purchases, then show her. After all, *he* had bought the ticket and won the lottery, not her. He picked up his phone and quietly slipped out through the front door, leaving it ajar, and walked down the pavement to the end of the street.

He dialled the number.

'I think I've won the lottery!' he stammered into the phone.

'Do you have your ticket?' a friendly voice on the other end asked.

After answering a few questions, it transpired that George had to go to the National Lottery headquarters in Watford with some identification to claim the money. They offered to come to his house to sort out the paperwork and verify his claim, but he had quickly said that his wife was very ill, and that he wouldn't mind coming to Watford.

'That's great, Mr Evans. I'm sorry to hear about your wife's illness, but may I be the first to congratulate you,' the voice on the other end had said.

'Hold on, hold on!' George nearly shouted into the phone. 'How much have I won?' In his excitement earlier, he had taken no notice of the actual prize amount.

'The jackpot itself was worth around three million pounds.'

George's stomach did a somersault.

'However, it's looking like there are about twenty winners.'

'Twenty winners?' exclaimed George, all thoughts of a luxurious existence going up in smoke. 'That's only a hundred and fifty thousand pounds each!' Years of betting on horses had sharpened his maths.

'It's still a lot of money, Mr Evans, and many people–'

'Yes, yes.' George ended the phone call.

He didn't want to hear any more. He walked back towards the house, his mind whirring. A hundred and fifty thousand *was* still a lot of money. He shivered, suddenly realising that he only had his pyjamas and slippers on.

When he got to his front gate, he looked up at the lit bedroom window where Pat was ironing and saw in his mind's eye the hundred and fifty thousand disappearing on stuff that *she* wanted. He slipped back through the open front door and stood quietly, pondering what to do next.

The sound of his wife walking along the landing to the top of the stairs galvanised his mind. He remembered that he needed identification for the lottery people, so he opened the drawer of the consul table in the hallway and took out his wallet, which contained his driving licence and some money, along with his passport. He grabbed his coat and hat and, softly closing the front door, slipped out into the night.

As good luck would have it, a bus came along just as he was walking along the pavement.

'Where to, mate?' asked the driver as George got on.

George had no idea. 'Where do you go to?' he asked lamely.

The driver laughed. George forced a laugh with him. 'Well, I can recommend Watford Junction.'

'That sounds perfect,' George said.

The lottery HQ was in Watford, and that was where he would pick up his winnings.

'How much do I owe you?' he asked, fumbling in his wallet.

'Don't worry about it, mate. Just take a seat.'

As they pulled into the station, rain was thudding against the roof of the bus. George could see the welcome lights of a pub across the road.

As he walked in, the man behind the bar looked him up and down. 'Is everything all right, sir?'

'Why?' asked George, then became aware that he still wore his pyjamas under his damp coat, and his slippers were sodden. This must have been why the bus driver had let him off the fare.

'Oh, I see,' he said, looking down at himself. 'My water tank burst and my whole house is soaked. I had to leave immediately. I'm looking for somewhere to stay while it all gets sorted out.'

George congratulated himself on his own quick thinking.

'Oh, what bad luck,' said the barman. 'What'll you have? It's on the house.'

A few pints later, the world had a very rosy glow as far as George was concerned. He was free – and he had come into money. He settled onto his bar stool. The barman had booked him into a local budget hotel where he would spend the rest of the weekend. Then on Monday, he would be a hundred and fifty grand better off.

He had a sudden thought. He put his hand into his pocket, then realised that he had left his mobile phone at home on the hallway table. Never mind, he thought. When I get the money, I'll be able to buy the very latest model, with internet and everything.

He spent most of the following day in his hotel room, feasting from takeaway delivery services and watching old movies on TV. The only time he went out was to buy some ill-fitting clothes and shoes from the local Sunday market stalls.

On Monday morning, he made himself as presentable as he could. The trousers and shoes he had bought just about fitted, but the arms of the jacket were about two inches too short, so he pulled the sleeves of his jumper down beyond the cuffs, hoping he'd look more respectable, and off he went to the National Lottery Headquarters.

He had a lovely day with lots of friendly people congratulating him. There was free food and champagne and, most importantly, the money would be transferred straight into his bank account.

The next day, he was travelling first-class on the train from Victoria to Brighton, where George Evans was looking forward to having the time of his life.

16

Will Kidman was looking forward to an evening with his wife, Angela.

The boys were being looked after by her mum, so Will had planned to take her to their local pub for a few drinks, and then onto an Indian restaurant.

As much as Will enjoyed working in the police force, he was always happy to be driving home at the end of the day.

Angela hated Will's career. She had told him on countless occasions that there would come a time when he would have to think about changing course and finding a different job.

He pulled into his road and noticed what looked like a bundle of clothes on the pavement. He frowned. Someone had dumped rubbish outside their house again. He slowed the car down and switched his lights to full beam. He could then see that it was a man, lying face-down.

Will swung the car across his drive and leapt out, running towards the inert figure, who let out a groan.

'Are you all right, mate?' Will asked, kneeling down.

Too late, he felt, rather than heard, something behind him. Then there was what felt like a hammer blow at the back of his head, which knocked him to the ground. The feel of the cold pavement against his cheek galvanised him into action, and he pushed himself up to face his adversaries, but a kick to his head sent him back down.

There was a scream in the distance, and Will was aware of lights coming on. He summoned every ounce of strength to do battle, but the odds were against him.

17

Harry came out of his local surgery, his head freshly dressed. He felt despondent. He'd had his first glimpse of what he was going to be seeing in his mirror for the next few months – or more – and hadn't liked it. It had almost been a relief when the fresh bandages had covered up the criss-cross of scabby, red, pink, and white patches and tiny tufts of sparse, furry growth.

'Will my hair ever get back to normal?' he had asked, at the same time feeling ungrateful. After all, he could have died.

'It's hard to say,' the nurse had said sympathetically. 'We'll know more in a few weeks.'

His first reaction was to consider drowning his sorrows at The Saracen's Head – after all, this was supposed to be a day off. He glanced at his watch. They weren't open for a while; it was still early. He decided to get something to eat instead.

The Fred and Ginger coffee house was just around the corner from his flat. He ordered breakfast, then sat on a wooden stool that faced the window, through which he could watch the world go by.

He'd often popped in here for a coffee and a muffin, just to sit and think. Harry didn't really know what to do with himself when he had time off. His work and social life revolved around The Job. That had been a problem when he was married. When duty called, Harry Black had answered. Despite her calm and positive disposition, there was only so much that Harry's wife, Maria, could take.

The final straw came one Christmas when Harry and Maria had arranged to fly to Barcelona during the festive period. Maria had been particularly looking forward to it, as she had relatives living there. Their suitcases were packed and the taxi to the airport was booked, but then there had been a shooting incident right outside the station where Harry was based. Harry had been called into work, and he'd gone, promising Maria that he would make amends. But Maria had had enough.

She had travelled to Barcelona on her own, where she enjoyed the company of a local flamenco guitarist. On her return, she informed Harry that she was moving out and that divorce proceedings were already underway.

Harry had taken the news philosophically. The relationship had been drifting anyway, and he knew that he'd been at fault. As a result, he had treated Maria generously, probably out of guilt, and after the divorce had just enough left to afford his small flat.

His life now felt pretty much the same as it had done with Maria, but with less clutter and much less guilt. Maria had always liked having fresh flowers and photos around. Harry just wanted the basics – somewhere to wash, eat, and sleep. He missed female company in many ways, but he didn't see how he could sustain a relationship outside of The Job.

His thoughts were interrupted by his phone ringing. It was Mainwaring.

'Ma'am?' he answered cautiously.

'Good morning, Harry. I hope I didn't disturb you.'

'Not at all.'

Harry. She'd called him Harry, and she was being nice – that was a concern.

'It's not good news, I'm afraid. Will Kidman is in hospital.'

'Will? What happened to him?' Harry was already out of his seat, pulling his jacket on.

'He's been beaten up, but he's conscious and is asking for you. I know the two of you are close.'

'How bad is he?' asked Harry.

'He has a fractured skull and other injuries, but he seems to be a tough cookie. Doctors are saying he'll be fine.'

'Do we have any idea who would have done this to him?'

'Nothing officially, but there is a suspect.'

'Who?' Harry asked.

'I'll let DI Kidman tell you what he knows, then we can take it from there.'

'I'm on my way.'

18

George Evans missed his wife. He was getting bored seeing the same faces in the Hop Poles, even though they were so nice and jolly. In his heart, he knew that the fact that he was paying for most of their drinks was probably helping.

He had wandered around the many other pubs in the area, but the Hop Poles was the nearest one to his hotel, and George wasn't that keen on exercise.

It was as though the same people followed him wherever he went. The word "Freeloaders" came to mind.

The excitement of having a few days by the sea with plenty of money in his pocket was losing its appeal. The days had become dull – boring even. The hotel staff were friendly enough, and the breakfast was adequate, but it wasn't home. Perhaps he would call it a day, and return to Pat. She would be angry, but she would forgive him. She always forgave him.

He was missing the routine, and he missed the life direction that Pat provided. He even missed being told what to do.

After eating at the hotel, he decided to take his customary morning walk along the shingle beach before going to the pub. He loved the combination of sea air, the gulls, and just being at the seaside.

A blast of cold air hit him square on, and he stepped back, the shifting pebbles nearly causing him to lose balance. He pulled his collar up and crunched down nearer to the water's edge where he looked out at the grey, choppy sea, his thoughts miles away.

This was real. His pub friends were fake. His wife was real. Oh God, he was missing her...

'Are you all right, mate?'

The voice belonged to a man wearing a dark coat and a leather hat. He was accompanied by a boisterous Alsatian, who was having a good sniff around George's ankles.

'Yes, yes, I am. Why?'

'I thought you were looking sad, you know, depressed.'

'No, I'm all right, but thanks.' George had a sudden thought. 'I wasn't going to drown myself.' He forced a laugh. 'I'm sure.'

The man joined him looking out at the waves.

'It's going to be stormy later, I reckon.'

'Yes,' George said, agreeing for the sake of it. He wished the man and his dog would go away. He had things to think about.

'Have you got family?'

'I have,' George said, feeling a wallop of guilt hitting his stomach.

'You're so lucky.'

Then the man was off, leaving George puzzled by the exchange. However, the man was right; he had family, and he was very lucky.

He slipped and slid his way back up the pebbles, grateful when his feet touched the uncompromising surface of the promenade. When he reached the Hop Poles, he heard the door being unbolted. He was convinced they were opening early just for him. A few minutes later, as he sat in the leather chair he had become so fond of, the door opened and one of his new drinking buddies came in.

'Morning, George.'

'Oh, hello, Arthur.'

Arthur ordered a pint at the bar, then looked over at George expectantly.

'Shall I put this on your tab, George?' called Dave, the barman.

George nodded absently, a part of his brain wondering how Arthur always came into the pub just after he had entered.

A few minutes later, the Crouch twins appeared, closely followed by Mo and a few other regulars. George bought them all drinks. He even bought drinks for two men wearing black, woolly hats, even though they were complete strangers. They accepted their pints of Guinness with surprise and raised their glasses to him.

He raised his glass back and looked into the fire.

'Are you all right, George? You're unusually quiet,' asked one of the Crouch twins.

'I'm fine, thanks,' he replied, smiling automatically.

But he wasn't. He carried on staring into space for a while, oblivious to the chit-chat around him. Finally, he stood up and pushed his way through the now-busy pub to the counter.

Dave saw the look on George's face. 'You look like you need a little livener,' he said, pouring out a large whisky. 'This is on the house. What's up, George? You look as though you've got the weight of the world on your shoulders.'

'I wouldn't put it like that, Dave,' George said, fiddling with a beer mat. 'Thing is, I'm not supposed to be here.'

'How do you mean? Where are you supposed to be, then?'

George downed his whisky and put his hand in his pocket.

'How much do I owe you altogether?' he asked.

'Well, you're all up to date, apart from today,' Dave said, 'so that's eighty-five pounds forty-nine, please.'

The two men wearing the woolly hats were still at the bar. They looked interested as George handed over three fifty-pound notes to Dave, and told him to keep the change.

'That's very generous. Are you sure, George?' Dave asked.

'Listen, I've had a few days' holiday and I've really enjoyed myself, but now's the time to be moving on. I'm missing my wife and can't wait to get the train home.' George walked to the pub door, turned, and gave a theatrical wave to the rest of the pub then left. His buddies didn't notice him leave and carried on drinking, unaware that their source of free booze had just dried up.

George retrieved his belongings from his hotel and then made his way up the hill to the railway station, unaware that he was being followed.

19

When Harry arrived at the hospital, Will was easy to find; his laugh could be heard along the corridor. To Harry's relief, he looked fine. He was propped up in bed, his face bruised and his head bandaged, chatting to a nurse.

'Don't you be taken in by him,' Harry said to her. 'He's got a wife, a mistress, and nine kids.'

'Harry, it's good to see you.' With a wince, Will pushed himself further up the bed. 'It's lovely here, but there's no bar service.'

The nurse looked over at Harry with a flicker of concern. 'Aren't you also a patient here?'

'I was until recently, but today I'm an official visitor. I think Will and I are taking it in turns to reside here. How is he?' Harry asked, gesturing towards Will.

'We didn't need to operate, which is good. He may have a bit of pain for a few days and then the skull will heal itself after a while. Apart from the cuts and bruises, he seems fine. I think he'll be back with his family soon.'

Harry perched on the plastic chair next to Will's bed. 'You look all right, considering.'

'I feel all right, considering.'

Harry pointed to Will's bandaged head. 'Are you just trying to look like me?'

'Heaven forbid. My standards would never sink that low.'

They had set about Will with baseball bats. Will had somehow kept conscious after the initial blow and had hit back, connecting a few times. He'd also sank his teeth into someone's neck.

The whole thing had only taken a few seconds. His attackers wore dark balaclavas. But, as he was being beaten, he heard one of them say, 'That's for our brother, you fucking pig.'

Angela had been looking forward to their night out and had been watching out for her husband's arrival. She had seen him being attacked. She had shouted through the open window, then put the outside lights on before running, screaming, into the driveway. Her actions may have saved Will's life.

'Another few seconds, I might have been dead,' he said to Harry. 'I'm really pissed off with myself. I wasn't quick enough – I must be getting old.'

'We all are,' agreed Harry, 'but it sounds like you nearly gave as good as you got. So you think it must have been the Graftons?'

Will nodded. 'But I don't know which ones. Their faces were covered.'

Angela and the boys arrived. The boys ran over to their father and gave him a hug. Angela, who had sat by Will's bedside most of the night, looked tired and drained.

Harry gave her a hug. 'He'll soon be out of here, don't worry.'

'Oh, I'm not worried, Harry. He'll be fine. I know that you'll get the bastards.'

Harry nodded. 'I'm on it.'

THE GRAFTONS LIVED ON A SMALL, disused farm. It was easy to find, despite Harry's dodgy satnav. He drove up a long, stony drive and parked by the house. The property was surrounded by rusting, old cars, bikes, and assorted scrap metal. Outbuildings that had once contained animals, straw, and farm vehicles were now disused and in a state of disrepair.

Next to the front door was a huge ship's bell with a cord attached. *A redeeming feature*, Harry thought, giving it a tug. The resulting jangle was startlingly loud and went on for ages. A dog barked, which set another one off in the distance.

The door was eventually opened by a small woman with grey hair pulled back into a bun. She looked up at him. 'Can I help you?'

Just as he was about to answer, she was shoved to one side by a youngish man with dark, curly hair and a sullen expression. 'What do you want?'

'I'm DI Black,' replied Harry, showing his credentials. 'I'm investigating the attempted murder of a police officer.'

Harry said this for maximum effect, observing the man's face. He wasn't disappointed. The man's eyes widened, and he looked nervous.

'And you are?' asked Harry.

'Barry Grafton.'

As the man edged further out of the door, Harry noticed a large plaster on his neck. *Good boy, Will, you got him*, he thought.

'What happened to your neck?' Harry asked.

'Nothing,' Barry Grafton said, pulling his collar up. 'I had an accident shaving.'

'Strange area to shave. Who else lives here?'

'Me, my mum Hilda here, my brother–'

'What's going on?'

Two men had appeared – Ron Grafton, who Harry recognised from the pub, and another man who had blue eyes and reddish hair.

'I take it you must be James,' Harry said.

'That's right, and who are you?'

'He's Old Bill,' Barry said, 'and he's saying he's here about a policeman who was murdered.'

'No. I said that I was here about the *attempted* murder of a police officer.'

'What's that got to do with us?' Ron Grafton said. 'The only person who's been murdered, as far as I'm concerned, is my son Eddie.' He peered at Harry. 'Hey, you're that guy from the pub the other night. You were causing trouble.'

'No,' Harry said, 'the only person causing problems the other night was your son. Nobody murdered him, as I'm sure you know. According to his medical records, and the tablets found on his person, he already had heart problems. Too much booze – and drug use – wouldn't have helped him.'

'Your police officer assaulted him,' James said, running his fingers through his thick, red hair. 'Everyone knows it. Even the barmaid at The Blue Orchid said so.'

'You know that's not true,' Harry said, turning to the younger man. 'If you've spoken to the barmaid, I hope that you also spoke to the forty-seven customers who were there that night. They witnessed your brother having his heart attack, as did our own police officers, one of whom tried to save his life – in fact the same officer who was nearly beaten to death last night.'

James looked abashed, but Ron Grafton was having none

of it. 'You lot all stick together. If you hadn't had a go at my son in the pub, he'd still be here now.'

'That's ridiculous, Mr Grafton. Anyway, I'm here to find the people who tried to murder my colleague. Now, who wants to tell me where they were between eight and nine o'clock last night?'

Harry looked around at the Graftons. They were all in on it, of that much he was sure.

'What about you?' he asked James.

'I know nothing.'

'Very original. But you do know something. Our desk sergeant remembers someone matching your description making enquiries about the officer who was attacked. I'm sure he'll remember your face and your hair, and we'll have you on the station CCTV footage. What do you reckon?'

Harry turned to Barry Grafton.

'And although I've already asked you about your shaving accident, what if we match DNA taken from the officer to the wound on your neck, what do you think we'll find?'

Harry was gratified to observe another flicker of concern cross the younger man's face.

'And you,' he said to Grafton senior, 'where were you between eight and nine?'

'Me? I was with my boys, wasn't I, lads? And they were with me.'

'And where, exactly, were you all?' Harry asked patiently.

'Right here at home, weren't we, Hilda?'

'That's right.'

Harry could have predicted this outcome. Although the Graftons could all alibi each other, this made things easier. If he could prove that just one of them hadn't been with the rest of their family the previous night, then their entire story would collapse.

'Do you mind if I have a look around?' Harry asked.

'Not at all,' Ron Grafton said, waving an arm expansively. 'We've nothing to hide.'

Accompanied by Grafton, Harry walked around the property. He had a good look in the outbuildings and around the old farm but nothing seemed amiss at first glance. Amongst the rusting cars, there were a couple that were covered with a tarpaulin. They look interesting, Harry thought. Why are they covered and not the others?

'Would you mind if I took a look around the house?' Harry asked.

'I think that's search warrant territory,' Grafton replied.

'So do you have something to hide?'

'No, we just like our privacy.'

Harry made his way back to Farrow Road, with plenty to think about.

The Graftons were as guilty as hell, that much he knew. But trying to prove it was going to be another matter. It would be almost impossible to get a search warrant based on a hunch.

Back at the station, Harry looked for any paperwork, reports, or anything that featured the Graftons. But apart from a couple of assault charges and a newspaper cutting about a local farmer who had been killed, there was very little.

James Grafton was squeaky clean. Barry had a string of petty offences to his name – several charges of assault, of being drunk and disorderly, and plenty of drug-related charges.

Harry sighed. He was getting nowhere, and other work was piling up. There were two murders and that bloody missing man to deal with, plus the usual daily issues.

He thought back to the Graftons. He knew that he would have to return – perhaps unofficially.

20

George Evans was on the train looking forward to getting home. He cursed himself for not buying himself a mobile phone to replace the one he'd left at home. He desperately wanted to call Pat. He wanted to hear her voice – even if it meant being told off.

For the first few days of his escape from normal life, he hadn't thought about Pat once. Now he couldn't stop thinking about her.

He reached over and picked up a newspaper a previous passenger had wedged into the side of his seat. He scanned the pages, his mind not taking anything in.

It was then that he noticed it. Near the bottom of the page, between an article about immigration and an advert for a hearing aid, was a photo of him, headed by the words "Missing Man."

Bloody hell, he thought, *I'm in the papers!*

He read on.

"Last Saturday evening at around 8.30 p.m., Mr George Evans disappeared from his home. He is 64 years old with receding, grey hair. He was last seen wearing striped pyjamas, slippers, and a grey hat and coat. If you have seen this man or have any information on his whereabouts, please call this number."

George was dumbfounded. He was famous.

He looked around at the other occupants of the carriage, but nobody gave him a second look. *Typical*, he thought, *I'd love to be recognised.*

At the next station, the woman who had been sitting opposite him got off. Almost immediately, her seat was filled by two men who seemed to be too big to sit side by side.

One of them nodded in George's direction. 'Look, it's that nice man who bought us a drink earlier.'

'Did I?' asked a bewildered George.

'Yes, at that pub in Brighton.'

George vaguely remembered the two men at the bar. 'Oh yes, didn't you have woolly hats on?'

One man turned to the other. 'I don't know. Did you have one on?'

'I might have done. My head was cold.' The man felt in his coat pocket and pulled out a woolly hat. 'I did! Here it is.'

'Then I must have worn one as well.'

'Well, that's definitely us, then.'

George laughed at their silliness, settled back in his seat, and closed his eyes. He felt exhausted after his few days of extreme alcohol intake. Now that he knew he was on his way home, he felt a kind of relief that Pat could once again take over running his life – or was that *ruining* his life? He smiled at his own cleverness and drifted off to sleep.

An ear-piercing screech of metal awoke him, as the train changed tracks as it arrived at Victoria Station.

He was conscious of one of the men opposite looking directly at him. 'Where are you off to then?'

'I'm going home to my wife.'

'That's nice. Have you been married long?'

George beamed at them. 'Forever!'

They all laughed.

One man leaned forward and tapped George on the knee. 'When we get off, we are going for a few beers at a couple of excellent pubs. As you bought us a drink earlier, we would consider it our privilege to buy you one in return.'

George couldn't see any problem with that – in fact, he was enjoying the banter. 'I'll only accept a drink from you if I can buy you another one straight back,' he said, his face mock-serious.

The two men laughed again. 'You're on!'

George and his new buddies started their evening by enjoying a few beers at a pub near Victoria Station. The two men had introduced themselves as Duncan and Colin. They told George that they had been working down in Brighton but were now going back to their families in North London.

The pints went down quickly, and before long they were drinking shots.

'So, George, what made you go down to Brighton?' asked Duncan.

'I came into a bit of money, so I went to my favourite place to drink some of it.'

'Fair play. How did you come into money? Did a relative die or something?' Colin asked in a sympathetic tone.

'No, I won the lottery.'

'Really?'

'Well, I sort of won it – had to share it with some others.'

'Still, a share of three million isn't too bad, is it?'

'Not bad at all, George,' Colin replied, giving a low whistle. 'We wondered what you did for a living when we saw you in the pub buying everyone drinks. We thought you must be a millionaire or something.'

The two younger men looked at each other, then Duncan

picked up his whisky and downed it. 'Come on, George, drink up. There's a better pub around the corner.'

21

Harry was back on the Grafton farm. This time he was in black from head to toe and had smeared shoe polish on his face. A beanie-style hat pulled down over his forehead made him unrecognisable – and covered his bandages.

Harry was aware that this might not be one of his cleverest ideas. He knew he was risking his job, but he was determined that the Grafton family should somehow pay for what they had done to his friend. The Graftons had always had a reputation for being slippery and untouchable, so he needed something, anything, that would enable an official search to take place.

It was half past midnight. Dense cloud had obscured the moon, making it easier for him to fade into the shadows. He had cut across the fields to the farm and was moving past the back of the house, hoping that the dogs he had heard barking on his previous visit wouldn't raise the alarm.

He saw light through the chinks in the curtains and thought someone might still be up. He peered through the gap, but could only see an empty lounge. He pulled away, feeling more like a peeping Tom than James Bond, and silently made his way across the garden.

Harry looked into the various outbuildings adjacent to the main house. The light from his torch revealed nothing of any significance, so he turned his attention to the collection of old vehicles that lay around in various stages of disrepair. Four of the scrapped cars were side by side, almost as if a race was about to start. Harry concentrated his efforts on the two that were covered with tarpaulins. From his belt, he pulled out a long screwdriver and worked on the boot of one of the cars. The lock swiftly gave way, allowing the boot to swing open with a sudden grinding sound.

He caught the lid and held his breath. Luckily nothing stirred, except for an interested cat which nearly gave him a heart attack as it twined around his legs.

'Piss off!' Harry hissed, and the animal stalked off, tail in the air.

He pulled out his torch and examined the contents of the boot. It was empty apart from a roll of cable and some old tools.

Harry closed the lid carefully, waited for a minute, then set to work on the boot of the next car.

This time, he had more luck. Inside there was a long, tent-style bag. He pulled it out. It contained two shotguns wrapped in a bin liner. Harry couldn't believe his luck. This at least gave him and his colleagues an excuse to make an official search of the Graftons' house. He replaced the guns and quietly closed the boot.

He heard a car engine and froze. He peered over the top of the scrapped car and could see twin pinpricks of light become larger as a vehicle came up the long drive. It stopped under a carport next to the house.

Harry ran over to a nearby hay barn, where he stopped and looked back towards the house. He could hear car doors opening and closing, and the sound of excited dogs, who must have been in the vehicle.

He sat on a hay bale and waited for them to go inside so he could leave. Finally, he heard what sounded like the front door of the house being closed. He relaxed. He moved around the barn, shining his torch.

I'm wasting my time here, he thought, picking up and examining a broken pitchfork.

Suddenly a blast of light shone into his eyes. 'Stay exactly where you are!'

Harry stood still. The man with the torch approached him slowly. 'Don't make a fucking move.'

At first, Harry couldn't make out who it was because of the powerful beam. He didn't know if the man had a gun or any other weapon.

'Barry, what's going on?' shouted a woman's voice in the distance.

'Fucking stay back, Mum. I've caught someone – get Dad here now!'

The man with the torch – who Harry now knew to be Barry Grafton – turned in the direction his mother's voice had come from, his torch wavering just enough for Harry to leap out of sight behind the stacked bales of hay. He knew he had to move fast before anyone else came. He ran behind the bales almost full circle, so he was just behind Barry, who was now shouting for help at the top of his voice, the beam of his torch all over the barn.

Harry swung the pitchfork at Grafton, catching him on the side of his head. As he slumped forward, Harry caught him with another whack to the back of his knees. *That's for Will.*

Grafton's torch flew through the air, burying itself in a mound of straw, and there was a soft thud as something else hit the ground and bounced near Harry. In the semi-darkness, he could make out the outline of a handgun. He grabbed it, stuffed it into his belt, then quickly made his escape.

By the time Harry got home, his thumping heart had slowed down to a beat that was nearly normal.

He placed the gun on the table and looked it over. It was a Glock – a popular handgun used by the armed forces and various police departments. What were the Graftons going to use it for?

He peeled off his latex gloves and opened a can of beer. He drank thirstily, then went into his bathroom and looked in the mirror. The mixture of sweat and shoe polish had made a bizarre marble pattern on his skin. He took off his beanie and looked with dismay at the black and grey streaks on his recently replaced bandages. Shit, that could give him away.

He started scrubbing at his face. When all the black grime had finally been flushed down the sink, he looked in the mirror again.

Harry, you are an idiot. During tonight's illegal search, you could have gotten yourself killed without witnesses or backup. In addition, you took Barry Grafton's gun. How are you going to explain that without revealing your illegal night-time search?

He reached into the mirrored cabinet above the sink, took out a reel of white bandage, then carefully wound it around the existing bandages on his head. He didn't have any gauze or ointments, so this was the best he could do.

When he was finished, he studied the result in the mirror. It wasn't too bad. The bandages were now much thicker around his head, almost turban-like, but at least they were clean and white. He hoped that nobody would notice any difference.

He then made a couple of phone calls.

A few short hours later, a horde of uniformed police stormed the Graftons' house and grounds where they found the shotguns in the car boot. The family members were taken away on suspicion of firearms possession.

Harry had a quick nap and then made his way back to the Graftons' house, this time, in his official capacity, and looking very different from a few hours earlier.

He'd had an idea about what to do with the gun. He wandered into the same hay barn where he had been the night before. Three uniformed officers were sharing a joke. Recognising Harry, they straightened, the smiles disappearing from their faces.

'Good morning, sir,' greeted one of the constables.

'Has this barn been searched yet?' Harry asked brusquely.

'No sir, we're just about to.'

'Make sure you search it thoroughly, Constable, even if you have to move every last piece of straw. I want to be personally briefed on anything that you might find.'

'Yes, sir.'

Around forty minutes later, Harry was approached by the same constable.

'You must have had a premonition, sir.'

'Why is that, Constable?'

'We've found a handgun, sir. A Glock.'

'Is that right? Well done, Constable. Good find!'

'Thank you, sir.' The constable went off, looking pleased with himself.

Harry justified his actions to himself because Barry Grafton had the gun in his possession in the first place; Harry had just returned it to where he'd found it.

Barry Grafton had been taken away by ambulance earlier with concussion and a leg injury. He had told police that he had been attacked by at least two men, but he didn't see them as they had attacked him from behind.

The ambulance brought Grafton to the same hospital as

Will Kidman. On hearing this, Will laughed, and said a quiet, 'Well done, Harry.'

They found the baseball bats they had used on Will at the back of a wardrobe. Both weapons had traces of dried blood and hair, which matched Will's, and fingerprints, which belonged to Barry and his father Ron. This came as a surprise to Harry. He'd have bet on James being the second assailant.

Apart from the baseball bats and guns, there appeared to be little to find at the Graftons' house. They found some weed in James's bedroom, but not enough to charge him with.

'There's something else here,' Harry said to Sandy, who was helping with the search.

'Why are you so sure?'

Harry shook his head. He didn't have an answer, just a feeling. The officers had swarmed all over the house and the outbuildings and had examined the surrounding land, but apart from the weapons there appeared to be nothing else. Harry and Sandy had checked the roof space – not an easy task thanks to the amount of junk that had accumulated throughout the years – but had found nothing. They came back down the loft ladder, covered in dust and dirt.

'What next?' Sandy asked, brushing himself down and spitting out a bit of cobweb.

'We keep searching.' Harry stopped a passing constable. 'Where's the cellar?'

'It's through that door. We've already checked, sir. There's nothing down there.'

'Thank you, Constable.' Harry turned to Sandy. 'We'll look again, just in case.'

Steep, stone steps led down to the cellar. At the foot of the steps was another door that had been partially eaten away by rodents and time. The grey wood was so rotten that a good shove would have probably reduced the door to dust.

They searched the cellar, their efforts lit by a bare bulb that dangled from the low ceiling, casting angular shadows.

Harry used the torch on his phone to get more light – and then saw something. It looked like an old, wooden frame that had been propped up against the wall.

'Give me a hand with this,' Harry said, grabbing hold of the frame.

They moved it to one side to reveal what looked like a hatchway set into the stone. Harry pushed the hatchway open, causing a chunk of rotting wood to come away in his hands. The opening was narrow, just wide enough for Harry to get his head through.

'Good God.'

'What is it?' Sandy asked.

'I think we're going to need some more light in here.'

'What can you see?' Sandy asked impatiently.

Harry pulled back and motioned for Sandy to take a look. Through the aperture was a cellar about six foot square. In the centre was a mound of earth, at the head of which were two wooden sticks formed into a cross.

'Bloody hell, guv. It looks like a grave,' Sandy said.

22

George woke up with a pounding head.

He was on a bed in a room that was barely furnished. Hung over the back of a chair was a threadbare, grey towel. A tatty, old Welsh dresser skulked against a faded wall.

Where the hell was he?

Why had he drunk so much? He groaned as memories of the previous night started to seep through his throbbing brain.

As well as drinking all evening, they'd been dancing with some women. George never danced, not even when drunk. Apart from that time, years ago, when he'd dressed as a ballerina.

He vaguely remembered downing shots at some bar, together with enough beer to sink a battleship. There had been a drinking competition where the barmaid rewarded the winner with a kiss and yet another drink.

Oh yes, there had also been those tequila slammers, followed by something green and blue.

He needed to pee. He blearily noticed a door that he hoped would lead to a toilet and started to slide off the bed.

To his shock, he couldn't move.

His hands were bound to the iron frame of the bed. He realised he was wearing nothing except for a pair of boxer shorts and his vest.

'Whoa, steady there, George.'

George looked in the direction of the voice. Duncan was sitting in a battered armchair staring at George, a strange look on his face.

'What's going on?' George asked, a tingle of fear starting to creep through his befuddled brain. 'Have I upset you somehow? Why am I tied to this bed?'

'No, you haven't upset us, George. It's as simple as this, me old mate. You have money, lots of it, and instead of buying us drinks we thought you'd like to share some of it. We don't intend to harm you, but if you cause us any problems, then...' He left the sentence hanging.

George groaned. This was like something out of a bad film, except it was really happening. 'You can't be serious.'

'We would like the number for your bank card. If you're a good boy, then we'll all have a nice time and nobody will get hurt.' Duncan smiled, almost looking like a benevolent uncle.

'Where am I?'

'You're in a room above a pub, Georgie boy, owned by my cousin. It's a busy London boozer, so you can shout as loud as you want. No one's going to hear you.' Duncan's face went serious again. 'The pin number now, George, if you don't mind.'

23

The cellar was unrecognisable from when Harry and Sandy had discovered the grave.

A power supply had been set up and bright halogen lights illuminated the jagged, grey walls. A plastic material covered the floor, which was mainly comprised of broken flagstones and earth. Some old bricks had been removed between the cellar and the little antechamber to allow proper access. The forensic team, dressed in their white disposables, were applying chemical tests, carefully scooping away the earth and placing it into a container so that it could be analysed at a later date if required.

There could be the bones of a beloved pet buried here, or cash hidden from a heist. Or there could be nothing. The grave was far too small to contain an adult.

Harry was taking in the scene when he was approached by a member of the white-suited forensics team.

Harry wasn't sure who it was until the white hood was pushed back, and the mask removed.

'Rosko, how's it going?'

'Harry, you're going to want to see this.'

Rosko led the way back to the cellar and then extended an arm towards his team, who were moving an old, wooden box from the antechamber.

'Perhaps this may be another mystery for you.'

They placed the box carefully on the ground. The lid had already been opened, so Harry could view the contents. At the bottom of the box, there was a bed of straw upon which were a cluster of small bones.

'What was it?' Harry asked. 'A dog or cat?'

'It's a baby,' Rosko replied. 'Or should I say was? The bones are very old.'

'Any signs of dismemberment or foul play of any kind?' Harry asked immediately.

'Not at first glance,' Rosko replied. 'If I had to make an assumption, I would suggest that because the bones are so small, this might be a stillbirth.'

'You're telling me that someone had a stillborn baby and hid it down here?'

Rosko nodded. 'That would be my guess.'

'But why?'

'That's for you to find out, Harry. It's above my pay grade.'

Harry looked over at the antechamber. 'Could anything else have been hidden in that same grave – perhaps under the box?'

Rosko shook his head. 'No, we checked. There's nothing else.'

A couple of minutes later, Harry was on the phone checking to see if a birth or a stillbirth had been registered at the Graftons' address.

Meanwhile, Inspector Liz Mainwaring had arrived at the Graftons' property. She had been told that that the media would be present, so she was there to field any questions. However, on her arrival, the only reporter present was Ralph Masters, who had apparently worked for the News of the

World as a clerk until its closure. He was now covering sports and community incidents for the local rag.

'Detective Chief Inspector, what can you tell us about this child's body that has been discovered?'

'At this stage, we are keeping all options open.'

'Could it be a murder?' Ralph asked, an expectant look on his face.

'We are currently looking at all possibilities and ruling nothing out.'

'Thanks,' said Ralph, scratching his head, clearly wondering what he was going to write. However, when he saw a wooden box being carefully carried to a waiting vehicle with blacked-out windows, he ran across to ensure that he at least got a picture.

The next day, a huge photo of the box took up most of the front page of the local paper, with the headline, "Child's Body Found at Farm!" The fact that these were actually the remains of a baby, rather than a child, didn't seem important, as far as the newspaper was concerned.

Another day later, the picture was bought by an agency and used by a couple of the big nationals. More press reporters descended on the area and discovered that there was no real story, so they decided to lump the discovery in with the two unsolved murders, giving rise to headlines such as: "Bodies piling up – police resources stretched to the limit!" and "Can police cope? Multiple deaths, no arrests!"

This is going to be like a nightmare for the DCI, Harry thought.

Word had it that Liz Mainwaring had never enjoyed raising her head above the parapet, but now she had to indulge both the paparazzi and also her bosses who, because of this publicity, would obviously now want in-depth daily information from her, together with swifter action and results. As a result, no one would have blamed her if she was feeling a little stressed.

Harry Black had been summoned to her office for an update. 'So where exactly are we with everything?' She looked at Harry enquiringly, glasses perched at the end of her nose.

'You already have my report.'

'Yes, but I want to hear from you directly. There are still two unsolved murders, and my boss wants to know what progress is being made.' She cupped her hands under her chin and waited for Harry to speak. It gave her a girlish quality, Harry thought.

'Our main task is to identify and catch the person or persons that committed the murders of Paul Hamilton and Kevin Stock.'

'Yes, yes,' she said impatiently. 'I know this already.'

'Both of their wives had a motive, in that their husbands had affairs, but both wives have an alibi for the period when their respective husbands were murdered.'

'Right. Now what about this Herg thing?'

'The Herg thing? It might be a red herring, but I don't think so. I believe that the murderer is trying to tell us something or send us a message. What or why, we don't know yet.'

'So, what's next?' Mainwaring asked, fixing Harry with a cool stare.

'I plan to focus on the two wives for the time being, and to look at all prospective purchasers of the house where the first murder took place.'

'Well, that sounds reasonable. Can we inject some urgency into this investigation? My bosses are demanding daily updates at the moment and, frankly, I have little to give them.'

'As much as we can, ma'am.'

'Well, carry on, Inspector. Don't let me keep you.'

'Thank you, ma'am.' Harry got up and went to the door.

'Oh, Inspector...'

Harry looked back at her.

'It looks like DI Kidman will be off work recovering from his injuries for a while.'

'So I understand, ma'am.'

'I've arranged some assistance for you.'

'Assistance? No need. I can watch over DI Kidman's case-load and his team, no problem.'

'I have no doubt, but we need all the help we can get, especially since we have the press to deal with – and extra pressure from above. Alex Jackson will arrive tomorrow morning from Scotland.'

'Would you like me to show him around?' Harry asked.

'It's a "she," Inspector.'

Harry sighed. He'd done it again. The last thing he wanted was to appear sexist, but the problem was the force had always been male-dominated, so it was an easy trap to fall into.

'Sorry, ma'am. I just thought that with the name Alex... Anyway, would you like me to show her the ropes?'

'That's the idea.'

'Why bring someone in from Scotland?' he asked.

'Lots of reasons.' She stood up. 'Cross-fertilisation of ideas, Inspector. Our Scots colleagues have had a number of successes with various initiatives such as knife crime, so we thought it would look good for us to use someone from across the border.'

Ah, there it is, thought Harry. *It would look good. She never seems to waste a chance to shine politically.*

'Ma'am, surely the Scottish police have no jurisdiction down here?'

'That's correct. Alex Jackson will be here in an advisory

capacity, with a view to perhaps transferring later on, depending on how things go.'

'How things go?'

'All you need to know is that she's had a tough time in recent months. I'll let her tell you her own story – if she wishes.'

As Harry left the office, he wasn't one hundred percent sure, but he felt that Mainwaring was warming slightly towards him.

24

George was feeling distressed. It had all gone wrong, and it was his fault, he decided. He was being punished by God for being greedy and selfish and wanting to enjoy himself to the exclusion of his wife.

What must Pat be thinking? She must be beside herself with worry.

He looked down and examined the ropes that bound his wrists to the iron bedstead. There must be a way of escaping.

Duncan and Colin suddenly returned with a bottle of water and a pack of sandwiches, which they placed on a china plate. 'Here you are, Georgie boy, lunch is served.'

George couldn't possibly have eaten anything. His stomach felt as if it was full of concrete. However, he was thirsty, and tried to grab the bottle, but the rope held him back.

'Now, now, George, manners! What do you say?'

'Please may I have some water?' George asked.

'I don't know,' Duncan said. 'What do you think? Has he been a good boy?'

'He's been a very good boy,' Colin replied, waving George's bank card around. 'It's just a pity we can only withdraw three hundred pounds in one day.'

George saw an opportunity. 'If you let me go, I'll transfer a load of money to your bank account.' The proposal sounded naive even to his own ears.

The two men laughed. 'Sure, you will, Georgie boy. Of course you will!'

'But if you're only taking out three hundred pounds a day, I'll be here forever.'

'Yes, well over a year, in fact,' Colin laughed. 'But that's not the plan.'

Duncan untied George's hands so he could drink. He rubbed them briskly to get some feeling back. 'What do you mean, not the plan? What are you going to do with me?'

'With you? Nothing. Your wife, however...'

'My wife! What's she got to do with it?' George tried to get off the bed.

'Easy now, George, easy.' Duncan put a restraining arm on his shoulders. 'George, you see, we're not stupid. As soon as they discover that you're missing, they are going to use various means to find you. They'd probably track you by using the signal from a mobile phone, but as you haven't got one, I reckon their only option is to track you by withdrawals from the cash machine.'

George groaned inwardly. He had already thought of this and had seen it as a potential saviour.

Duncan put his hand in his trouser pocket and pulled out a wad of notes. 'So this will be our last withdrawal from the cashpoint. Tomorrow we will contact your wife, who will be pleased to pay for your return. At least, I hope so, for your sake.'

George, while beside himself with worry that they were

planning to involve his wife, suddenly realised that neither of these men were particularly bright, and somehow or other, there may be a way out for him. All he had to do was work it out.

25

Harry knocked on Will's office door. It felt weird, almost as if he were calling on a stranger.

'Come in.'

The female voice had a pleasant Scottish lilt to it. Harry pushed open the door and greeted the person who was sitting in Will Kidman's seat.

'Alex Jackson?'

'Ah yes, you must be the famous Harry Black.'

'Famous?'

'That case in America? We all heard about it – great bit of work.'

'Thank you. It's a pleasure to meet you,' Harry said warmly.

Alex Jackson had short, brown hair and attractive features. She wore a hint of mascara that accentuated her sea-green eyes. 'Your chief said that you'd be showing me around,' she said.

'It'll be my greatest pleasure to show you the delights of North London and the Home Counties...'

'Is this the English version of sarcasm?' Alex asked.

'No, there'll be plenty of that later.'

She laughed and stood up. 'Have you got time to give me a quick tour now, or shall I hang on?'

'No, now is good.'

Harry showed Alex around the station and introduced her to the team. They later found themselves having coffee and fruit cake in the police cafeteria, which they had to themselves. Crockery and cutlery were being cleared away after the lunchtime service.

'What made you want to come down here?' Harry asked, scooping the last crumbs from his plate.

'I guess the top brass thought I looked as if I needed a holiday,' Alex answered, looking impishly at Harry.

'All right, you don't have to tell me if you don't want to,' he said with a grin.

'I don't mind telling you. I suppose you could find out anyway with a quick phone call to Galashiels.'

'Find out what?' Harry asked, intrigued.

'I'll tell you later, if you don't mind. I will not spill any beans about my murky past within the first half hour of meeting you,' she said. 'I'll wait until we've known each other at least an afternoon.'

Harry laughed. 'Fair enough, I suppose. Anyway, I ought to bring you up to speed with everything that's been going on down here.'

They went to his office where he updated her with the recent events – the murders, the missing man, and the situation with the Graftons, leaving out his clandestine visit.

'Who gave you the tip-off about the guns being at the Graftons' house?' Alex asked.

Harry was impressed. Not even the DCI had asked him that – not that she would have got an honest answer.

'It was anonymous.'

'Of course,' she replied.

Harry couldn't tell if she believed him or not, but carried on telling her about the discovery of the grave in the Graftons' cellar.

'And where are the Graftons now?' she asked

'We're questioning them,' replied Harry. 'We have enough to charge Ron Grafton and his son Barry because their prints are on the baseball bats, but we can't really keep the rest of the family locked up just because an old grave was found in their cellar.'

'And what about this missing man, George Evans? Have you tried to locate him by his phone signal?'

'No. Unfortunately he left his phone at home.'

'Did he use it before he vanished?'

Harry winced. 'I didn't follow that one up. Well done.'

Alex smiled. 'Well, there's my contribution to the English police team. I can return to Scotland now with my head held high.'

'No, you can't,' Harry said. 'You've got a couple of murders to help solve yet.'

'Oh, that'll take me another five minutes at least.'

Harry laughed. He decided that he was enjoying having Alex around; she was funny and very astute. She was attractive too, Harry thought, like a younger version of Annie Lennox. Not normally his type, but what *was* his type? That woman on the plane hadn't been his type either, but he'd fancied her nonetheless.

'Is there anything else you'd like to see, or know more about?'

'No thanks, Harry, not for the moment. Although...' She pointed to the two folders on Harry's desk that related to the two murder victims. 'Can I borrow these? They'll give me some night time reading in my hotel room. Talking of which, I'd better find out where I'm staying and organise a car.'

'Don't worry,' Harry said. 'I'll arrange a fleet car for you for tomorrow. In the meantime, when you're ready, I'll drop you off at your hotel.'

They arrived at the lodge-style accommodation, which was cheap and cheerful – and not particularly well managed, judging by the sticky remnants of old Christmas decorations along the tops of the glass doors and windows.

'Budget constraints are in force down here,' apologised Harry. 'I'll see if there's anything else around if this is too dismal for you.'

'Don't worry. We have exactly the same cost issues at home – everything has been cut to the bone. At least this one has a bar, *and* there's a pub next door. Actually, I can feel a glass of wine coming on. Would you like a drink?'

More than you'll ever know, thought Harry wistfully. Booze and work seemed to sum up his existence in recent times. 'I won't tonight, if you don't mind, but I'll take a rain check – whatever the hell a rain check is.'

'See you tomorrow, then.'

Harry drove home, for once not enjoying the prospect of his lonely flat; he wished he had stayed for a drink with Alex. *I've only known her for five minutes, but I already know that she's going to be an asset*, he thought, immediately feeling a stab of disloyalty to Will.

Harry had been to see Will most days. In fact, most of the nurses now recognised him. One jokingly asked if he would like some permanent accommodation at the hospital.

Because Will's hands were still bandaged, the nurses had to assist him with some day-to-day requirements such as feeding and helping him to dress.

'Your Angela will never do a better job than those nurses when you leave here,' Harry had joked one day.

'She will in one department,' Will had returned with a straight face, and then smirked like a naughty schoolboy.

Harry arrived home, still thinking about Alex. He could see the enticing down-lighters of the local pub beckoning to him in the distance.

He resisted the temptation to extend the evening and went indoors to bed instead.

26

The next morning, Alex found Harry at his laptop, tapping busily.

'You're early,' she said.

'You know what they say about the early bird and all that. There's a lot happened that we haven't yet got a handle on, and it's all getting a little frustrating. It doesn't help that the media are asking questions about the unsolved killings, and there are rumblings from upstairs.'

Alex put the folders she had borrowed the night before on his desk. 'I've looked through these,' she said. 'You've been thorough, but what about the rope that was used to strangle the victims?'

'It's been identified as jute. It's quite common. You can easily get it online.'

'Yes, I saw that. I mean, were there any traces of acids that could have come from the murderer's skin? I appreciate that the killer must have worn gloves at the time of the murder, but maybe when they cut the rope in preparation, they may have used their bare hands, in which case there could be traces of DNA.'

'The rope is being analysed, but don't forget you might also have the DNA of the person who sold it to the killer, not to mention the DNA of the person who originally cut the rope to length, plus anyone else.'

'Yes, I suppose you're right,' Alex said. 'Okay, so what about the victims' phones? The report states that in both cases the victims made calls to numbers that now no longer exist.'

'That's right,' said Harry. 'It looks as though burner phones were used in both cases. In Kevin Stock's murder, there was a card lying near the body. On it was written the name "Sam" together with a phone number. Stock had called that number a few days earlier. Unfortunately, that number is also discontinued.'

'Were there any fingerprints?'

'Yes, belonging to an Amos Carling, the guy who discovered Kevin Stock's body,' Harry said, wincing at the memory.

'Kevin Stock must have been given the card at some stage. So he either met or knew the killer, or met someone else who knew the killer.'

'That's right, but it's an impossible task,' Harry said. 'You'd have to establish Kevin Stock's whereabouts for all the weeks leading up to the murder, then get video footage of all the people he met during that time.'

'Okay, so what can I do to help? There's no point in you having Scotland's finest at your disposal, then not using me.'

Harry grinned. 'You can see where we are on the George Evans case – you know, the missing man. You had the bright idea about checking the last phone calls he made from his mobile. In the meantime, I'm going to see Hilda Grafton to see if I can get more on the shotguns that were found, and also there is the small matter of the old grave.'

'Have they released her?'

'Yes, there wasn't enough to keep her. James will be

released as well, although I'm told he won't be out until a bit later. I want to get her on her own. I'll take Sergeant Koorus with me.'

When Harry and Dawn arrived at the Graftons' house, the door was wide open. They called out, but received no response.

They went in and looked at the surrounding destruction. Carpets had been ripped up to allow access to the floor-boards underneath. Bits of plaster had fallen from the ceiling where searches had taken place under the floors above. Contents were spilled from cupboards. Even a radiator had been yanked from the wall, spilling its dirty residue on the floor. The team had done a good job searching, but the effect was one of devastation.

In the middle of this was Hilda Grafton, a diminutive figure surrounded by mayhem.

'Who's going to put this right?' she cried out.

If the officers had any sympathy, they didn't show it. 'That's the consequence of keeping illegal weapons on your premises, Mrs Grafton.'

'Fuck you. What do you want?' she asked.

'Just a quick chat,' Harry said. 'We'll be gone before you know it.'

'Yeah, right. Once you lot get your claws in, you don't let go.'

'Let me make you a nice cup of tea,' Dawn said.

'Fuck the tea,' Hilda Grafton said. 'Just say what you've got to say and then piss off.'

'All right then.' Harry found a clean spot on the sofa and sat down. 'Tell me why shotguns and a Glock pistol were found on your property.'

'They already asked me all this at the station. I told them I know nothing about them.'

'I don't believe you. Your husband Ron knows exactly what the guns have been used for.'

'My Ronnie wouldn't have said anything to anyone,' Hilda replied, misinterpreting what Harry had actually said. 'He's old-school.'

'So, you're suggesting that he's too clever,' said Harry.

'That's right.'

'If he, or in fact your boys, are that bright, why didn't they clean their fingerprints off of the baseball bats, Mrs Grafton? If they had, the chances are that they'd be home right now, because we wouldn't have anything on any of you.'

Hilda Grafton opened her mouth to say something and then thought better of it.

Harry went on. 'As it is, we have to believe that either a crime has been committed with those guns, or they're about to be used. Which is it?'

Hilda Grafton's face, which had been tired and drawn, flushed. 'I don't have to answer any more questions.'

'No, you don't legally. But think about this, your husband and your son Barry are being held on attempted murder charges. Whether you like it or not, they will go to prison, probably for some time. Eddie is dead, which just leaves James. If he is linked to those shotguns, or the baseball bats, then he could also be put away, which would leave you living on your own.'

Harry paused and looked directly at her. 'This is assuming that you are not involved in any way, otherwise you could be in prison too, leaving your house and all of its cherished memories to the mercy of squatters.'

Dawn was looking sideways at Harry, open-mouthed.

'Mrs Grafton, all I want you to do is tell me about those guns. Then, depending on your involvement, you can carry on with your life. We won't bother James anymore and the pair of you can continue with your lives.'

Harry stood up.

'A mother's first duty, Mrs Grafton, is to protect her children. Isn't it about time you started to protect yours? After all, you couldn't protect the one that we found downstairs in your cellar.'

27

'How the hell did you know?' asked Dawn as they drove back to Farrow Road.

Harry hadn't known. Call it a policeman's instinct. Call it anything – whatever it was, it had paid off. His statement to Hilda had absolutely floored the woman. She had stood there, unable to speak for a while, but when she did, the words had tumbled out, as had the tears.

It turned out that the rumours had been true. Yes, she had an affair with a local farmer, Graham Hopkin. Ron Grafton had found out and gone to "sort it out," which had resulted in Hopkin being found dead in his field. Although it had looked like a farming accident, the police had been involved and had been suspicious. After all, how do you get mowed down by your own farm vehicle? However, farm accidents happen all the time and the police closed off the investigation.

Ron Grafton had been questioned only because he had been seen in the vicinity of the Hopkin farm, but that had been the end of it.

Even though this had taken place some thirty-odd years ago, there was still a record of the event in the police archives.

There was also a picture of Graham Hopkin, who looked quite a distinguished character, with red hair, a red moustache, and wide, blue eyes. Just like James Grafton.

Harry Black had done some research before he and Dawn came to visit Hilda Grafton but had taken a chance when he mentioned the grave in the cellar.

Even he was unprepared for the emotional outburst that came pouring from Hilda Grafton.

'Yes, that is my baby,' she had said, her voice trembling.

'Tell me everything that happened.'

Hilda Grafton flopped into a chair and the complete story had come tumbling out. She'd had a long-term affair with Graham Hopkin, which resulted in a pregnancy, and baby James arrived. Ron had no reason other than to assume that it was his, although he wondered slightly why his first-born looked so different from the rest of the Grafton family, who were dark-haired. That Hilda had auburn tinges in her hair and that her father had blue eyes probably eased any suspicion.

Then Hilda fell pregnant again. Ron was overjoyed, but in true family tradition, they kept the news to themselves. The Graftons had their roots in Bulgaria, where some considered it bad luck to announce the arrival of a baby until it was nearly due.

So, it was with equal degrees of surprise and suspicion that Ron Grafton was asked a question by the landlord of his local pub. 'How's the missus then? I hear she hasn't got long to go.'

'What do you mean?'

'I mean the baby that's coming along soon.'

'How do you know she's pregnant?' Grafton had asked sharply.

Apparently the pub landlord looked like he could have cheerfully bitten off his own tongue. Faced with Grafton's intense stare, he had no alternative but to carry on. He told Grafton that he'd overheard two local farmers discussing the Graftons' impending arrival and had assumed it was common knowledge.

'Which two farmers?' Grafton had asked.

'Old man Jenkins and what's-his-name, Hopkin.'

'Graham Hopkin?'

'Yes, him.'

He'd ordered two large brandies, which he downed immediately, and then left the pub to confront Hopkin.

Years later, when Grafton finally told the whole story to Hilda, he admitted that he had stopped the car on the way to Hopkin's farm and had cried for the first time since he was a boy. He told her that he'd felt as though his guts had been wrenched out.

He left the car at the side of the lane and walked towards Hopkin's farm.

He could see Hopkin's combine harvester was being driven around his field, through a gap in the hedgerow. He observed Hopkin behind the wheel as he passed and felt an uncontrollable rage which suddenly gave way to an icy calm, as he realised what he had to do.

He walked onto the field and flagged the vehicle down, pointing to the ground as if there was an obstacle.

Hopkin halted the vehicle and climbed down, looking surprised to see Ron Grafton seemingly appear out of nowhere.

'Hello, Ron,' he had said. 'What brings you here?'

Grafton had looked at him for a few seconds and then said, 'You've been fucking my wife.'

Hopkin had tried to say something, but his face had told Grafton everything he wanted to know.

He had hit Hopkin several times, hard in the face. Hopkin had lain on the ground, his arms outstretched, pleading for

Grafton to stop. But Grafton, white-faced with fury, had then lashed out with his boots, kicking Hopkin repeatedly in the face until he was unconscious.

Something told Grafton that if he left things as they were, Hopkin would recover and still be a threat to his marriage. The police would inevitably get involved and Grafton could be imprisoned, leaving Hopkin to continue his relationship with Hilda. The thought snapped him into action. He pulled himself up into the combine harvester.

By the time Grafton left the field, it would have been impossible to knit all the pieces of Graham Hopkin together; the farm vehicle had done its worst.

When Grafton got back home, Hilda was hanging out washing in the garden. He noticed that her bump had increased in size, but he didn't feel paternal love. He felt rage.

'Leave that and come with me,' he demanded.

'I'm busy – can't it wait?'

'I'll give you busy, you bitch. Come here now!'

Even at that young age, Hilda was a tough cookie, but that didn't stop her trembling uncontrollably. She had a good idea what might be wrong, but she couldn't imagine what her husband was about to tell her.

He led the way into the house and pointed at an old, wood-framed leather seat. 'Sit.'

She perched on the chair, looking like a bird ready to flee. He told her everything he had done that day. Everything.

When he got to the part where he had murdered Graham Hopkin, she let out a noise that sounded like she was being strangled, and ran from the room.

Grafton started after her, then heard the toilet door being slammed, and the lock turned. He heard a window being opened, but didn't take any notice, until something prompted him to look outside.

There, in the field adjacent to their house, was Hilda, stumbling toward Hopkins' farm.

Grafton ran after her, easily catching up with her. By now, she was more staggering than running. Her hair was matted with perspiration and tears were cascading down her cheeks.

'Please don't kill me,' she pleaded, backing away from him. 'I just wanted to be happy.'

'I'm not going to kill you,' he said, realising what he had done and what he might lose.

They went back to the house in silence, Hilda still shaking. She went straight to the kitchen sink and was violently sick.

Afterwards, she washed her face with cold water and patted her skin dry. As she went to the kitchen to get a glass of water, she felt giddy, then fell to the floor.

Her baby was stillborn. He was tiny, with wisps of gingery hair. Hilda lay in bed watching her husband remove the little bundle. Right then, something seemed to die inside her.

There seemed no reason to tell the authorities about the baby's death, because nobody had officially known about Hilda's pregnancy.

Ron Grafton buried the baby in the cellar, then built a wall in front of it, using the old bricks that were lying around. He left an aperture so that Hilda could see the grave when she wished.

As far as the murder of Graham Hopkin was concerned, the police eventually put it down to accidental death. They were suspicious of Grafton and interviewed both Hilda and Ron, but the pair put on a united front.

The landlord and a couple of the pub regulars were also interviewed, but it's one thing enjoying a bit of local gossip, and quite another being involved in a murder enquiry. So apart from the occasional hushed whispers, nobody said anything, and the secret had remained a secret until now.

When Hilda had finished telling the story, her shoulders had slumped, and she was bent over in the chair as if she was reliving the experience.

Dawn had tried to imagine the burden that Hilda must have been carrying around and went over to her, putting an arm around her shoulder.

Hilda immediately pulled away. 'Get away from me, I don't need pity.'

Dawn backed off. 'I'm sorry, I just wanted to–'

'There's nothing that anyone can say or do to change anything,' Hilda said. 'I made my bed, I've had to lie in it, and that's that.'

28

'Well done, you,' Alex said to Harry. 'But what happens now?'

'Ron Grafton will be charged with the murder of Graham Hopkin, together with the assault or even the attempted murder of DI Kidman. They will probably charge Hilda Grafton with perverting the course of justice because she concealed the facts for so long, and they will both be charged with concealing the birth of a child. When Barry Grafton is released from hospital, he will also face charges of assault, or attempted murder.'

'Won't Hilda's confession help her in any way?' Alex asked.

'It's possible that the judge may decide that Hilda Grafton is treated with a degree of leniency after her admission of guilt and pointing the finger at her own husband.'

'Dawn Koorus was very impressed with you,' Alex said. 'She told me you were like Columbo and Poirot rolled into one when you were interviewing Hilda Grafton.'

'More like Inspector Clouseau,' Harry said. 'You know, it's incredible how the whole thing started. Have you ever heard of the butterfly effect? Where one small thing starts a chain of much larger events?'

Alex nodded.

'Well, that's what happened in this case. Had Eddie Grafton not kicked off in the restaurant that night, then the whole Grafton family would be at home happily watching television, not stuck in a hospital or a prison cell.'

'Talking of which, what's happening with James Grafton?'

'He was released a little while ago. His mother asked if we could arrange for her and James to meet as soon as possible. She wants to tell him about his real father.'

'Oh my God,' Alex said. 'Poor man! He's lost nearly all of his immediate family and is about to be told about the death of one he didn't even know about.'

There was a tap on the door. Dawn Koorus came in. 'How would you like an update on the Grafton case?'

'An update?' replied Harry. 'What more can there possibly be?'

'Hilda Grafton has made a further confession.' Dawn eyed the room like a magician about to explain how a trick works. 'Remember the two shotguns? She says that she'll do a deal that will implicate her husband and others in a post office raid that took place twenty years ago. She says that her husband bought the handgun more recently, but it hadn't been used.'

'Seriously?' said Harry. 'Did she say why they held onto the shotguns?'

'She didn't have an answer for that, so probably just stupidity. But it gets better.' Dawn went on, 'Remember the old car where the guns were found?'

'You are joking,' said Harry, already starting to smile. 'Surely it's not the same car that was used in the raid?'

'Bang on, guv.'

'What, they didn't dump it?'

'Looks that way.'

'Unbelievable.' Harry thumped the desk with his fist. 'Thank God for other people's stupidity. This has made my day. I'm going to take Will some grapes and share the good news. This will cheer him up no end.'

29

The manager of the hotel had advised Lucy that Mr and Mrs Smith had extended their booking of the room to three days, and had asked not to be disturbed under any circumstances.

'What? They don't want their room cleaned for three days?' she had exclaimed.

'Lucy, you must remember that the customer is always right,' he had replied, his finger wagging as if imparting great knowledge.

She later spoke to the concierge who knew everything about everyone. He had seen the woman come downstairs and ask to speak to the manager. When the manager had arrived, she had pushed some money into his hand and had explained that as they were on a religious fast, they couldn't be disturbed under any circumstances. The manager had accordingly instructed the staff to respect their wishes.

Despite knowing this, Lucy had a feeling that all was not well. Her roles in the hotel included room service, and when she was delivering room service orders, the Smith's room was always in darkness. There was never a strip of light under their door.

Lucy wasn't generally nosy, but one morning, she was cleaning the adjoining room and peered through the keyhole of the connecting door. She could tell that the curtains were open by the amount of light in that room, but there was nothing to be seen. No movement, nothing. The feeling that something was wrong inexplicably got worse, but she consoled herself with the thought that the couple were due to leave the following day.

At eleven the next morning, Lucy tapped on the door. Guests were supposed to check out by ten, so this was an hour later. There was no way that she could be told off by management. There was no reply, so she inserted her skeleton key and pushed the door inwards. She took two steps forward and stopped dead at the sight that confronted her.

Her screams were heard all over the hotel. The duty manager and a waiter came running up the stairs to see what was wrong and pushed into the room beside her. By this time, Lucy had stopped screaming, but her mouth still hung open in shock.

Mr Smith gaped hideously at her, with lifeless eyes staring out of a purple face. He looked as if he was standing up, but his body, which leant against the bathroom door, was being supported by a rope around his neck. The rope was hoisted over the top of the door and tied to the handle on the other side.

And there was blood. There was a gash on one side of his head. A dark red stain had spread over his collar and down the front of his shirt.

Lucy couldn't take in anything more. There was a loud clump as she fainted.

The duty manager pulled out his mobile. With shaking

hands, he dialled 999, before throwing up all over the hotel room carpet.

The police arrived minutes later. The first officer on the scene was nearly sick as well, especially with the smell of vomit that was already in the air, but he pulled himself together before radioing Control and getting an urgent message sent to DI Black.

Harry arrived to find that, despite the gruesome setting, the first officers on the scene had done exactly as they were expected to. The area, including the front of the hotel, had been taped off and officers were in the process of interviewing hotel workers.

What he hadn't expected was what lay before him. Not the body of Phillip Greening, although that was pretty horrendous, but a word on the wall which looked as though it had been drawn in blood with a finger: "Her."

Her? Harry mused. Was it supposed to have said Herg?

His thoughts were interrupted by the arrival of Rosko and his team, closely followed by Alex Jackson.

'Rosko, Alex, welcome to the murder mystery party.'

'Lovely,' Alex said, looking around the room. 'Very pretty. Surely the killer could have made it look even more gruesome.' She looked distastefully at the vomit on the floor.

'Would you two luvvies kindly come back later?' Rosko said politely. 'There's probably been enough contamination of evidence in here. If you've seen what you need to see for now, then please bugger off.'

'Fair enough,' Harry said, and they went downstairs to join their colleagues.

The staff had been separated so that one person's account of events didn't taint another's. How several people can see exactly the same scene but recollect a different version always perplexed Harry. There was even one staff member who was able to describe Mr Smith in detail, even though he had never seen him!

Harry and Alex spent a couple of hours assisting with the interviewing of the staff. Later, they found themselves hunched over a table at a café across the road from the hotel.

'This murder is different from the first two,' Harry said, unwrapping the little biscotti that had arrived with his coffee.

'In what way?'

'There's a slight change in direction. For example, they didn't use the rope to form a word, this time, but wrote on the wall instead. The victim was stood up, propped against the door. Why didn't they just leave him on the bed? That would have been a lot less hassle.'

'You said they – what makes you think that there was more than one involved in the murder?' Alex asked.

'The girl, Lucy, said that the couple who checked in were a thick-set man in his forties or later and a slim, attractive woman in her mid-thirties. Lucy didn't believe they were really married. If that's the case, and supposing that the woman was the killer, she couldn't have hoisted up Mr Smith with the rope on her own. She must have had an accomplice.'

'Or maybe it was the accomplice who did the murder, and the woman was an unwilling accessory.'

Harry nodded. 'Maybe. Anything is possible at this stage. It's unfortunate that there's no CCTV in the hotel corridors or the main entrance.'

'So we seem to be looking for a double act of some sort – maybe a couple?'

'It appears that way, although we can't be totally sure. The other thing is that word that was scrawled on the wall in blood. Her. Why Her and not Herg like the first victim?'

'Perhaps they were interrupted.'

Harry looked across the road at the hotel. The first reporters were just starting to gather. Harry recognised a few.

'My, your hacks are slow to get to the scene down here,' remarked Alex. 'Back home they would have arrived before the murder was even committed!'

'I'm sad to report that violent crime is getting a bit commonplace down here,' remarked Harry. 'Murder is not quite as newsworthy as it once was.'

Harry's phone rang. It was Rosko.

'What have you got?' Harry asked.

'It's about your Mr Smith. His name isn't Smith, surprise, surprise. His real name is Phillip Greening. According to a credit card receipt in his pocket, he was supposed to be staying at a different hotel. There were photos and other items found in his wallet that suggest that he has a wife and family.'

'And what are your early thoughts about the murder itself?' Harry asked.

'Plenty of thoughts but no actual evidence, unfortunately. However, between you, me, and the gate-post, I would put my mortgage on the fact that Phillip Greening was murdered on his first night at the hotel. There are early signs indicating that he was drugged, then strangled, like the others, but I'm guessing that during the process he must have woken up prematurely, which perhaps caused the killer to panic and knock him out, which would account for the gash on the side of his head.'

'Any idea what he was hit with?'

'A cosh, maybe? A blunt object of some sort. Whatever was used definitely wasn't in the room.'

'Okay. Thanks, Rosco. Keep me updated.'

Harry updated Alex on his telephone conversation.

Alex had been listening. 'It's got to be a weighty object to knock someone out,' she said. 'What do hotels have that are heavy enough? A vase, perhaps, or a small fire extinguisher?'

Harry's face lit up. 'I think I might know,' he said. 'Let's get back to the hotel.'

The Gaumont was still a hive of activity, but the wholesale panic had been replaced with an almost eerie calm. Harry found the head housekeeper, who obligingly unlocked the door to the bedroom where the murder had taken place. He then asked her to let him into the bedroom next door. She had reluctantly complied. 'I hope I don't get into any trouble over this.'

After a quick look in both rooms, Harry had a trace of smugness on his face.

'Come on, let's see if I'm right,' he said to Alex. 'If I'm wrong, I'll buy you dinner.'

Alex followed him outside, part of her wanting him to be wrong. They walked onto the grass at the side of the hotel and past shrubbery that had been pruned into spherical shapes.

'What are we looking for?'

'Have patience, Watson.'

'Who?'

'Watson. You know, Sherlock's... Ah, here we are.'

Harry had stopped by a flower bed. He reached in his pocket, pulled on a pair of disposable gloves, and bent down. When he stood up, he was holding two pieces of heavy china.

'What's that?' asked Alex.

'This, my dear Alex, is either going to turn out to be the murder weapon, or the weapon that knocked Greening out before he was killed. Or it's here because someone doesn't like china animals in their hotel room.' He put the two pieces together where they became an almost life-sized, black-and-white cat.

'They used to use ornaments like this as bookends – we had some when I was a kid. When I went into the bedroom where the murder happened, there was only one china cat on the mantelpiece, so I checked next door, and that room had two.'

'Well done, Sherlock,' said Alex. 'Let's hope there are fingerprints.'

'Let's hope indeed.'

30

Alex Jackson was enjoying her secondment down south in The Smoke. She felt she had seen more action in the last few days than she had done in the past year in Galashiels.

She entered her office and put her briefcase on the floor just in time to answer the phone. It was Control looking for DI Black. They had an important call for him.

'I'll take it,' she said. 'Inspector Jackson, can I help?'

'Hello, this is Dave at the Hop Poles in Brighton. It's about your missing man, George Evans. I assume that he's still missing?'

'Why do you ask?' Alex said.

'Because I've just read something on the internet that says the police are looking for him. The thing is, he left here a few days ago saying that he wanted to get back to his wife, so I don't understand why he should still be missing.'

'You'd better tell me more,' Alex said, pulling across a pad and grabbing a pen.

Dave told her about George's generosity to the other patrons of the pub. He said he thought George might be an eccentric millionaire who had lost his marbles until he had read the online article.

'When did you last see Mr Evans?'

'Saturday. There's something else. When he left here, I think he was being followed by two men.'

'Are you sure?'

'It was a lunchtime session – people don't normally knock back pints during the day, but these two did. Then they made a rush for the door straight after George left. I wondered what was happening, so I looked outside and saw that they had slowed down right behind him. They definitely looked like they were following George.'

'Can you tell me anything about the two men?'

Dave gave a rough description.

'Anything else?'

'No, not really.' Dave thought for a moment. 'They'd been in a couple of times before and I remember one of them asking how business was and telling me he had some interest in a pub in London. I think he mentioned it was near a railway station like Victoria, or somewhere like that.'

'Doesn't the train from Brighton end up at Victoria?' Alex asked, making notes on a desk pad.

'Yes, it does, and George definitely said that he was catching a train.'

Alex pressed Dave for as much detail as he could remember, but there was little more he could offer apart from a vague recollection of what George was wearing.

'Thanks again, Dave. I'll get someone to come and see you and take a formal statement.'

In the meantime, Harry had driven down to Horsham in Sussex. He had received a phone call from the nursing home saying that his mother was asking for him.

He didn't hesitate. His mother had never asked for him before, and so he had sped off towards West Sussex.

The sister was waiting for him by the front doors when he arrived.

'How is she?' he asked.

'Would you mind stepping into the office where we can talk?'

Harry, who was already concerned, became anxious. 'What is it, Sister?'

'I've tried to contact you – have you been in hospital or something?' The sister asked, staring up at Harry's bandages.

Harry was grateful for the potential excuse but didn't use it.

'It's been a busy time, and I was in America for a couple of months. This was just an injury at work,' he said, pointing at his head.

'Nevertheless, you only have *one* mother.' The reproach was calm and well-meant.

Harry could only nod.

His mother was nearly eighty and had been blessed with a sharp-witted intellect throughout her life.

After Harry's father had died some ten years earlier, she had led an industrious life, busying herself by helping others and getting involved in the local church and charitable events.

Her health had deteriorated in recent times, and she now could not look after herself properly.

'I'm afraid her dementia is getting worse,' the sister told Harry. 'It may get to a stage where she might not remember who you are. I'm just warning you. It can be upsetting when this happens.'

'I can imagine,' Harry said. 'Can I see her now?'

'Of course. If you need anything, let me know.'

His mother was seated on the edge of her bed. She greeted him with a huge smile, her blue eyes shining with delight.

He kissed her softly on both cheeks and pulled up a chair.

'Where's Maria?' she asked, looking around.

'Maria left a long time ago,' he said gently.

'Left for where?'

'She left for good, Mum.'

'That's sad.' She sat, looking through the window, watching the brown leaves being blown around the grass outside before magically forming themselves into piles. A further gust of wind pushed splashes of rain onto the window, temporarily obscuring the autumnal setting.

Harry watched with her. He wasn't sure what his mum could understand or take in, but he spoke softly of his childhood memories, his eyes distant and sad. Every so often, she turned her head and looked at him fondly.

31

George Evans rubbed his aching arm with his free hand. His captors, perhaps assuming George to be docile and too scared to even attempt to escape, had allowed him to have one arm free. They had also provided him with a pot to pee into, plastic bottles of water, and a plate of sandwiches and biscuits, all of which were accessible with his free hand.

Although fear had numbed George's brain, his intellect, although lazy at times, was currently working at full steam. He had made himself appear far more vulnerable to the men than he actually was, and he could feel that he was in a far better position to escape. But how exactly?

In a flash of inspiration, he saw a way. With his free hand, he grabbed the china plate that the sandwiches and biscuits were on, and tipped them onto the bed. He then swung the plate against the bedhead, smashing it into three pieces. Picking up the largest piece, he placed the broken edge of the plate against the rope that tied his other hand and started to saw, stopping every few seconds to listen for any sign of his captors returning.

At that moment, Colin and Duncan were in the vicinity of George's home. They were about to visit Pat, who was enjoying a cup of tea with her niece, DCI Liz Mainwaring.

Mainwaring was telling her aunt that she had put her best man on the case to find George, and it was just a matter of time before he was found, when there was a knock on the door.

'That'll be the window cleaner for his money,' Pat said, taking a twenty-pound note from under the clock where she kept a small emergency stash.

Liz Mainwaring took the opportunity to excuse herself and use the upstairs bathroom, where she then sat in quiet contemplation. *Bathrooms and toilets are great*, she thought. *No one can come in unannounced, so they're the best place in the house. No one can get to you.*

There was a pot of geraniums on the windowsill. As she washed her hands, she scooped some water into the pot to wet the dry soil. She smiled as she did so, and then caught herself. *Idiot – who smiles at plants?*

She unlocked the bathroom door, went out onto the landing, and froze.

She could hear a harsh male voice coming from downstairs, followed by her aunt's voice, which sounded shrill and anxious.

'I don't know what you're talking about! I'm telling you, you've kidnapped the wrong man. We haven't won any lottery! Do I look rich?' Pat was holding out the material from the comfortable, old cardigan she was wearing for them to inspect.

'Your husband's name is George, isn't it?' Colin asked.

Pat picked up a photo from the mantlepiece and showed it to them. 'Is this the man you've kidnapped?'

'That's him.'

'Well, that's my husband, and he definitely hasn't won the

lottery. You're not very good at this sort of thing, are you?' Pat said, peering at them disdainfully.

The men shuffled and looked at each other. Something had gone wrong.

'So, how much have you got?' Duncan asked.

'I don't know. My pension doesn't come in until next week.'

'Well, what have you got on you right now?'

Pat looked at the twenty-pound note that was still in her hand, then peered under the clock. She retrieved the remaining notes and thrust them at the men. 'There,' she said. 'There's forty-five quid there. Can I have my husband back now?'

'For forty-five quid?'

'Yes. That's all I've got.'

Colin and Duncan looked at each other again. Doubt was written across their faces.

'Mrs Evans, we're going to leave you now. If you breathe a word to anyone about our visit, we will hurt your husband. Badly.'

'Okay, I promise,' Pat said fervently.

Liz Mainwaring had heard enough. She tiptoed back to the bathroom, thanking her lucky stars that she had her handbag with her, which contained her phone. She sent a text message to the police control room – "Send help, we are being robbed," together with her aunt's address. As a backup, she dialled 999 and whispered, 'Police,' when prompted.

The operator at the other end said, 'I can't hear you very well. Would you mind speaking up?'

She hissed again, 'Police, dammit.'

She could hear further noises downstairs, so she threw the phone back into her handbag, went to the landing, and leaned over the bannister.

Duncan and Colin were by the front door, about to leave.

'Don't forget, Mrs Evans, if you say anything to the police, you'll never see George again.'

'I understand. You already have my word and–'

Her words were cut off by the sound of Mainwaring's police radio, which was in the pocket of her coat, hanging up next to the two men.

'All units, 38 Marlborough Terrace,' the voice crackled. 'Suspects still on site.'

Duncan and Colin jumped. Duncan rounded on Pat. 'What's that? How do they know about us?'

'My friend, who's a police officer, accidentally left his coat there,' Pat said. 'Perhaps they were listening in. You'd better go now. Quickly!'

From her position upstairs on the landing, Mainwaring mentally congratulated her aunt on her quick thinking. Then her own phone rang from her handbag. It was the control room reacting to her message.

Downstairs, the men had heard her phone ring. 'There's someone else in the house!' one of them exclaimed.

'Shit,' Mainwaring exclaimed under her breath. What should she do now? The men might come upstairs and investigate.

She went with her instinct. Attack was definitely better than defence.

She took a deep breath and hollered at the top of her voice, 'Okay, officers, get them. Now!' Then she loudly clomped down the stairs towards the two startled men shouting, 'Police! Do not run!'

The two men, flummoxed by this turn of events, did exactly that. They dashed through the open front door and took off down the street. Mainwaring ran after them. As she ran, a patrol car slowed down beside her.

'Everything all right, ma'am?'

She pointed ahead. 'Never mind about me. Get them!'

The patrol car sped forward, its lights flashing. Liz could see the two men in the distance. They had stopped and were both doubled over, holding their stomachs. When the police reached them, they seemed to accept their capture, and were driven away.

After making the necessary statements to her officers, Liz Mainwaring sank down on her aunt's settee, shaking with a mixture of adrenaline and triumph.

'Jesus Christ.'

'Well done, you,' Patricia said. 'I'm very impressed. I can now see why you're now a senior police officer.'

'Really? Thank you!' Mainwaring took this as a major compliment, especially from her aunt. In truth, she'd had an easy ride to get to her position as a DCI and her mettle had never really been tested. Now that it had, at least to some extent, she realised that she had actually enjoyed it.

'Well done yourself,' she said to her aunt. 'You were so cool-headed.'

'Do you think we deserve a drink?'

'Make it a huge one. All we have to do now is locate George. I have a feeling that those two little bastards will be only too willing to tell us everything.'

'I do hope he is okay,' her aunt said, fiddling anxiously with her beads.

BACK IN THE upstairs room at the pub, George had been busy sawing at the rope. He had just managed to cut himself free.

But there was no escape through the locked door and the only window was a skylight, which was much too high for him to reach, even if he stood on the chair.

George went to the Welsh dresser at the side of the room, grabbed a knife and fork, and set about using them to prise up a floorboard. His idea was to take up a few floorboards, then wait until darkness, when he could knock out the boarding under the flooring and drop onto the floor below. He didn't know how high the drop would be, but he was willing to take a chance.

George discovered that prising up the heavy oak boards armed only with cutlery was hard work, but he worked diligently into the evening, pausing every so often to wipe the sweat from his forehead. He kept listening out for the two men, who he was convinced would return soon. They had taken his trousers, leaving him only with his shirt and an ill-fitting pair of white underpants, which were now a filthy grey. Not that George cared what he looked like; he just desperately wanted to be out of this situation and back with his wife.

The first floorboard was the most difficult. If he could remove that one, he knew he'd have a better purchase on the second and third. He dug in with his makeshift tools and was rewarded as the bits of wood splintered away and the gap widened.

A couple of hours later, George sat back on his heels, exhausted but exhilarated. He'd managed to remove three floorboards. The gap was now just wide enough for him to squeeze through. He wiped his dirty hand across his sweaty forehead and waited until his breathing was normal and the beating in his chest had calmed down. Christ, he hadn't done this much manual labour for years.

He could hear a muffled announcement down below, followed by music.

He smiled to himself. A disco, or a party, perhaps. Brilliant – there would be lots of people. Surely no one would harm him in front of witnesses.

He put his bare foot through the gap he had created and

pushed on the boarding underneath. It felt rigid enough to take his weight.

He pushed against it again. Nothing. It didn't give. He stamped on it. Nothing.

He put his other foot on top of the boarding so that he was effectively standing on the ceiling of the room down below. It still felt firm enough. He jumped cautiously up and down a few times, thinking that whatever was underneath was never going to give.

And then, with a loud crack, the wooden batten holding the light fitting underneath gave way, taking the plaster ceiling down with it. George fell through, stopping abruptly as his upper body and arms got wedged between the joists of the floor. He gasped for breath. He couldn't move. He was trapped. Unable to see what was happening below him, all he could do was dangle, his feet in mid-air, and listen to the music which was now much louder.

On the floor below, nineteen-year-old Charlotte Hansen had her eyes closed as she danced to an old sixties track by The Four Tops. Her body swayed in time to the beat.

The DJ was lifting the crowd. 'All together now. Reach out, reach out...'

She did just that. She reached out, her bare arms high in the air.

'Reach out... Reach out.'

Suddenly, her fingers touched warm, hairy flesh.

She looked up and screamed. Suddenly, everyone was screaming, including the bar staff and the DJ, who abruptly cut the music.

In the middle of the room, dangling from the ceiling, surrounded by plaster, was the lower body of a man, whose underpants had fallen down around his ankles, exposing his aged genitalia, just inches away from Charlotte's face.

The floating disco and mirror lights only served to make the vision even more surreal in the now-silent room.

Just then, the doors burst open and half a dozen police officers rushed in. They stopped abruptly, joining the shaken revellers, who were staring at the dangling body.

Behind them was Detective Inspector Harry Black. He looked up towards the ceiling with amusement.

'Mr Evans, I presume?'

32

'Unbelievable.'

Harry and Alex sat in the lounge area at her hotel. The barman was behind the counter, his attention on his phone.

'Unbelievable,' Alex said again. 'You put in man hours and effort to find George Evans's abductors, and the whole thing just falls into Mainwaring's lap.'

'You'll be saying "It's not fair" next...'

'But it isn't fair! Mainwaring's going to be even more impossible now. The word is, she caught them single-handed.'

'If she did, fair play to her.'

'You're too charitable. I've only been down here for five minutes and even I know that she's known as the Führer behind her back.'

Harry laughed and knocked back his pint. 'Another?'

She looked at her wineglass and made a face. 'Oh, go on then.'

He went to the bar where the barman was still engrossed

with his phone. He looked up at Harry and put it away with barely concealed impatience.

'Sorry to interrupt your enjoyment, but could we have the same again?' Harry asked.

'That's okay,' said the barman, without a trace of embarrassment. 'I had nearly finished watching the video, anyway.'

Harry shook his head in wonder. How had customer service become so unimportant?

He put the fresh drinks on the table and sat down opposite Alex. 'Okay, so tell me about your life in Scotland and why you left it.'

'Are you sure? Okay then. I'll just give you some of the highlights, although you can have some lowlights if you wish.'

'Go on,' Harry said, taking a sip of his pint.

'As you know, I was sent down here from Galashiels, but the reason was because I was being victimised by some of my colleagues.'

'Why?'

'I was seeing a fellow inspector at the same station. He got promoted and then ditched me. I was obviously too low a rank for him, because he then took up with the new head of Human Resources. Although I suspect that he had been seeing her at the same time as me.'

She took a sip of her wine and placed the glass back on the table.

'I was really pissed off, because we'd been quite serious about each other, and had started to make plans. But he had insisted we keep our relationship secret. He said that it would be bad for our careers to tell our colleagues.'

'We've got a couple of sergeants in a similar situation,' Harry said, thinking of Dawn and Sandy.

'Right. So, one evening, I saw my ex with his new girlfriend in a Thai restaurant in Selkirk, and decided that I wanted some sort of revenge.' She saw a look on Harry's face. 'No, don't you dare judge me!'

'I'm not,' protested Harry, putting his hands up. 'It's just that I've just seen so many casualties of so-called revenge. Go on. What happened next?'

'I went into the restaurant, walked up to their table, picked up his wine, and poured it over his head. I then threw his dish of, I think it was Pad Thai, all down his front. He just sat there looking at me. She stood up and shouted at me, so I pushed her back down into her seat, which tipped back against the next table and spoiled *their* meal. Suddenly there was a bit of a fracas going on, so I left them to it.' Alex smiled at the memory.

'Remind me not to upset you. Go on.'

'Well, that was it.' She shrugged. 'The next day, I was summoned to his office for a dressing down. It was awful – he treated me like a complete stranger. She was sitting by his side making notes, and then afterwards she gave me a lecture about keeping my emotions under control, and how I might need counselling for stress. To be fair to her, I think she felt sorry for me.'

'So why did your colleagues victimise you?' Harry asked.

'Because they didn't know about our relationship before he was promoted, so they assumed I was a bit of a nutter attacking him out of the blue like that. Perhaps they're right. Maybe I am a nutter!' Alex said with a wink, before taking a generous swig of wine.

Harry looked at her. 'From what little I know about you, you seem to be a stable, resourceful, and confident person who deserves better.'

'That's very kind. How much have you had to drink?' she asked in a teasing voice.

'Too much to drive,' he said, looking at his watch. 'It's a taxi for me.'

'You can stay, if you like. There's a spare bed in my room,' she added quickly, a flush appearing on her cheeks. 'I'm not trying to seduce you. Life is complicated enough.'

'No, I'm okay, thank you. But that's very kind of you.' Harry didn't know whether the offer to stay had been a veiled invitation for something more, but, as Alex had said, life was indeed complicated enough. Harry didn't have much of a love life, apart from the occasional fling, and even if it had been an offer, his instinct and heart would have said no. At least not tonight.

Harry slept fitfully at his flat. He picked up his car from Alex's hotel the next morning and made for the nearest cafe for breakfast. He'd thought about inviting Alex, but she had a day off, so he let her be. Hungrily, he downed a full English with a pot of tea and toast, while scanning one of the tabloids that had been left on the table.

"Murder hunt continues" was one of the headlines. He read on, without real interest. The story covered the death of Phillip Greening, with a picture of a younger version of Greening and a human-interest story about the staff member who had found his body, Lucy Hayes.

Towards the middle of the newspaper was "Jackpot! Missing man found in lottery riddle!" with a short paragraph and a photo of George Evans.

I'll bet he got into some hot water with Patricia, Harry thought with a smile.

The thought of Patricia Evans made him think about the book about Greek mythology she had shown him. Zeus's wife had wreaked her revenge – there was that word again. Revenge. Alex had talked about it last night. What was it about women and revenge?

Women and revenge... Somehow that was the link. He was sure of it.

It was time to speak to Phillip Greening's wife.

Harry arrived at the Greenings' house thirty minutes later.

'Thank you for seeing me at such short notice.'

'That's okay,' said Sarah Greening. She had long, mousey hair and was wearing a light green top and jeans. 'Tea or coffee?'

'No thanks, but you go ahead.'

The kitchen featured an island in the middle, containing a cooker hob and a sink. There were stools around the perimeter. Harry took a seat while Sarah filled the kettle.

'I know that you've already given a full statement to my team, but I do have some other questions, if that's okay?'

'Fire away,' she said.

'As you know, your husband was in the company of another woman when he arrived at the hotel where he was killed.'

'Yes, that's right.' She glanced away towards the window as she replied.

'And he met that woman near the hotel that he was *supposed* to be staying at.'

'So your officers told me.'

'Mrs Greening, did your husband have many extramarital affairs, as far as you know?'

Sarah Greening looked grim-faced. 'I've no idea. It's not important now, is it?'

'You said to my officers that your husband went to conferences twice or three times a year. Are you aware of any conferences that he might have genuinely attended?'

There was a long pause. 'Not really, I suppose.'

'In all these years, he never discussed any aspect of these conferences with you, and you never asked him about them?'

'Yes I did, but he was always very vague, and if I pressed him about them he always got cross, so I gave up.'

'But you *were* suspicious?'

'I suppose so,' she said, examining her nails.

'Mrs Greening, isn't it probable that your husband had many secret affairs or sexual liaisons during your marriage, using these conferences as an excuse?'

'Yes, all right, it's very probable.' Her face had turned pale and her eyes glistened. Tears had formed and were about to fall down her cheeks.

'And how do you feel about that?'

'Obviously I hate him for it.'

'Enough for you to want to kill him?'

'Don't be so ridiculous!' she exclaimed. 'Anyway, your officers have already asked me where I was during the time when Phillip was supposed to be at the conference.'

'And what did you tell them?'

'The truth. That I was with someone I've been seeing.'

'Another man?'

'Yes,' Sarah said, an angry flush working its way up her neck. 'I've known about Phillip's activities for a few years. If he can have some fun, then why can't I?'

'Mrs Greening, in that case, did you get someone else to murder your husband?'

'Like who? That's just stupid.'

Harry drove away from the Greenings' house, unconvinced.

He called Sandy Sanders.

'Sandy, we're onto something, but I'm not sure what. Can you arrange for the wives of the first two murder victims, Laura Hamilton and Lisa Stock, to come to the station to be re-interviewed?'

'Yes, no problem. What are you thinking?'

'I'm thinking that Mrs Greening had a clear motive to murder her husband, and we know that Hamilton and Stock also have a similar motive. This has got to be more than coincidence. I believe it's possible we may be able to link them all to a third-party assassin. Someone they commissioned to commit murder on their behalf.'

'Bloody hell, Harry. Any idea who?'

'No. This is something that I have to get my head around. The only links seem to be this blasted Herg and the card with Sam's name on it. Apart from that, there is very little. Everything is conjecture at the moment, so I'm hoping that we'll get something more from the wives.'

Harry's next stop was the Kidman residence. Will was out of hospital and back at home.

Holding aloft a bottle of single malt and a bunch of flowers, Harry was warmly greeted by the family and by a recent addition to the family – a cocker spaniel called Alfie.

'Well, mate,' he said to Will, extricating himself from Alfie who was jumping up at him, 'how are you feeling now?'

'He's feeling much better,' said Angela. 'And less stressed.' She looked pointedly at Will.

Will looked abashed. 'I'm fine and looking forward to getting back to work,' he said firmly, looking back at his wife. 'I heard that our DCI solved our riddle of the missing man.'

'Near enough. She collared the two kidnappers single-handedly,' said Harry. 'We'll probably never hear the end of it.'

33

It was the first time that the team at Farrow Road had ever seen Liz Mainwaring this happy. It was as if someone had unlocked a confidence button within her, allowing a new inner self to shine through.

'Heard you apprehended two violent criminals by yourself, ma'am,' became a daily mantra from junior staff eager for promotion.

Mainwaring seemed to have a renewed zest for her job, and this spilled over onto her team, even onto Harry, who she summoned to her office.

'How are you, Harry?' Mainwaring asked.

Harry nearly fell out of his chair. 'Fine, thank you,' he said, eyeing her warily.

'How's your head? I see the eyebrows are growing back.'

He rubbed them self-consciously. 'All good, ma'am.'

She asked how the Kidman family were, before getting down to business. 'So, bring me up to date with our murder enquiry.'

'I'm pursuing several angles at the moment, ma'am. We

still believe that the best way forward is through the wives of the victims.'

'I agree,' Mainwaring said. 'Keep pursuing the Herg thing too.'

'I will, ma'am.'

'And how are you getting along with Alex?'

'Fine ma'am. She seems a very capable officer who deserves to go far. She has already made some valuable contributions.'

'Glad to hear it. I think my opposite number in Galashiels will be interested in your comments. Well, keep me informed, Harry, and keep up the good work.'

Keep up the good work? Bloody hell. Why was she being so nice?

Harry walked back to his office, not knowing whether she'd had a bang on her head, or whether he was about to be fired.

His phone rang. 'Guv, Laura Hamilton and Lisa Stock can be available tomorrow morning.'

'Thanks, Sandy, that's perfect.'

The next day, Harry arranged the soft interview room to his liking. He felt that he had one shot at this and wanted to get it right first time.

He wanted a second person to sit in on the interviews. He would normally have used a sergeant, but he found himself hovering outside Will Kidman's office.

He tapped and went in. There was no doubt about it, there was definitely a tickle inside his system each time he saw Alex.

'Good morning to you.' She smiled. 'How may I be of assistance?'

'You can start by sharing some of that coffee,' Harry said, almost gruffly, his eyes on the machine behind her.

'My pleasure, your lordship. Would sir like me to prepare the house bean speciality?'

He ignored her banter, instead filling her in on the events of the previous day and his plans for that morning.

'I think you should interview Lisa Stock first and Laura Hamilton second,' Alex said, 'because I believe that Laura is the more vulnerable of the two women, given the fact that she tried to end her life. That way, you can use any info you get from Lisa Stock to open Hamilton up.'

'That's a good plan,' said Harry. 'Although Lisa has a bit of a temper and seems to have a drink problem. How would you like to sit in and monitor the interviews? I know you're busy and I would normally use one of the–'

'Just you try to stop me,' Alex said, jumping up and putting on her jacket.

Lisa Stock looked moody as she was led into the soft interview room. 'Why have I had to come here? I've already answered your questions. Why can't I just be left alone? Things are still difficult, you know.'

'I'm sure,' Harry said in a soothing voice. 'Have a seat, Mrs Stock. These are just routine questions. As you know, we are still trying to find your husband's murderer. The same person, we believe, has possibly committed at least two other murders.'

'Then you should be out there looking for them, instead of talking to me.' She sat with her arms folded, looking anywhere but at Harry and Alex. 'Do I need a solicitor?' she asked finally.

'Why? Do you think you need one? This is not a formal interview, as I said, these are just routine questions. Nothing more.'

'Well, go on then, hurry up. I've got things to do.'

'Mrs Stock, the last time I saw you, I asked you whether your husband had had any affairs. You answered no. In fact, you got upset with me for even suggesting it. Do you recall that conversation?'

'Of course I do. Do I look stupid?'

Alex glanced at Lisa Stock's pink hair, but said nothing.

Harry continued, 'Then how do you explain the fact that the police were called one night to a disturbance outside your house, Mrs Stock, after which you kicked out your husband because he'd had an affair with your babysitter?'

'They weren't having an affair – it was just casual sex. All men think with their dicks. Everyone knows that.'

'You were upset enough to be involved in a shouting match to which the police were called.'

'Yes, but I took my husband back. It was all her doing, the dirty slag.'

'Whichever way you dress it, Mrs Stock, your husband cheated on you. Now I ask you again, did your husband have any affairs apart from the one with the babysitter?'

'Or did he have casual sex with anyone else?' Alex cut in.

'Why are you keeping on about my husband having affairs?' Lisa asked.

'Because,' said Harry patiently, 'the person who killed your husband must have had a motive to do so, and the motive might have been revenge.'

'What, me? You think I did it?' Lisa almost shouted.

'No, not necessarily, Mrs Stock. The murder could be linked to one of his extra-marital relationships. For example, the babysitter, or the parents or a friend of the babysitter. That's why we need to know about his other liaisons, and that's why we are asking you these questions. It's nothing personal.'

Lisa unfolded her arms, looking slightly mollified. Perhaps a touch relieved, Harry thought.

'I've got nothing more to add. You know everything.'

'Okay Mrs Stock, thank you for coming down. Just one more thing.'

Lisa Stock had already stood up to leave and was adjusting her hair over her collar.

'What does the word Hera mean to you?'

Alex leaned forward towards Harry. 'Harry, it's Herg, not Hera,' she said in a low voice.

Harry ignored her and waited for Stock's answer.

'Hera? Nothing... Who is Hera?' she replied. However, her hand stayed on the back of her collar as if she'd forgotten it was there.

'You've never heard of Hera?'

'No.'

'Are you sure?'

'I've just told you, haven't I?'

After Lisa Stock had left, Harry turned to Alex, 'Well, what did you think?'

'I think that you are a devious shit. What are you up to? How come we seem to have moved from Herg to Hera, and why does no one else seem to know about this apart from you?'

Harry ignored her question. 'Did you see Lisa's reaction when I mentioned Hera?'

'Yes, of course. It was obvious. A child of three would have picked that up.'

Harry reached in a drawer, pulled out a book, and placed it in front of Alex. 'We have to thank the DCI's Aunt Patricia for this.'

Alex picked up the book. 'The Legend of Zeus. How is this relevant?'

'Zeus's wife had a nasty jealous streak. Zeus often cheated on her and she used to exact revenge in the most horrible fashion... Sometimes using poison and strangulation.'

Alex looked bemused. 'Don't tell me, her name was Hera?'

'Correct. I realised the rope that was used on the first victim, Paul Hamilton, had been twisted in such a way to form what looked like Herg when it might actually have been Hera. Perhaps someone moved it accidentally, or we just misread it.'

'And you weren't completely sure until you mentioned Hera to Lisa Stock?'

'Exactly. This all adds to the revenge angle. I'm willing to bet that all three women have heard of Hera.'

'Laura Hamilton is waiting outside. You won't have long to see if you're right.'

Laura Hamilton looked very different from when Harry had last seen her. Her blonde hair was now darker, and it was bundled into a brown-and-yellow, woollen bobble hat, which matched the scarf around her neck. She wore a large pair of sunglasses, which, with her hat, made her look as though she was about to go skiing.

'Have a seat, Mrs Hamilton.'

'Now *you*, of all people, can call me Laura.' She looked at Alex. 'He saved my life, you know.'

Alex nodded. 'I know. And you can repay him by helping us today.'

Laura removed her dark glasses. She looked as if she'd aged ten years since Harry had last seen her. 'How can I help?'

Harry stood in front of her and folded his hands. 'You can help us by coming clean about everything. You told us about your husband's affair when we spoke before, but guess what? It turns out that you're not the only one.'

'What do you mean?'

'Laura, we've spoken to the wives of the other two men who were murdered. Their husbands were also unfaithful.

You're in good company. In fact, we've just interviewed Lisa Stock, and she has told us everything she knows. Now it's your turn.'

Laura looked as though she was going to be sick. 'You know everything?'

'Not quite. We need to know exactly how *you* came across Hera.'

Harry knew that he was slightly misleading Laura in order to get to the truth, but there was a killer to be found.

'I found Hera in a newspaper,' she said, sounding almost resigned.

Harry and Alex hardly dared speak. This was the breakthrough.

'I was so angry with Paul over his affair, I wanted desperately to hurt him somehow. But not to kill him!' she said quickly, looking at the two officers. 'But I wanted to know that he would never be unfaithful to me again.'

Harry kept his expression neutral. Alex nodded and smiled encouragingly.

'So, I saw an advert in the personal section of one of the Sunday papers. It said something like, "This simple trick will stop your man from ever cheating again," and it had a website address.'

Harry resisted the urge to ask for the web address at this stage, but simply nodded as if he already knew. 'So you contacted them via the website. What happened then?'

'I just filled in a form with my contact details, then a couple of days later, a woman phoned me.' Laura stopped and cleared her throat. 'May I have a glass of water, please?'

'I'm sorry, I should have offered when you arrived. I'll get you one now,' Alex said, and went off.

While she was away, Laura asked Harry, 'How much trouble am I in?'

'It all depends on how much you admit to, and how much you can help us.'

'Okay,' she said. 'I'll do my best.'

The water arrived, and Laura drank thirstily. She put the glass down and wiped both her hands on her knees.

Harry prompted her to carry on, 'You were saying that a woman phoned you. What did she say?'

'She said that I was one of many unhappy women whose partners had cheated, and that they had a hundred percent success rate in stopping partners from cheating. I know what that means now.'

Tears started to appear. Alex pushed the tissue box over to Laura, who blew her nose noisily.

'She wanted to know where Paul worked, so I told her. She told me not to worry. She said that everything would be taken care of.'

'Did she mention any form of payment? Or was this a free service?' Alex asked.

'I asked her that. She said that once I was satisfied that my husband would never stray again, I could make a donation towards their cause. I asked her how she was going to prevent my husband from straying. She said it was a ground-breaking technique, simple and effective. Those were her exact words, "Ground-breaking." Do you see?'

Harry and Alex saw. A play on words... Perhaps indicating a burial.

'Did she give a name or say where her organisation was based?' Alex asked.

'She told me to call her Sam.'

Sam, the name on the card Amos Carling had found near Kevin Stock's body.

'Have you paid your "donation?" yet?' Harry asked.

'No, not yet.'

'Did she say how much it would be?'

'She asked if Paul was insured. I told her he was. She said that it would be five thousand pounds, but a lot of that money would go towards helping women in my situation who didn't have the means to pay.'

'This sounds more like a charitable mission rather than a murder contract,' Alex exclaimed. 'Did she mention how payment should be made?'

'She said it would have to be cash, but she said that, for everyone's safety, I would never know where or when the handover of the money would be, and that I would just have to keep the cash on me until the time was right.'

'Okay, now I need some more details from you, starting with the website address,' Harry said.

Laura gave an appreciative nod. 'I just realised. You didn't actually know a lot of the stuff I just told you, did you?'

Harry smiled. 'Look, our job is to catch the bad guys, in any way we can.'

'I don't mind,' she said. 'In fact, I feel better already. Am I free to go?'

Harry nodded. 'For the time being. I'm afraid there will be plenty more questions in the near future.'

After Laura Hamilton had left, Harry picked up the phone. 'I want Lisa Stock and Sarah Greening picked up and brought here now. If they resist, arrest them for wasting police time.'

When Harry replaced the phone, it immediately rang again.

'Guv?'

'Sandy, what is it?' Harry asked impatiently.

'Another body has been found. Same as before – rope and everything.'

'Please tell me you're not serious!' Harry fell back in his seat, frustrated. He had known it would only be a matter of time before the killer struck again. But this was quick.

34

Harry arrived at the scene and got out of the car. A watery sun cast a surreal yellowish light on his surroundings.

He could identify the property where the murder had taken place by the van parked outside with "Scientific Research" emblazoned on the side. There was already some neighbourhood interest, with small gatherings of people looking in the direction of the property. The house had a Fox's "For Sale" sign on the front lawn.

Harry picked up his phone. 'Sandy, grab some of the team and get down here. I want a thorough door-to-door to see if anyone saw anything.'

'Right, guv.'

Harry walked round to the back of the property. 'Good morning, Rosko. What have we got?'

'It's a Mr Jeremy Baxter. Looks like he was drugged and then strangled with a rope, just like the others.'

'Can I take a look?' Harry asked.

'You can. I'm nearly done here.'

Harry ducked under the “Do Not Cross” tape and examined the body.

He was younger than the other victims. In similar style to the others, he was splayed out on the patio with a rope around his neck. The long end of the rope had been carefully formed into a word.

Harry’s eyes narrowed. ‘When do you reckon this happened?’ he asked Rosko.

‘I’m not a betting man, but I would say sometime yesterday between eight and ten in the evening.’

‘And the body wasn’t discovered until late last night.’

‘Yes, by a pizza delivery boy, as I understand.’

The “pizza boy” was actually a man in his late thirties. Mo Khan was now something of a celebrity at the take-away outlet “Super-Fast Pizzas.” He had clearly got over the upset of discovering the body. Harry almost had to prise him away from the two reporters who had somehow got wind of the story.

Mo led him into an office.

‘So you discovered the body at the back of the house,’ Harry said.

‘Yes, I did,’ Mo said, almost proudly.

‘You were delivering leaflets.’

‘That’s right.’

‘The letterbox is on the front door. Why did you go around the back?’

Mo looked uncomfortable. ‘I wanted to go to the toilet, so I went around the back of the house to look for somewhere. I was desperate. That’s when I found the body.’

‘How did you see it in the darkness?’

‘I was wearing my head torch. We need them so we can see where the letterboxes are.’

‘Right, now think carefully. When you discovered the body, did you move anything?’

'No, definitely not.'

'Did you see that there was a word formed by the end of the rope that was around the victim's neck?'

'Yes, I thought it was strange.'

'This is very important. Did you touch the rope – even slightly?'

'No. I swear I didn't. I delivered the leaflet through the front door, saw the place was in darkness, and looked for somewhere to go to the toilet. I went around the back and saw the body. I stared at it for about a minute, because I didn't believe what I was seeing.'

'What did you do then?'

'I phoned my boss at the takeaway.'

'What?' said Harry incredulously. 'You didn't think to phone the police first?'

'That's what my boss said. Then I phoned you guys, and I waited around, then the police cars came and I was asked lots of questions, then they let me go home.'

'Okay, Mo, thank you for now. You've been a great help.'

'That's okay. Do you want a pizza on the house? The boss won't mind.'

'No thanks,' Harry said reluctantly, realising that he was hungry, despite his earlier breakfast. But there was no time to eat. There were things to do.

35

Fox's Estate Agents was busy with Saturday afternoon enquiries. Although there was a nation-wide slump in the housing market, properties in the area were selling well and Fox's was the main estate agency. Harry waited his turn, whiling away the time by perusing details of the various properties that were displayed on the inside of the agency windows. He was seriously considering moving house because the road outside his flat was getting noisier.

'Hello, Inspector. What can I do for you on this bright and cheery afternoon?' Don Fox stood there, suited and suave, his silver hair immaculate. 'Is this business, or can I help you search for a property?'

'Business, I'm sorry to say. Is there somewhere we can go to have a chat?'

'Of course, Inspector. Follow me.'

They went to Fox's office, where the obligatory tea and custard creams appeared. Harry allowed himself to wolf down a couple of the biscuits and sipped the tea gratefully.

'So you're telling me, Inspector, that this homicidal

maniac has killed again. When are you ever going to find this murderer?'

'That's an excellent question,' said Harry.

Still munching, he looked around Fox's office. *Now he's a real family man*, he thought. Photos were everywhere – Don Fox with his children, grandchildren, and extended family. One picture took pride of place; it was in a thick, silver frame and was a photo of Don Fox and his wife at the centre of a family group, looking lovingly into each other's eyes. *I can't see that ever happening to me*, thought Harry, with more than a touch of envy.

Harry put down his cup. 'Mr Fox, it appears that this latest victim was discovered behind yet another property that is on your books.'

'It must be a coincidence. It wouldn't make any sense otherwise, would it?'

'It wouldn't,' agreed Harry. 'I just wanted to know if you've had any potential buyers visit the property in the last couple of weeks, particularly the last few days.'

'Ah yes, I see where you're going with this, Inspector. The same procedure as before. Let me consult our records.' He came back with a ledger. 'This is our signing in and out book,' he said. 'When one of my team takes a potential client to a property, they have to sign for the keys and write in the client's name.'

'Do you mind if I borrow that?' asked Harry.

Back at the station, Harry trawled through the ledger looking for anything that might help, but there was nothing of any significance. He put the ledger in his drawer and stretched out his arms behind his head.

There *was* something new.

The last murder had been different because the body had been strung up over the bathroom door, and that the victim had been hit on the head with an ornament. But this one was different again. This victim didn't have a wife. He had lived alone, which seemed to skewer the revenge angle.

Harry flipped open his laptop and searched various social media platforms. It was no good. His concentration was waning. He was exhausted. He finally gave in and went home.

There, he lay on the couch, recent events playing in his mind. He switched on the television and allowed himself to be sucked into a soap drama.

He was awoken the next morning by a persistent knocking on the front door. Struggling off the couch, Harry stumbled down the hallway. He opened the door to see Will holding aloft a paper bag.

'My contribution to your breakfast requirements, sir.'

'Hello, Will, it really is good to see you. You're looking so much better.'

'You look bloody awful, Harry. Get the kettle on.'

'You're always saying that. What brings you here? Not that you need a reason.' Harry filled the kettle and shook out the contents of the paper bag onto a plate. 'Ah, croissants and pain au chocolat, excellent. A healthy start to the day.'

'I'm here to tell you something, Harry. I wanted you to know first.'

'Are you pregnant?'

'Would you ever stop taking the piss? I'm leaving the force.'

The grin left Harry's face. 'What? You?'

'Yes, I'm afraid so.'

'Any particular reason?'

'Angela and the kids, mainly. The Graftons' attack on me really freaked them out. They want me to do something normal.'

'What are you going to do?'

Will helped himself to a croissant. 'I'm going to set myself up as a private investigator.'

'Of course, that'll make you so much safer than being a copper,' Harry said.

Harry's sarcasm wasn't wasted on Will. 'I know, I know. But my family thinks that it's going to be better, and they'll get to see more of me.'

'And that's a blessing for them?' Harry laughed.

'What about you, Harry? When is some unfortunate lady going to make an honest man out of you?'

'Never going to happen, Will. Tried it once, it didn't work.'

'But that was because Maria didn't realise what it's like to be a copper's wife. Is there no one at Farrow Road that you fancy? What about my replacement, Alex?'

'I wouldn't inflict myself on anyone, especially looking like this,' Harry said, pointing at his head. 'Anyway, she's not your replacement. She's down here from Scotland just to help. She's not allowed to play an official role in the English force.'

'All the better, then – there wouldn't be a conflict of interest. What's she like, this Alex?'

'Oh, you know. She's okay, a good officer.'

'What about as a person?'

'She's all right.' Harry said, handing Will his tea with a slight grin.

Will laughed. 'You can't fool me. There's something there, whether you admit it or not.'

Harry quickly changed the subject. 'Fancy a pint, Will? I've got a day off and I could do with chilling out somewhere.'

'Tell you what, I'll grab Angela and the kids. I know a pub by the canal that does a great lunch.'

'Will, it sounds perfect, but there is one condition. No more talk about getting me married off.'

'All right then, just as long as you don't start going on about my change of career.'

'Done.'

36

The War Room was full. Everyone around the table was looking towards Harry.

'So, as you all know, the killer has struck again. The body of a Jeremy Baxter was discovered behind a house by a pizza delivery man.'

'Does this murder bring us any fresh evidence?' Dawn asked.

'It's too early to tell. However, it looks like the same MO as the others.' Harry paused and looked around the table. 'I reckon that we have two options. We can either wait until there has been a full investigation into Jeremy Baxter's death to see if anything comes up that will assist our enquiries, or we can act now before another murder takes place. I say we act now.'

'I agree,' Alex said. 'We can't afford to lose a minute on this. I vote that we concentrate only on what we know to be fact.'

'Right,' Harry said. 'So, for the time being, we will discount Jeremy Baxter and concentrate on the murders of Paul Hamilton, Kevin Stock, and Phillip Greening. We're looking for connections to people that call themselves Hera rather than Herg, which now makes sense, certainly as far as the revenge angle is concerned. And remember, the name "Sam" is also in the frame somewhere.'

'How can you be certain that there's more than one person involved in this Hera thing?' Sandy asked.

'I'm not certain. But it seems unlikely that Phillip Greening's murder could have been carried out by just one individual. He was a big, heavy man who was killed then propped up against a door.'

'What about Hera? What do we know?' Dawn asked.

'Not much,' Harry admitted. 'All our information about Hera came from Laura Hamilton. We re-interviewed Lisa Stock and Sarah Greening, both of whom flatly deny that they contacted anyone prior to their husband's deaths. We've only got Laura Hamilton's account of the lead-up to her husband's death and how she found Hera.'

PC Stephens, the officer who had discovered George Evans's striped pyjamas in the dustbin, leaned forward and nervously put his hand up.

'No need for protocol here, PC Stephens,' Harry said. 'If you have a question, ask away.'

'How sure are we that Laura Hamilton's account is accurate?'

'It's a fair question,' Harry answered. 'However, I would put my mortgage on the fact that she is telling the truth. After all, why would she lie? She has nothing to gain and everything to lose. Besides, she gave us the address of the Hera website.'

Alex put her hand up.

'You as well, Alex? Are we back in the classroom?'

'If it's good enough for PC Stephens, it's good enough for me.'

There was a burst of laughter which had the effect of

easing any tension around the table. PC Stephens shot her a look of gratitude.

Alex continued, 'Our options are limited. We could put further pressure on the wives, but that would only confirm what we think we already know. Or we could wait until one of the wives has been contacted for payment, which means that we might be waiting for a month of Sundays, during which more murders may take place. Or we could take a more proactive approach.'

'I favour the proactive approach,' Dawn said. 'Have you got anything in mind?'

'Yes,' Alex said, looking at Harry. 'We have the germ of an idea that might work.'

Harry leaned back and put his fingertips together. 'Our only decent lead is this website address. Everything else is just fluff at this stage. We don't even have a proper description of the woman in the floppy hat and sunglasses who was with Phillip Greening at the hotel.'

'Can't we get their name and details from the website address?' PC Stephens asked.

'You'd think so, wouldn't you?' Sandy said with an exasperated look. 'I spoke to the new cybercrime department in Leeds. They tried to trace the website owner, but with no luck. They said something about bouncing gateways and IP addresses, all of which is beyond me. It means that when you try to identify the origins of the domain name, you get bounced around the web on a wild goose chase.'

'That's why I believe we only have one option,' Harry continued. 'One of us has to pretend to be a cheated wife and attempt to make contact with this Sam or Hera, or whatever the hell she likes to be called.'

'That's a great idea,' Dawn said, excitement in her voice. 'I volunteer to play the part of the cheated wife.'

'Don't be too quick to put yourself forward,' Alex said. 'They may want to meet you at your home.'

'That's fine, I can make that work. I have my own house. I live on my own, well, most of the time,' she said, glancing at Sandy. 'I'd be perfect for the role.'

'Perhaps I could play the part of the husband?' PC Stephens said.

Sandy made a face. 'I think I should be the husband.'

Harry cut in, 'No, I think PC Stephens – sorry, what's your first name?'

'John.'

'John Stephens will be ideal. Sandy, with respect, you're too close to Dawn. This has to be done extremely professionally, with Dawn and John learning their roles with no emotional entanglement.'

Sanders looked as though he was about to protest, but he shrugged instead. 'I suppose you're right.'

Harry looked across at Sandy. 'I'll need you to put together the electronic communications for this whole process. There's a lot to cover. All the main rooms in Dawn's house, the kitchen, lounge, and hallway. You can use my office as the base control.'

Sandy nodded, looking mollified.

Harry looked at the assembled officers. 'Okay, ladies and gentlemen, are we all agreed on this strategy?'

There were nods around the table. 'In that case, let's get on with it.'

37

When they arrived at the pub after what was a long meeting, it was early evening.

After the earlier unpleasant incidents at the Moon, they had decided to visit a music pub on the outskirts of town instead. Amplifiers, loudspeakers, and parts of a drumkit were being ferried onto a makeshift stage in preparation for the scheduled live music. Door staff were getting ready for the evening shift, and there were only a couple of dozen customers, a handful of which were Harry's officers.

Harry paid for the first round of drinks and was just about to sit down when someone tapped him on the shoulder.

'Inspector Black, do you mind if I have a word?'

Harry's heart sank when he saw that it was James Grafton. Their idea of choosing a pub well away from the town centre hadn't worked.

Harry forced a smile. 'Hello, James. Haven't seen you for a while. How's it going?'

'Don't worry, Inspector, I'm not going to give you any grief. I just wanted to ask you a favour.'

'A favour? Are you sure? After all the trouble your family has–'

'Inspector, please hear me out.'

Harry appreciated the fact that as James said "Inspector," he lowered his voice. Not everyone is a fan of the police.

'How can I help you, James? And please call me Harry, especially in here.'

Harry noticed that James was looking smart; his ginger hair was cut short and he was wearing a designer shirt and jeans.

'Harry, I know that me and my family haven't seen eye to eye with the law up until now–'

'I think that's an understatement.'

'However, bearing in mind that I personally haven't caused any trouble...'

'Go on,' Harry said, feeling as if he was about to be coerced into something.

'I just wondered if you would put a good word in for me. I'm applying for a job.'

Harry thought of several "good words" he could use, but then he realised that despite the problems and violent behaviour that the Grafton family had caused – including the vicious attack on Will Kidman – there was no evidence that James Grafton himself had been directly involved.

'I may be able to do that,' Harry said slowly, sipping his pint. 'What sort of job are you applying for?'

'I want to become a police officer.'

Harry nearly spat out his beer. 'Are you serious?' Harry looked at James incredulously. 'What do you think your family will say? Especially your father.'

James smiled sadly. 'As you know, most of my so-called family are inside, and I think we've established beyond any doubt that Ron Grafton isn't my actual father. I've accepted the fact that I was born as the result of my mum's affair and, in a way, I'm relieved.'

'Relieved?'

'Yes. I wasn't exactly proud to have Ron Grafton as my father.'

'Yes, but even so...'

'Look, Harry, before all this blew up, I knew that I was different to the rest of the family. I just went along with their ideas because I had to, but I haven't got a police record. All I've done is associate with known villains, and I didn't have much of a choice about that.' James took a sip of his pint and stared into the distance. 'When I discovered that, apart from my mother, my family wasn't my family, I felt as though I'd been set free to be the person I wanted to be.'

'You're certainly different to the rest of your family, son, especially when you speak like that. You mentioned your mother, how is she going to react to you going into the force?'

'My mother will be like any other mother, she won't judge.'

That's true, Harry thought, making a mental note to see his own mum again soon.

'The other benefit of having me in the force is that I know how criminal minds work. I grew up with it. If I could ever make detective, I know I'd be brilliant at it.'

He's got a good point, Harry thought. 'Well first things first, son, let's try and get you recruited onto the force.'

'Thank you, Harry.'

They shook hands, and James went back to his friends. Harry stood for a moment, thinking about the twists and turns of life, while watching some of his officers let their hair down and dance to the live music which was in full swing.

38

Dawn logged onto Herascircle.com. The site looked amateurish and badly put together. The screen featured a red banner with white lettering – “Are you an unhappy wife? Allow us to renew your life!” *How cheesy*, she thought. The page scrolled down to “Does your husband need the kiss of Hera?”

MAYBE THE KISS OF DEATH, she pondered.

She filled in the details on each webpage, carefully making sure that the information she was giving wasn’t over-egged or too vague. This was the first time that Dawn had been involved in an operation of this magnitude, and she found to her frustration that, as she typed, her hands had a slight tremble. When she had finished, she called Harry to give it the once-over.

‘That’s fine,’ he said, after scrutinising the screen. ‘Just the right balance. All we can do now is wait.’

Harry had had his regular update meeting with Mainwaring. She had consistently been happier and kinder to her team since being involved in the capture of George Evans's abductors.

'Have a seat, Harry. Would you like some coffee?'

'No thanks, ma'am. I've just had one.'

She put her spectacles on the desk in front of her and folded her arms. 'I just want to make sure that this plan that you and your team have come up with is safe for all the individuals involved.'

Harry felt that her concern was justified – it was a hell of a risk.

'I believe that we've been careful enough,' he said, 'but it's obviously difficult to cover all eventualities.'

'I know, but that's our job. What do you think are the potential threats?'

'The immediate threat is that we frighten off Hera and lose our advantage. This is the best opportunity we've had to catch these people, so we can't blow it.'

'I agree.'

'The next threat is when they respond and ask for details of the fictitious husband. We have to be careful to ensure that we give them the right information. We don't want to put our man in danger. We don't want them trying to murder our fictitious husband before it's supposed to happen, if you see what I mean, otherwise we might not have a back-up in place.'

She nodded. 'I understand. So where are we now?'

'At the moment, we're waiting for them to make their move. Dawn has put her details on their website to let them know that she needs their services. She'll play the part of a wife whose husband is having an affair. PC John Stephens will play the husband.'

'Not Sandy Sanders?'

Harry smiled. It was clear that Mainwaring had heard the rumours.

'No, Sandy will be far more valuable doing what he does best, which is installing then controlling the communications between us and Dawn's house. Don't forget, he has a vested interest in keeping Dawn safe. He'll probably want to monitor the comms twenty-four hours a day by himself!'

'And what about PC John Stephens, is he up to this task? Is he going to cope?' Mainwaring asked.

'In the beginning, his part is minimal. His job is to come and go from the house until he is contacted by the Circle.'

'The Circle?'

'Hera's Circle, ma'am. That's what they appear to be called.'

'So what happens if they just kill him straight away?'

Harry stroked his chin. 'That's very unlikely. We believe that after the wives had initially contacted the Circle, someone from the Circle then made a physical contact with each husband before the final meeting when the murders took place. That's what we hope will happen with John.'

'So you reckon they'll contact our fake husband first to entice him to a rendezvous?'

'Yes,' Harry said. 'The second victim, Kevin Stock, had a business card on his person from someone called Sam, which he received prior to his death. Phillip Greening was approached by a woman just before he was enticed to a local bar and then brought along to the hotel where he was killed.'

There was a long pause as Mainwaring looked into the distance. She looked back at Harry. 'Okay, I can't think of a better plan. Are you going to use fake names for Dawn and John?'

'We thought about that,' Harry said, 'but we decided it would complicate things. It just takes someone to use the wrong name at the wrong time, and everything goes up in smoke. Apart from that, if the Circle decides to check Dawn's details, they'll find that the house is registered to her, along with anything else they decide to look into, such as utilities.'

'So you think they will make contact with Dawn first and get her to tee up her husband?' Mainwaring said.

'Something like that, yes.'

'And then they'll make a play for John.'

'That's right. Then we can nab them and hopefully bring down the entire house of cards.'

Mainwaring didn't look happy. 'I'm sorry if I keep going over it, it's just a very risky operation.'

'It is, ma'am, however, we have complete surveillance of the house and we'll be with John every step of the way.'

Mainwaring gave a thin smile. 'Let's just hope that it goes to plan, for all of our sakes.'

'Yes, ma'am.' Harry went to the door and looked back at Mainwaring, who was putting her glasses back on. 'Ma'am?'

'Yes, Harry?'

'I just wanted to say that I very much approve of the *new you*.'

Mainwaring looked quizzically at Harry for what seemed an eternity. 'Good,' she said finally. 'What was wrong with the old me?'

'Nothing, ma'am,' said Harry, hurriedly leaving her office.

Mainwaring looked at the closing door and smiled.

39

They made contact just over a week later.

Dawn had received an email saying that they would contact her by phone and asked her what time was best for her. She didn't respond instantly, trying to not to appear over-eager. She also forwarded a copy of the email to the cybercrime department, who still couldn't trace the source.

She said that the following day would be best for her, and although she was expecting the call, when it happened, it sent shivers through her body.

'Are you alone?' an electronic voice asked.

'Yes.'

'You are at home?'

'Yes.'

'Good. I want you to go to the kitchen window and wave.'

'Wave? Why?'

'Just do it. Now, please.'

Dawn went to the kitchen window and waved. She could see the main road and the houses opposite. She couldn't see anyone looking in her direction. There were flats in the distance – perhaps someone was watching her with binoculars.

'Okay, I can see you,' said the voice. 'I just like to know that people are where they say they are.'

'Oh, okay.' Dawn couldn't think what else to say. At least she knew now that they were being watched.

'Tell me about your husband.'

'What, describe him?' Dawn said. 'Or tell you about his habits and personality?'

'Yes. All of that.'

'Well, he's about six foot tall–'

'About? Don't you know?'

'Sorry, yes, of course I know,' Dawn said, wiping perspiration from her brow. 'He is six foot one inch tall, broad chested, with dark hair.'

'I'll need you to send me a photo of him,' the voice said. 'Tell me more. Is he a drinker? What are his hobbies and his habits? What sort of women has he been going with?'

In front of her, Dawn had a pad listing everything that she needed to know about her fake husband. 'He only drinks Guinness and brandy – not at the same time, obviously!' she added with a nervous laugh. 'His women all seem to have blonde hair, not like me, and his hobbies are computer games, which he plays incessantly. He also likes golf, football, and ornithology.'

'Orni-what?'

'Ornithology. He studies birds, the feathered variety, as well as others.'

They had put this on the list because it was one of PC John Stephens' genuine pastimes.

'What about his habits?'

'He's got this habit of being a womanising shit,' Dawn shouted into the phone, really getting into her role, 'and I want to see the bastard suffer.'

It seemed to pay off. There was an electronic laugh at the other end of the phone. 'You shall have your wish. The next thing I need from you is two or three places where he will definitely be over the next couple of weeks.'

'But I don't know where he's going to be,' Dawn said.

'Then you'd better find out.'

The line went dead.

Dawn stared at her phone. She waited for a full minute before looking towards the ceiling and saying, 'Did you get all of that?'

'Yes, all good. Well done Dawn. You did really well,' Sandy's disembodied voice crackled around the kitchen.

The phone was linked to a digital voice recorder at the office at Farrow Road station, and microphones and mini-speakers provided two-way communication.

The next few days at Dawn's house were strange for Dawn and John. They were living a fake life, like actors playing a part. They had to assume that someone was watching them night and day, so they went out shopping together, like a married couple, making sure that they didn't look *too* happy together. On one occasion, they went to a restaurant. They sat outside, the chilly night air warmed by outdoor heaters. After their meal, they deliberately picked a fight with each other, which resulted in Dawn storming off into the night, shouting insults at John.

The phone rang the next day. The number was withheld, as before, and the electronic voice was unmistakable.

'Are you alone?'

'Yes, I am.'

'Dawn, you must learn to control your temper.'

'I'm sorry?' Dawn said, feigning ignorance.

'At the restaurant last night. Now, if we are going to help you deal with your little problem, we don't want people pointing at you, saying that you had an unhappy marriage and you were rowing in public, do we?'

'No, you're right. Sorry.'

Dawn's hands were shaking. It was one thing playing a part to the outside world, but to find that the people she was trying to deceive had actually been watching her made it very serious. Sweat was running down the back of her neck.

'I have some locations where John will be,' she said, almost wanting to appease the voice.

'Tell me.'

Harry and the team had preselected three locations, carefully considering which one the Circle was most likely to choose.

'He's playing golf this Tuesday, he always goes to a local pub on Friday nights, and he is going to watch his team play football on Saturday at Vicarage Road,' Dawn said, reading from her notepad.

'Tell me which pub, and what time he normally goes,' the voice said.

'The Red Lion in Nash Mills. He always leaves home after dinner, at around eight.'

They had chosen the Red Lion with John's safety in mind. There were always plenty of customers at that time on a Friday, and there were areas where plain-clothes officers could hide, or pose as customers.

'Sounds good,' the voice said. 'We'll be in touch.'

After the call, Dawn stood, her hands resting on the sink, and tried to gather her thoughts. Her brain felt scrambled and her hands were still shaking.

'Are you all right?' Sandy's voice asked.

She jumped. She had momentarily forgotten that the house was being monitored. 'Yes, I'm fine thanks. I just felt shaken. It's all becoming real. The place of contact looks like it's going to be the pub, rather than the golf club or the football stadium. So, we'll concentrate our efforts on the Red Lion, Nash Mills.'

'I'll update everyone.'

Sandy got straight onto the covert surveillance team, who would arrange the hidden cameras and sound equipment, and told them the target and address. Then he updated Harry, who phoned the Red Lion to make the necessary arrangements.

40

PC John Stephens pulled up at the Manor Golf Club. He was out of uniform and wearing casual clothing. He had joined online a few days earlier and was now a fully-fledged member. Now he knew that he was going to be targeted at the Red Lion, he was looking forward to a pleasant, relaxing afternoon with no pressure, just whacking a ball around the green. How hard could that be?

He had to be at the golf course, just in case anyone from the Circle was keeping watch to ensure that Dawn was telling the truth about his whereabouts.

He was walking towards the golf shop when a woman jumped out of a buggy and ran towards him.

'Can I help you?' she asked.

She was dressed in a green-and-gold jumper with the Manor's motif across the front and a matching baseball cap. Strands of blonde hair peeped out from underneath.

'I'm John Stephens,' he replied. 'This is my first time here.'

'Ah, brilliant,' she exclaimed. 'I'm Samantha James. My job is to show new members around and introduce them to the club rules and etiquette. I'll also get you some vouchers entitling you to all sorts of benefits – free training sessions, free buggy hire, discounted golf club hire... Loads of stuff. You even get a free T-shirt and discounted meals and a drink on the house in our restaurant.'

'Blimey, that sounds great!'

'Come on, let's start,' she said excitedly. 'Jump in and I'll give you your personal tour.'

Samantha drove the buggy expertly through the paths around the golf course and pointed out the various greens, giving John a history of the club at the same time. She was a warm, engaging character with a wonderful sense of humour. She had a slight accent to her voice that John couldn't quite place.

After about twenty minutes, the tour ended. Samantha drove them back towards the clubhouse, but instead of dropping him off where she had picked him up, she drove the buggy to the rear of the hotel.

'I hope you don't mind, but you're the last of the morning, so I'm putting the buggy to bed until later,' she said. 'After this, I'll take you to the bar for your free drink and T-shirt, and I'll get you some vouchers.'

They drove down a ramp to a cavernous area right underneath the hotel that housed the buggies, sit-on mowers, and a host of heavy-duty tools.

'Wait here a moment,' she said. 'I've just got to lock up. Then I'll call the lift that'll take us upstairs to the clubhouse. When I close the doors, it will be dark because there are no lights down here, so don't move. Don't worry, I'll be back before you know it.' And then she was running off, back up the ramp to shut the doors they had just come through.

As Samantha had predicted, when the doors closed it was pitch black...and silent.

John Stephens sat still in the darkness. Normally this

wouldn't have worried him, but recent events playing on his mind had heightened his sensitivity. He tried to calm himself. What did he have to worry about? He was in the capable hands of the delightful Samantha. Samantha, an unusual name for a young woman these days, he thought. And didn't it sometimes get shortened to Sam?

He stiffened as the thought struck him. His heart started to pound.

Sam. That was the name written on the card found on Kevin Stock's body. God, how stupid he was. He had literally walked into the lion's den. His brain froze with fear and a sense of self-preservation came over him. He stepped out from the golf buggy and tiptoed through the darkness along the concrete floor, carefully feeling his way among the machinery and tools until he came to the parked golfing carts.

He stopped and listened. He could hear nothing.

John kept going until he could feel a cold brick wall blocking his route. He moved along the wall until he came to a wooden door which was ajar. He slid behind it and softly pulled the door closed. He stood for a moment in the darkness, his heart pounding.

He could hear Sam calling out his name. Her voice was getting louder as she drew nearer. Shakily, he pulled out his phone. The illuminated display showed that there was no signal. Of course, they were underground. So now what?

He didn't want to give away his position by using the torch on his phone, but the dim light of the display showed him another door along to his left. He moved towards it. He could hear movement behind him. She was definitely getting closer. John started to panic. Hurriedly, he pushed the door open and stepped forward into nothing.

He hit the concrete floor of the disused boiler house some

six feet below, knocking all the air out of his body. He lay there in agony, watching helplessly as the boiler house lights came on. He had completely missed the concrete steps.

Samantha stood on the ledge above him. As he faded into unconsciousness, he could hear her shouting for help.

41

How the bloody hell did this happen?' Harry demanded. 'Talk about the best-laid plans.'

'Look, Harry,' said Alex, 'it was nobody's fault. John thought the courtesy girl, Samantha, was our murderer and panicked. Her name certainly didn't help.'

'Have we finished checking her out yet, to make sure she isn't involved?'

'Yes. Samantha has worked there for ten years, since she was sixteen. Before that, she lived with her mum in Italy. There are no doubts as to who she is.'

'John has bollocked up the entire operation,' Harry said, frustrated.

Alex shook her head slowly. 'No, he hasn't... In fact, we are possibly better off now.'

Harry looked at her. 'Better off? Really? How?'

'Now we have just one place to watch. Before, it could have been the pub, the golf course, or the football stadium. Now all we have to do is concentrate on the hospital where John is.'

'Of course,' Harry said, slapping the side of his head. 'How stupid of me.'

'Also,' Alex went on, 'if the Circle had any suspicions before, I'm sure this will help. It may well be that one of the Circle could have been at the golf club to see John being taken to hospital.'

'Shit!' Harry exclaimed sharply, thumping the desk with his palm.

'What is it?'

'If what you just said is true, and the Circle know that John's at the hospital, then that means they don't have to contact John to try to get him somewhere where they can kill him. All they have to do is go straight to the hospital, where he's a sitting duck.'

'You're right. They could pretend to be a visitor or a member of staff. There's no security, so it would be easy for them. They could even be on their way there now. We need to move quickly!'

Harry grabbed his phone and made several calls in quick succession. His final call was to Dawn.

'You still need to act like John's wife. Visit him, stay by his bedside as much as possible, but if you see anyone – or anything – suspicious, don't take any risks, just shout for help.'

'If I have to shout for help, who will come running?' Dawn asked.

'You'll be surprised,' Harry replied.

APART FROM THE PAIN, John Stephens was feeling like a complete and utter idiot. He lay in the hospital bed feeling that he'd single-handedly wrecked the operation and let Harry and the team down. Dawn, playing her part, had visited and told him of their plans, which he felt had thrown him a lifeline.

He looked around the ward. It was now difficult to tell who were the nurses and who were the undercover police officers. Anyone visiting the hospital would have thought that all budget constraints had been removed. There seemed to be an excess of porters, reception staff, and nurses who had appeared out of nowhere, all at the same time.

The existing hospital staff were told what was happening on a "need to know" basis. They were only too happy to have extra assistance. The undercover police officers were also pleased to be doing something different; they were enjoying the pretence of being a doctor, nurse, or porter.

John looked at the chair at the foot of his bed and smiled. It was piled with different coloured polo shirts and hats, all stitched with the golf club logo. Samantha had visited him frequently. He was always pleased to see her; she was always bright and cheerful, and at least he knew that she wasn't playing a role, unlike the staff at the hospital.

The previous night, a man with a white coat and scruffy hair had been wandering around the ward with a clipboard. John had called him over. 'I don't mean to be rude,' he had said, 'but I think you should make more of an effort to look like a doctor.'

'I beg your pardon,' said the man. 'What exactly do you mean?'

'I mean that you're too scruffy to be a doctor. At least comb your hair and smarten up. You're letting the side down by not having the same personal standards as an actual doctor.'

'But I am a real doctor!' the man said, looking affronted.

'Oh.' John put his hand to his mouth in embarrassment. 'I'm so sorry, I thought you were one of them. What I mean is...'

The man in the white coat stared at him icily. Then his shoulders started to shake, and he doubled over with laughter.

'Don't worry,' he said. 'I'm no more a doctor than you are.'

He went off giggling, and John wondered how many of his other colleagues he would tell before the end of the shift.

He settled back down against his pillows. Even with all these people who were there to protect him, he felt vulnerable and, if he were honest, scared witless.

Dawn either visited John at the hospital or stayed at home ensuring that her phone wasn't too far from her. Although the Circle hadn't been in touch, Dawn had an uncomfortable feeling that she was being watched.

Then the phone rang.

Dawn was washing up. She nearly dropped the receiver into the bowl in her haste to answer the call.

'How are you coping on your own?' asked the voice.

'How did you know I was on my own?' Dawn asked innocently.

There was that electronic chuckle from the other end.

'What happens next?' asked Dawn.

'What happens next is now up to me. I suppose, as far as you're concerned, you can make plans for a rosy future.'

'But could I –'

There was a click.

'Bollocks, she's gone!' Dawn stopped as she realised she was being overheard. 'Sorry!' she said to the empty room.

'Don't worry,' Sandy said, from his listening position at Farrow Road.

'What now?' she asked.

'We wait, I suppose.'

A couple of days went by. The team of officers, in their roles as hospital workers, were growing bored with the day-to-day routines. It had all been a novelty at first – helping with the patients, scrubbing the corridors, and assisting with the catering. But now the team felt that it was all starting to wear thin, and they were getting frustrated.

Harry recognised the potential danger in this and attempted to rally his troops. 'Come on, guys, now is the crucial time. You must keep vigilant. If you take your eye off the ball and something happens to John Stephens, you'll never forgive yourselves – and we'll be back to square one.'

They all knew this to be true and went back to their roles with renewed enthusiasm. However, when a woman with a floppy hat pulled down over her face walked through the hospital corridors mingling with scores of other visitors, no one seemed to take any notice.

When she got into a lift that took her to the wards, she was the sole occupant. She locked herself into a visitor's toilet cubicle, and a few minutes later re-emerged wearing a nurse's uniform, wig, and spectacles. No one paid her any attention because the genuine nurses assumed her to be an undercover officer, and the undercover officers assumed that she was a nurse.

In effect, she had the run of the place.

She walked briskly down the hospital corridors clutching a clipboard, smiling and nodding to any passing staff.

At the outer door of the wing where John Stephens was, she tucked her clipboard under her arm and squirted sanitiser on her hands. She rubbed them together to dry them, before pushing the green button that opened the doors.

She smiled at the nurses who were at their station and marched through the ward, even pausing briefly to exchange pleasantries with some of the patients.

She got to the end bed where PC John Stephens was resting. Then she stopped and pulled out his chart from the foot of his bed, looking as though she was cross-referencing it with her clipboard.

'Good morning, Mr Stephens,' she said brightly. 'I believe it's going to be a heavenly day.'

In the next bed, a heavily bandaged man with a white beard had been sound asleep. He opened his eyes when he heard the nurse.

'I need help. Can you help me?' he asked in an anxious tone.

'I can only deal with one patient at a time,' she said, a trace of annoyance in her voice. 'I'll see to you after this gentleman.'

She pulled the curtains around Stephens' bed and looked down at him.

'How are you feeling, Mr Stephens?' she asked in a soft tone.

'I'm fine, thanks. It's very painful though.'

She looked down at his plastered leg. 'When did you last have a painkiller?'

'Last night, about ten.'

She pulled out a bag and produced a syringe. 'It's time for another one then. This will be an excellent relief for your pain. You'll feel as if you are floating on air.' She squirted some liquid out of the syringe, then pushed the material of his hospital gown up his arm. She moved the needle closer to his skin. 'It's okay, John. You'll just feel a tiny scratch, and then sweet dreams.'

Stephens' eyes opened wide as realisation hit him, and he tried to pull his arm away.

At the same time, the curtains were yanked open. Standing there was the bandaged man from the next bed, staring balefully at the woman. He was removing a microphone and earpiece from around his neck.

'I asked for help, but you ignored me. Thankfully, this lot heard me,' he said, pointing up the ward.

She looked up. There was a whole line of nurses, doctors,

janitors, and hospital workers standing there, all barring her exit. She looked at the old bandaged man as if dumbfounded, then suddenly jabbed the needle into Stephens' hand. He yelled out in shock.

The confusion gave her a head start. She leapt across the ward and hurled herself through the open window.

The bandaged man cursed. He chased after her, following her through the window and landing on the soft grass below.

Harry threw off the fake bandages, leaving the genuine ones around his head, and took off after the woman, who was about thirty yards ahead. He was cursing himself for allowing that bit of theatre back in the ward; he should have grabbed her immediately. Now John Stephens might be in danger, depending on what he had been injected with, and how much. *That's a mistake I'll never make again*, he thought, as he pounded across the grass. His feelings of guilt gave him added strength in his legs, and he closed in on the woman.

He chased her around the outside of the hospital and across the hospital car park. Passers-by looked astonished to see what looked like a pretty nurse being chased by an old man in a hospital gown. Then two passing men decided that it was their duty to help the nurse by rugby-tackling Harry.

'I'm the police!' Harry shouted, as he fell to the ground.

'Of course, you are,' one of the men said.

'He's a nutter,' the other one scoffed. 'Look at his head.'

Harry was wearing a hospital gown over his shirt and trousers, and there were bits of fake beard flapping around his chin. His appearance was compounded by the fact that the bandages around his head had begun to unravel, making him look like something from a horror film.

'Lads, I know what I must look like, but please take my wallet from my trouser pocket and you'll find my police identification.' Harry said this as calmly as he could, but he was staring anxiously towards the figure escaping in the distance.

The woman looked back at the man chasing her. She was in a state of shock. Events had overtaken her and all she wanted now was to get away. Who was the old, bandaged man? There was something familiar about him...

She slowed down as she approached the front doors of the hospital. Her plan was to retrieve her normal clothes from where she had hidden them, then ditch the uniform and the wig. She was sure that nobody would expect her to return to the hospital. She would just hide in plain sight again. She entered the building, and once again went into nurse mode, striding purposefully along the corridor.

Ahead of her, the lift doors opened, and out came a stream of nurses. She faltered for a moment and then carried on walking, smiling and nodding. She in turn received smiles and nods from the group. As they passed, two of the female nurses broke away from the rest and grabbed her, swiftly pinning her arms to her side.

'You're going nowhere,' one of them said.

'What are you doing? Get off me,' she said, struggling.

'You're being arrested for having a bad hair day,' said the other.

'What?' She caught her reflection in the mirror tiles that decorated the lift area, and could see that her wig was askew. She looked at her captors. One was black and petite with long hair tied into a ponytail; the other was white with short hair and had a Scottish accent.

'I see you've met my colleagues, Koorus and Jackson,' a voice said.

The nurse looked round to see the man who had been chasing her. His fake beard and moustache had now come off altogether, and he was trying to rearrange the bandages around his head. He still looked familiar somehow.

Harry removed her glasses and wig, and then stepped

back and looked at her in shock. He had recognised her straight away.

'Jane Cooper, or Sam, or whatever your blasted real name is, I'm arresting you for murder. You do not have to say anything–'

'Amy,' she said. 'My real name is Amy.'

42

AMY'S STORY

Amy and Mary's parents, Eileen and Patrick, were of Irish origin. Because of the economic crisis in the 1980s, they had followed other family members to the USA. They then moved back across the Atlantic and chose Kilburn in north-west London to be their home.

Both of their children were sweet-natured and intelligent, with long, blonde hair and blue eyes. Although three years separated them, apart from their heights, they looked like twins. Amy was fiercely protective of her younger sister and battled other kids in the playground if Mary was bullied.

Amy also protected Mary at home. Their father Patrick had a short fuse and would lash out, physically and verbally. When Mary accidentally broke an expensive vase, it was Amy who took the blame – and the consequential beating.

Their lives changed when Amy was twelve. Her mum had sent her to the shops to get some groceries. When she returned and was letting herself in through the front door, Mary was sitting on the bottom stair, white-faced. She could hear her father shouting and her mother screaming. Amy ran through the house to the kitchen where her mum stood with one hand to her face, the other holding onto the back of a stool to steady herself. Blood trickled from her nose. Her father stood back. His fist was still clenched.

'Mum, what happened?' Amy asked, panic in her voice.

'Nothing for you to worry about,' her father said in that certain tone that always struck fear in her heart. 'Get upstairs now and take your sister with you.'

'But Mum's bleeding.'

Her father started towards her. 'Don't you dare answer back to me. I said, get upstairs!'

She had learned long ago the penalties of arguing with her father. She grabbed her sister's hand and almost dragged her upstairs to their bedroom.

'Are you okay?' she asked Mary, as they sat on the bed.

'Dad hit Mum...' Mary said in a strange, distant voice.

This was nothing new. Mum and Dad were always fighting and arguing, but this was different. This was the first time that Amy had seen blood on her mother's face, and the first time her sister had mentioned it. Perhaps it was because she was getting older and was more aware of what was happening.

'Don't worry, I'll always look after you,' Amy said soothingly, stroking her sister's hair. But Mary didn't seem particularly upset about the incident; she just stared straight ahead, as if in another world.

After that, life seemed to return to normal. However, their father showed signs of guilt over his recent behaviour by being overly nice to his family, and some extra treats appeared on the dining table.

Then, one Sunday, their father arrived home from the pub drunker and louder than normal. He had been celebrating the landlord's birthday and had enjoyed many whiskeys on the house.

He was in great form, swinging Amy and Mary around by

their arms and smacking Eileen hard on her bottom. 'Ooh, stop it, Patrick, not in front of the girls.'

'If I can't grope me own feckin' wife,' he roared, his Irish brogue even thicker after the copious amounts of Guinness and Jamesons.

Eileen had cooked Sunday lunch and had done her best to keep the food warm while waiting for Patrick to return from the pub. The family settled around the big, oak kitchen table looking on with anticipation as Eileen carved into the roast chicken, which was just starting to dry out after being kept in the oven for so long.

'Jayzus, Eileen, what do you call that? That's not fit for the pigs.' Patrick still had a smile on his face, but his eyes had darkened.

'If you hadn't been so long in the pub, our meal would have been perfect,' Mary said, looking directly at her father.

A silence descended over the table and the smile disappeared from Patrick's face as he stared at his daughter.

'What did I hear you say?' he said softly, half getting out of his seat.

Mary didn't flinch. 'I said that if you hadn't–'

'I'm sure she didn't mean it, don't forget she's only nine,' her mother said quickly, also rising.

'I don't care how feckin' old she is, she doesn't talk back to me like that – not now, not ever!'

Patrick slammed his fist on the table, knocking over the gravy jug, his face purple with rage.

'Calm down, Patrick,' Eileen said, desperate to smooth things over. She could see the signs that it was getting out of hand.

'Don't you tell me to calm down!' he shouted. He swung round to Mary, who was looking at him without emotion. 'You're going to apologise to me now, you little piece of shit.'

'Patrick! Language, please! Stop this now – you've had a drink...'

'Shut up Eileen!' He lurched towards Mary. 'Say you're sorry and make sure you feckin' mean it!'

'But I'm not.'

Suddenly, he swung his clenched, meaty hand through the air and caught the back of Mary's head. The force snapped her head forward so that her face smashed into her full plate, scattering her meal across the table.

A terrified hush fell over the table. This was far worse than things had ever been.

Slowly, Mary lifted her head from her lunch, bits of food stuck to her face, and looked at her father defiantly, without a trace of fear.

Patrick leaned forward, his hands supporting him on the table, and shoved his face next to his daughter's. His beery breath made her recoil. 'You're going to apologise to me now, you little–'

'Dad, leave her alone! You're a bully. She's only little.' Amy had run around to Patrick's other side to defend her sister.

Patrick turned his head towards Amy. Just as he was about to unleash a torrent of abuse, Mary stabbed her fork hard into the back of her father's hand.

Patrick roared with pain and staggered backwards, looking disbelievingly at the utensil stuck in his hand and the blood running down his fingers.

Eileen was amazed that her daughter had the capacity to drive the fork so deep into his flesh. She knew Mary was strong, but she hadn't realised how strong.

Amy and Mary had leapt out of their seats and ran to the furthest end of the dining room where they held each other, shaking with fear.

With a yowl, Patrick pulled out the fork and hollered,

'You feckin' little pair, come here now!' He lunged towards them.

They sped out of the room and down the hallway. They fumbled with the lock on the front door, and got out of the house into the street where they waited, trembling, ready to flee should their father appear.

Inside the house, Patrick was still shouting, 'This is your doing, Eileen. You're a useless mother, you've spoilt those girls, and now they're a pair of disobedient brats.'

Eileen was stunned at how the situation had escalated; one minute, they were sitting down to a cheery lunch, and then all of a sudden, violent chaos had ensued. But one thing she knew; she'd had enough. She'd had enough of the endless rows, the drunken taunts, the sleepless nights, Patrick's bullying, his aggression. This was the first time that her husband had actually used his fists on one of the girls. Having felt those fists herself over the years, she knew that this had to stop now. She knew that even if he promised on his mother's grave that he would never hit her again, it would still happen. It was how he was made. Now was the time.

She put her hands on her hips defiantly and looked up at him.

'Patrick, listen to me–'

'Shut up, woman, and make me a sandwich. The dinner's not fit for a dog,' Patrick said, attempting to bind his hand with a tea towel.

'You're getting no sandwich. In fact, you're getting nothing more from me ever again. You and I are finished. Is that getting through your thick, drunken brain? We are finished.'

'Don't be so stupid, woman.'

'I'll show you how stupid I am. I'm about to call the police and report an assault.'

'You'll do no such thing.'

'What are you going to do, Patrick? Are you going to

batter me with those big hands of yours – again? You've just punched a nine-year-old child in the head. What do you think the police are going to say? In fact, what are your friends down the pub going to think when I tell them that you've just bashed a little girl? Do you think the landlord will give you any more free whiskey?'

Patrick sat down heavily on a dining chair. Eileen could see that his alcoholic fog was starting to clear, and perhaps there was a growing realisation of what he had done. A tear rolled down his cheek.

'Oh, Eileen, I didn't mean it. You know I didn't mean it. I'll never do it again. You know I love my family, I just–'

'You can stop all this self-pity. I mean it this time, Patrick. You and I are finished. Either leave now, or I'll call the police.'

Patrick looked at her pleadingly, but Eileen had her arms folded and a look on her face that meant business.

'Don't bother saying anything else. If you don't leave right now, I'll make sure that your reputation is ruined in all the pubs in Kilburn and with your friends and family back in Ireland.'

Patrick's departure from the family home left them in financial difficulties at first because he had been the main bread winner. But Eileen took on extra cleaning jobs, Amy started a little business walking the neighbours' dogs, and Mary helped out where she could. Despite these minor hardships, their home felt calmer and happier.

Then, two years later, Eileen met someone.

"Flash" was the first thing that came to her mind when she clapped eyes on Tony.

She was at the supermarket checkout about to pay for her shopping, when she heard a crash behind her. She looked around to see a bundle of arms and legs on the floor, together with the smashed remains of some wine bottles.

She helped him up and picked out the bits of glass that had caught on his jacket. 'Are you okay?'

'Thank you, yes.' He looked at her with heart-stopping, smiley eyes.

Eileen straightaway thought he was a beautiful man; he had jet-black hair with a quiff, a black leather coat, and a gold chain that hung around his chest. *Yes, flash*, she thought. *He's got trouble written all over him*. Despite that, she was smiling as she walked out of the store.

A couple of weeks later, she was invited by one of the women she cleaned for on a night out. She hadn't been out socially for a very long time and had some reservations.

'Just go, Mum,' Amy had insisted. 'I'll look after Mary. Go and enjoy yourself – you deserve it.'

Not that Mary needed much looking after. She had looked like her sister a couple of years earlier, but now she was looking very different; she had filled out, and her hair was cut shorter, whereas Amy still wore her hair long.

'I won't know anyone,' said Eileen.

'You'll never know anyone if you don't get out more,' Amy said. 'Go on, it'll do you good.'

So out Eileen went. She had a great time. They had met at a nearby pub and then had gone into town.

Wine slipped down their throats as if it was in short supply and they had eventually found themselves at the National, a live music venue on the Kilburn High Road. Eileen hadn't danced for years; Patrick had never really been the dancing type. She had really missed having a jig around, and the fact that she was slightly drunk helped as well.

The band started to play one of her favourite songs. She looked up at the stage in appreciation and was surprised to see the man from the supermarket there, playing guitar. He was looking cool with his quiff, gold chain, and his gorgeous, smiley eyes. She manoeuvred herself to the front of the stage and gave him a drunken wave.

He noticed her straight away and nodded and smiled at her. When the song finished, he leaned down to ask her if she wanted a drink after their performance. She didn't need much persuading. His twinkling eyes had already worked their magic.

He moved in a fortnight later.

At first, the girls were resentful of Tony since they had had Eileen to themselves for so long, but like their mother, they were soon charmed by him. Eileen was blissfully happy. She was getting what she hadn't had from Patrick – attention, intimacy, and respect, and she was thriving. The girls had never seen their mother seem so content.

Most evenings, Tony was out performing with his band, touring around the various bars and music venues, and sometimes got home late. Eileen would bring him breakfast in bed the next day and fuss over him. Tony would look at her with those eyes and melt her already molten heart.

Tony was a few years younger than Eileen, and so quite enjoyed being mothered, cooked for, and having his washing done. He reciprocated by doing odd jobs around the house and contributing to the family's finances.

Family treats started to happen – trips to the cinema, holidays by the sea, and regular visits to McDonald's. Amy couldn't get enough of it, but Mary was a little more reserved. Since the hand stabbing incident, she had had periods where she seemed to be vacant and wander off somewhere in her head. Since Tony had arrived, those periods seemed more frequent and lasted much longer.

Eileen put it down to the fact that she was simply growing up. She was doing okay at school – she seemed to have nice friends and was otherwise quite settled.

Amy had also noticed the changes in Mary, but she was

now a teenager and had her own issues to worry about. She liked Tony very much – in fact, too much. Some of the girls at the school would hoist their uniform skirts up to show off their legs to the local boys and then smooth their skirts back down when they got home. Amy did the opposite. When she neared home, she would hoist her uniform like a miniskirt, so that Tony could get a look at her legs. She wasn't quite sure what she was doing or why, but it felt good. She felt powerful, as though she had some hold over him.

On a couple of occasions, he had entered the bathroom to find her wearing just a towel, and she would "accidentally" let it slip, giving him a brief glimpse of near-nakedness. He laughed at her, but she suspected that he was still having a peek.

This flirtation started to increase momentum. Amy constantly thought of Tony and even entertained the thought of taking him away from her own mother. The moral aspect didn't come into it. He became the subject of her fantasies, and she would wake up feeling hot after dreaming of him.

Then she decided to follow him when he went into town. Her plan was to accidentally bump into him. Then they would go for a drink and could talk like adults without being interrupted, and after that, who knew? Surely he felt the same way about her?

She followed him all the way as he walked to the town centre, carefully keeping a good distance behind him.

He went into Harps, a music shop. She watched him through the window as he picked up a guitar, swung it around his neck, and started to strum. He put it back, picked up another, and did the same again. He then chatted to the man behind the counter. Amy kept watching, her face wedged between the wall and the plate-glass window so that he wouldn't see her. A bit of brick dust went into her eye and she looked away, blinking furiously.

'Hello, you!'

Tony had come out of the music shop and was standing in front of her looking at her with his smiley eyes.

'What are you doing here? Shouldn't you be doing your homework?'

'I was on my way into town,' she said, feeling stupid and exposed, 'to get some things.'

She fervently hoped that he wouldn't ask her 'What things?' because her mind had gone blank, and she wouldn't have had a clue how to answer.

'Tell you what,' he said, 'let's get an ice cream.'

They sat in the ice cream parlour, long spoons scraping the cold sweetness. Amy felt tongue-tied in Tony's presence, so she kept her eyes looking down at the creamy goodness at the bottom of the glass. Tony didn't appear to notice her awkwardness. He told her about the band, about their rehearsal the other night, and stories about their past performances. He told her about the time when, at the end of a gig, the drummer had thrown his sticks out into the audience, only to find that it wasn't actually the end of the gig, because the band had decided to do one more song. The drummer had run out of sticks, so he had to go into the audience to retrieve the ones he had thrown.

She laughed hard at this, even though she hadn't been listening to much of his story. Her mind was too preoccupied by the fact that she was sitting here with Tony. Just her and Tony.

She leaned on her hand, gazing up at him dreamily.

'Would you like anything else?' asked the waitress collecting the glass dishes.

Amy scowled at the interruption.

'No, thank you,' said Tony, looking at his watch. 'I have to go to a rehearsal now.' He looked at Amy. 'Would you like to come along?'

She nodded eagerly, her face shining, her heart thudding.

The rehearsal room was just the converted garage of a large house owned by Ned, the drummer who, according to Tony's story, had thrown his sticks away prematurely, and his wife Linda. Tony gave Linda a kiss as she greeted them at the door and introduced her to Amy, who smiled shyly. They went to the rehearsal room, where the band were congregated.

'Who's this?' they wanted to know.

'This is my very special lady, Amy,' Tony said, putting an arm around her.

Amy beamed with delight.

The band went through their routines and tried one or two new songs until, all too soon, the afternoon came to an end. Amy and Tony walked home together, exchanging small talk. Amy desperately wanted Tony to show some sign of affection towards her – perhaps take her hand, or put an arm around her – but despite her infatuation, she was sensible enough to realise that this was impractical, at least for the time being.

'Amy, where've you been?' asked a worried Eileen when they got home.

'Oh, don't you worry, love,' said Tony twinkling at her. 'I've been taking care of her, we've had ice cream and she's met the band.'

Part of Amy was disappointed with this. Her secret few hours with Tony were now not so secret, and a bit of the specialness had been taken away.

That night, her dreams took on new and fuller dimensions. She and Tony were married and living in a house that was somehow exactly the same as Ned and Linda's. The rest of the band lived in the garage. There were lots of children around, all eating ice cream with forks. Suddenly her mother appeared, announcing herself as the cabaret act. She stood on a stage that had miraculously materialised in the kitchen and started to sing. A deafening, high-pitched sound came from her mouth, almost like a scream...

It was a scream.

Amy sat bolt upright in bed and fumbled for the bedside light. The sound was coming from Mary's bedroom. She rushed in to find her sister sitting up in bed, staring straight ahead, looking terrified. Her forehead shining with sweat.

'Mary, what's up? What's happened? Did you have a bad dream?'

Mary looked at her and whispered, 'Someone touched me.'

'Don't be silly, there's no one here,' Amy said, looking around the room.

'I'm sure someone touched me.'

'All right, what happened?'

'I'm not sure. I was asleep, and I woke up. I felt a hand moving up my thigh, so I screamed.'

'Could you have dreamt it?'

'Don't think so... Don't know.'

The door opened and Eileen came in, looking concerned, closely followed by Tony. 'Is everything all right, darling?'

'I think it was just a bad dream, Mum,' Amy said, looking hard at Tony.

Tony also had a worried look on his face, which seemed genuine enough. 'Perhaps you shouldn't eat so near to bedtime,' he said in a caring voice.

'Were you in my room just now?' Mary asked bluntly.

'Don't be silly, darling, he's been asleep with me. You must have had a bad dream,' Eileen said.

Everyone went back to bed.

Amy lay in bed thinking about the night's events. Mary must have been dreaming – nothing else made sense. She pushed the bad thoughts from her mind, turned over, and tried to get back to the dream she had been enjoying earlier.

The next day, no one mentioned the events of the previous night and life returned to its pleasant normality.

A couple of months later, the family were sat around the dinner table.

'You need to eat more,' Eileen observed, spooning extra potatoes onto Amy's plate. 'You're pale and losing weight.'

'I'm fine, Mum, really. You just think everyone needs feeding up.'

Tony pushed back his chair. 'Right, I'm off. See you later.'

'Where are you performing tonight?' Amy asked.

'At the White Hart. What are you up to?'

'Oh, just boring homework and stuff,' she replied.

'Okay, honeybunch,' he said, twinkling at her. 'Don't study too hard. See you later.'

'Try not to wake me up when you come in,' Eileen said, smiling lovingly at him.

After Tony had gone to work, Amy tried to concentrate on her homework, but it was no use. As usual, images of Tony's beautiful face came into her head. She knew this wasn't healthy, and her feelings were potentially dangerous, but he was like a drug. There was a permanent ache in her heart which she couldn't see being resolved until they could be together.

She closed her books and stood up. 'I'm going out for a bike ride.'

'A ride?' Eileen said. 'But it's getting dark.'

'Mum, I'm nearly fifteen, I won't be long.'

She got on her bike and set off for the White Hart. Even though she had only seen Tony that same evening, there seemed to be a big difference between seeing him "officially" and "unofficially." When he was at home, he was Mum's Tony, but when he was away from home – well, that could change.

She rode the few miles to the White Hart. After securing her bike, she stood across the road from the pub. The White Hart was a long, slim building which had latticed windows along its side. As a result, you could see everyone in the pub from the street.

Amy could hear the band's opening number, which was always an old sixties classic, "Satisfaction." Their version wasn't nearly as good as the Rolling Stones original, but the customers, particularly the oldies, always seemed to enjoy it. She waited for Tony's strident vocals to start. This was one of the songs where he played guitar and sang.

She crossed the street towards the pub to have a better look. The windows were steamed up, but she didn't need to see the band to realise that the singing voice wasn't Tony's. One of the other band members was singing. She rubbed at the windows and tried to peer in. Tony didn't even appear to be on the stage. Perplexed, she walked into the pub to find out why. The band came to the end of the number and Ned the drummer saw Amy and waved.

'How's Tony feeling?' he shouted across the crowd.

'What?' Amy shouted back.

'Tony, not well at home. Is he okay?'

Amy wasn't sure what to do or say. She stuck up a thumb and shouted, 'Yes, he'll be fine!' before leaving the pub quickly, feeling confused.

She got back on her bicycle and rode off, not knowing where she was headed. She knew something was up, but had no idea what.

She cycled around for half an hour, not wanting to go home yet. Somehow, she ended up outside Ned and Linda's house, where she had been with Tony. It brought back happy thoughts of when she'd met the band. She couldn't think what to do next. She stood astride her bike and stared at the house, which was in darkness. The night sky was cloudy, making it difficult for Amy to make out the details of the property. The street was so quiet, she could hear the gurgling of the drains which were still dealing with a recent fall of rain.

She rubbed her shoulders and legs. Her muscles were aching from riding. She decided it was time to go home and made to leave. She gave a last look towards the house and then saw a light come on downstairs. Amy froze. She could faintly hear voices coming from inside, one of which sounded familiar. Quietly, she lay down her bike. Something prompted her to move towards the house, her heart beating wildly as she tiptoed over the front garden. She cursed herself for even being there. What was she doing? This was really stupid.

She peered through a triangular gap in the curtains where she could see into the lounge. She could make out the back of someone's head sitting on the sofa, and judging by the hair, she knew it was Linda. Beyond, in the kitchen area, she could see someone else who was obscured by an open fridge door. As the door shut, she could see that it was Tony, clutching a bottle, walking back from the kitchen into the lounge.

He was naked.

Amy started to shake. Her heart pounded even more as Linda, who was also nude, apart from a thin, gold chain around her waist, stood up and embraced Tony. Tony responded by giving Linda a long, lingering kiss. Amy watched with a strange curiosity as Tony's penis twitched and grew.

Suddenly, Linda turned and walked towards where Amy was watching. Amy ducked down under the window and held her breath. A minute later, she allowed herself to resurface and take another look, but the curtain was now fully closed, and the light was off.

Amy stood in the darkness, which now felt still and hostile. She was feeling exposed and vulnerable, realising that if Tony and Linda looked out of the window, they could possibly see her.

She ran, crouching, to where her bike lay. After pushing it quietly along the pavement for a couple of minutes, she leapt on it and pedalled furiously towards home. After riding for a few minutes, she had to stop. Her legs had turned to jelly, and she was shaking uncontrollably.

It had started to rain again, and the raindrops seemed to merge with the tears that were cascading down her cheeks. She sobbed so violently she thought she was going to be sick. She felt as though her world had shattered.

Suddenly, she hated Tony. Everything that she had dreamt about and hoped for had been dashed into tiny pieces and swept away by the universe. She got back on the bike and rode, not quite as fast as before, but she wasn't paying attention to the road ahead; all she could see were the images of Tony and Linda, wrapped around each other.

Tears started to fall again, making her eyes sting. She raised a hand to wipe them away, obscuring her vision. She didn't see the car coming up fast on her right, or the look of horror on the face of the driver as he hit her. She was flung into the air for what felt an eternity, and then the ground came rushing up quickly to meet her.

43

They received the phone call from the hospital at three o'clock in the morning.

It had been an anxious night all round, beginning with Amy's disappearance. Eileen had made frantic phone calls to the White Hart, where Tony was supposed to be playing, only to find out that he hadn't turned up there either. There was a brief moment when Eileen considered the ridiculous possibility that the two might have run away together.

As a result, Eileen was relieved as well as angry when Tony arrived home at half two in the morning.

'Where've you been?' she demanded, as he tripped on the mat on his way through the front door.

'What do you mean?' he countered defensively. 'You know exactly where I've been – playing our gig at the White Hart.'

'You're a liar!'

'Why am I?'

'Because I phoned the White Hart, you creep, and do you know what they said?'

Tony shook his head, knowing what was about to come.

'They told me you weren't there, and that you were at home in bed, ill. Can you imagine how embarrassing that was?'

Tony nodded dumbly.

'So, where were you?'

Tony had had time to think. 'I was out with my mate. He's got marriage problems, and I was helping him sort them out. I didn't want to tell the rest of the band, so I made an excuse.'

'Why couldn't you tell me what you were doing?'

'I didn't think.'

'That's your problem – you never think. You haven't even asked me why I was looking for you, have you?'

'I was just about to,' Tony said, feeling that he was getting off the hook.

'Amy's gone missing.'

'Are you sure?'

'Yes. I phoned the police, but they said she'll probably turn up later and not to worry too much.'

'Didn't they send somebody out?'

'No, apparently it's been a busy night for them and she hasn't been missing long enough.'

'Have you checked her room?'

'Of course I have. She went out on her bike earlier and didn't return.'

The phone rang, making Eileen jump.

Amy had been found. They said that she had been knocked off her bicycle by a motor vehicle. The driver of the car had been breathalysed and had been arrested for drink driving. That's all they knew at this stage.

'How is my daughter?' Eileen had screamed down the phone.

'She's fine. She was very lucky. Just has cuts and bruises.'

'Can I see her?'

'Of course.'

When Eileen arrived at the hospital, Amy was sitting up in bed reading a magazine.

She looked up at her mum, delighted that she was on her own. She had been dreading seeing Tony after what was now imprinted on her mind.

'Tell me what happened, darling,' her mum said, sitting on the side of the bed.

'It was my stupid fault, Mum. I wasn't looking where I was going.'

'It wasn't just your fault, the man caused the accident by drinking too much.'

'Whatever, but it was still my fault.'

'You'll soon be home, darling,' her mother said, touching her cheek tenderly.

Amy nestled her head into her mother's shoulder. It would be wonderful to be home – despite Tony.

THE PREVIOUS NIGHT, Ned the drummer had still been at the White Hart when Eileen had phoned, helping put the sound equipment away. The barman had called across to Ned and asked where Tony was. Ned had replied that he was at home ill.

'No, he's not,' said the barman. 'His missus is on the phone asking where he is.'

Ned had just shrugged, idly thinking Tony was probably out shagging someone, and that he would be in trouble when he got home.

When Ned returned home, he felt like going straight to bed. He was tired and decided that he would move his drums and any other gear from the van back into the house the next morning.

He opened the garage door ready to put the van away and

saw rubbish spilling out the top of one of the wheelie bins, stopping the bin lid from closing. He opened the lid to push down the contents, and saw an empty champagne bottle, together with an empty wine bottle.

I don't remember buying that, he thought. He had his own wine collection, and always stuck to the same brand, so when he saw the local supermarket's label on the bottle, he was mystified.

The next morning, he woke up late and wandered down to the kitchen where his wife was preparing breakfast.

'Did you have a good night last night?' Ned asked.

'How do you mean?' asked Linda, looking uncomfortable.

'There was an empty wine bottle and a champagne bottle in the bin when I got home.'

'Oh, that,' she said. 'My friend Alison popped round last night for a chat and brought a couple of bottles. You remember Alison, don't you? She came to one of our barbecues once. You know, the woman with the piled-up hair and the thin neck. She looks like a bird when she walks.'

Ned didn't normally notice everyone who came to their barbecues, which were usually boozy, all-day events.

'Oh, right,' he said absently.

Linda's face relaxed. 'How did last night's gig go? Did you cope all right without Tony?'

Ned stiffened, as did Linda, as she realised her mistake. 'How did you know that Tony wasn't there?' he asked.

'I didn't, I mean... I know that Tony wasn't there because I saw him on his way home.'

'But he was supposed to be ill in bed.'

'That's right, he was just walking along the pavement when I saw him. He looked terrible – white faced and shivering. He said he was going straight home to bed.'

'Then why *didn't* he go home?'

'What?'

'He didn't go home. Eileen phoned the pub, looking for him.'

'Oh, I don't know, then.'

Ned left things there, but he was deeply unhappy. He had had some nagging doubts about Linda for some time, but had put it down to some silly paranoia. Now he was certain that there was something going on. But with Tony, his mate? Surely not.

He decided to find out the truth one way or another.

Ned *had* remembered Alison from the barbecue, mainly because of her bird-like stance that Linda had mentioned. He also knew that Linda kept her address book in the drawer in her bedside cabinet. He waited until Linda was out and found Alison's number.

'Hello?' A voice answered.

'Hello, Alison, it's Ned here.'

'Who?'

'Ned, Linda's husband.'

'Oh hello, long time no speak. How's Linda?'

'She's fine, thanks. When did you last speak to her?'

'Ooh, not since your last barbecue. Why do you ask?'

Ned pulled away from the handset and stared at it, his heart thumping, his world in sudden turmoil. Suspicion had become fact.

'Hello, hello... Are you still there?'

Ned ended the call.

AMY WAS home from the hospital. As a treat, Eileen had prepared a special tea and had bought Amy's favourite cakes and pastries.

Amy seemed calm; her anger and bitterness had turned into a cold placidity. She looked around the sitting room. Her sister seemed happy enough, cramming huge slices of Battenberg into her mouth, crumbs everywhere as usual. Her mum sat next to Tony, her hand lovingly placed at the back of his neck.

Amy desperately wanted to tell her mum everything she had seen the previous night, but was mature enough to realise that it would hurt her mum beyond repair, and the ensuing damage might break up the household.

The only person who was hurting at the moment was Amy, and she found that it was easier to deal with than she had imagined. She was just pouring herself another tea when there was a loud, aggressive knock at the front door.

Mary ran into the hallway to see who it was.

Amy could hear the deep murmur of a male voice, and then, suddenly, the sitting room door burst open. There stood Ned, his face white with fury. He pointed across the room.

'You are a fucking cheating lying bastard!'

'What? I don't know what you're talking about,' Tony replied, a tremor in his voice.

Ned hurled himself at Tony, throwing punches at him. He knocked him into the television set, which smashed into the corner of the room, scattering ornaments and upsetting a vase of flowers.

Ned got in a couple more punches before Eileen bravely put herself between the two men.

'What's going on?' she said. 'Stop it, you two!'

'Are you going to tell her, you piece of scum, or shall I?' Ned shouted, standing over Tony.

But Tony couldn't speak. His hand was covering his mouth where one of Ned's punches had landed, blood dribbling through his fingers.

'Tell me what's going on,' Eileen shouted again, her voice getting anxious.

'Your precious Tony has been shagging my wife. That's what's been going on.'

'Don't be so ridiculous,' Eileen said. 'You're mistaken. Tony wouldn't do that. Besides, he's with me every night. Don't you dare come into my house and accuse my Tony of filth like that. I thought you were supposed to be his friend. Now get out!'

Ned ignored her, his eyes still on Tony. 'Go on, why don't you tell her? Tell Eileen where you were last night... Tell her why you weren't performing with the band at the pub.'

'He already told me,' Eileen said in a patient tone. 'He was with a friend, helping to sort out a marriage problem.'

'No, he wasn't,' Ned replied. 'He was with my wife, *creating* a marriage problem.'

'Rubbish,' Eileen said.

'It's true, Mum.'

Everyone's eyes jumped to Amy. The room went deathly silent.

'What could you possibly know, darling?' Eileen asked her daughter.

Amy told them everything that she had seen at Ned's house. She also spoke fleetingly of her crush on Tony. 'I'm so sorry, Mum, I couldn't help it. I didn't know what was happening to me.'

'Don't worry, darling, these things happen,' Eileen said tightly, her face scarlet with emotion.

Amy looked at her mum with sadness. Although she was young, she instinctively knew how her mum would be feeling. To find out that the love of your life is a two-timing weasel was tough. She could relate to that from her own perspective, and her mother's. Her soul was screaming with anger, injustice, and heartbreak – not to mention guilt.

Her mum's face was calm, almost serene, as she said to Ned, 'Thank you for coming here tonight and letting me know what a complete shit my perfect boyfriend is. I think you can go now. I'll take it from here.'

Ned drove straight home. He resisted the urge to go the pub and get bladdered. He had things to do first.

Linda was in the bath when he got in. He went straight into the bathroom and stood looking down at her, his arms folded.

Linda looked terrified. She pulled her knees up and hugged them to her chest. She was clearly expecting something bad to happen. Alison had phoned her to find out what was going on with Ned after he had put the phone down on her earlier.

'So, are you going to tell me, or am I going to tell you?' Ned said, staring at her.

'I'm sorry,' she almost whispered, the tears starting to stream down her face.

'You're sorry. Is that it?' He looked at her with contempt. 'I've been to see Tony. He's going to have to eat on the other side of his face for the next few days. I don't want to see him again, because if I do, I swear I will fucking kill him for ruining my life.' He leaned towards her intimidatingly. 'And what makes you any different? I should also kill you. You've ruined my life as much as he has, you little whoring bitch.'

Linda cowered in the bath, quietly sobbing. 'I am so sorry.'

'Yes, I'm sure you are. You are dead to me. Pack your bags and get out before I do something that I'll regret!'

Ned turned on his heel and left the bathroom. He then allowed himself to do what he had been yearning to do for the last few hours. He got in his car and drove to the top storey of a multi-level carpark where there were no other vehicles or people around, turned the engine off, then put his head in his hands, and cried.

~

After Ned left the house, Eileen, Tony, and the girls sat in a stunned, uncomfortable silence. Tony sat on the chair, his head bowed, clutching a bloody tissue which he was using to dab his face.

Eventually, Eileen turned to Amy and said softly, 'Take Mary upstairs with you. I need to have a word with Tony.'

The two girls ran upstairs to their rooms, but Amy doubled back and silently crept down to the landing to eavesdrop. The living room door was shut, so she could only hear a murmur of voices. She padded down the carpeted stairs and listened at the door, holding her breath so she wouldn't miss anything.

'Come on, who else?' her mum was asking Tony.

'There's been no one else, I swear!'

'You're a womanising bastard, Tony, of course there were others. You even led Amy on.'

'No, I didn't. I can't help it if the stupid cow fell for me.'

'Did you two do anything?'

'No, I swear I didn't. Ask her!'

'Don't worry, I will, and if I find that you've touched her in any way, I'll cut your fucking balls off!'

Amy could imagine Tony flinching.

'And what about Mary?' Eileen went on.

'What about her?'

'That night when she thought someone was touching her in her sleep.'

'What about it?'

'When she screamed, I woke up. You were just getting back into bed. You said you'd been to the bathroom.'

'I had been to the bathroom,' Tony said, his tone defensive.

'Are you sure?'

'Of course, I'm bloody sure. What are you saying?'

'I'm saying that now that I know that you are a liar and a cheat, it calls into question everything else that you've said.'

'I've told you, I was in the bathroom that night.'

No, you weren't, thought Amy. She remembered passing the bathroom when she had rushed into Mary's bedroom. The bathroom door had definitely been wide open. She had a mental snapshot of that night.

The realisation made her sick inside. The probability was that Tony *had* touched Mary. She looked up through the stair-well towards Mary's bedroom to make sure that she hadn't been eavesdropping as well, and then went back to her own room.

44

Tony left that day. Over the next few months, Eileen went into a state of decline. She was listless, hardly ate, and her face was lined and pale. Conversely, Amy put on weight, and her face took on a healthy glow. Her schoolwork improved, as did her exam results. Mary, too, seemed more content. Amy had more time for her these days, and their bond was, if anything, stronger.

Other children kept their distance from the sisters and thought they were a little strange. This was more to do with Mary who would lapse into long, distant silences and had a cold, unblinking stare, which many found unnerving. However, the two girls had each other's backs, were content with their own company and family, and got on with their lives.

Until something happened that took those lives on a different course.

They came home from school one day, eager to tell their mother about a new teacher, Mr Forester, who, at six foot two and with brown, curly hair, was considered quite a hunk. They ran giggling along the hallway towards the kitchen at the rear of the house where their mum always was, only to find it empty. Amy noticed that her mum's knitting that had been started that morning hadn't progressed any further and was lying on the arm of her mum's chair.

'She'll be upstairs,' Amy said.

Their mother's bedroom door was shut, which was unusual. Amy tapped on the door and then let herself quietly into the room. Her mum was in bed, her eyes closed.

'She must have taken a sleeping pill,' Mary said, looking at the bottle on the bedside table.

Amy suddenly realised that something was wrong. She pulled the duvet down and shook her mother's arm, which was cold. She looked at Mary in horror.

'Phone 999, now!'

When the ambulance crew arrived, the girls were on either side of their mother, cuddling her, as if they could warm her back to life.

The funeral was a small affair, with just the two girls and the people who had employed Eileen to clean for them. The vicar, a huge, rotund individual with a bushy, black beard, gave a sermon in which he talked about forgiveness, then read from the bible, quoting Matthew's Sermon on the Mount. As he spoke, his baritone voice echoing through the church. The two girls looked at each other.

Mary whispered, 'An eye for an eye.'

Amy shushed her sister and turned back towards the pulpit.

When the service finished, the usher motioned for the girls to leave first. As they walked along the aisle, they spotted a figure in the back pew. It was Tony.

The two girls looked at him icily, then turned their heads away.

45

When Tony left, he had moved into a bedsit above a pub. Because of his affair with Linda, he had been kicked out of the band, and as a result, his income was limited. The landlord of the pub had taken sympathy on Tony and offered him free accommodation and a few pints in return for playing his guitar and singing in the pub. This suited Tony down to the ground; there was always some willing lady who would be tempted by Tony's smiley eyes. As far as he was concerned, everything was on the up.

One night, as Tony was nearing the end of his set, he looked up. His heart sank when he saw Ned, leaning by the bar, watching, a look of hatred on his face.

Ned drew a finger across his throat and pointed at him. Tony was so shaken, he played the wrong chord. He called an end to the set, and put down his guitar. He looked at where Ned had been, but he was no longer there. Relieved, Tony went behind the bar and poured himself a large vodka, and then walked towards the pub garden.

'Just going for a fag break,' he called to one of the bar staff.

The landlord Gerard and his wife were having a night off. They always took Thursday nights off; they were sacrosanct. They had enjoyed a wonderful three-course meal at a country pub restaurant a few miles away. They drove back, planning to have a nightcap at their own bar before going to bed.

As they neared their pub, they could see flashes of blue light that lit up the surrounding shops and offices. A police barricade was set up along the street, so they parked and walked the remaining distance, astounded to find that the blue, flashing lights belonged to police cars outside their own premises.

A policeman stopped them at the tape that was cordoning off the area, and said, 'I'm sorry, but you can't come through here.'

'But this is our pub – and our home,' Gerard said, a little crossly. 'What the hell is going on?'

'Come this way,' said the officer, and led them to a detective.

'Are you the business owners?'

'Yes, we are. Why?'

'Do you know a Tony Walker?'

'Yes, he lives here.'

'Not anymore, he doesn't,' the detective said wryly. 'He was found dead a couple of hours ago in the pub garden. He was murdered. Can you tell me where you've been this evening?'

The couple, now shaken and anxious to help, answered the detective's questions and asked some of their own. The detective told them that Tony hadn't returned from the pub garden. No one had noticed his failure to return until one of the punters had called out for the background music to be turned on. The barman had said no, because Tony was singing that evening, whereupon the punter had asked, 'Well, where is he?'

At that point, someone had run in from outside, shouting for the police to be called. There was a dead body in the car park. When the police arrived, they had found Tony's body near some dustbins.

He'd been hit on the head with a brick, then strangled with a rope.

46

Ned Chandler stood in the dock, Linda watching him from the public gallery. She had already given evidence. The barrister pointed dramatically at Ned, half-turning to face the jury.

'Mr Chandler, did you, or did you not, say to your estranged wife that you would kill Tony Walker?'

'I did, but–'

'Yes or no?'

'Well, yes, but–'

'And you also threatened to kill your wife Linda?'

'I did say things to her that I didn't actually mean.'

'But you did threaten her?'

'Sort of, yes, but I was angry and–'

'In addition, Mr Chandler, on the night of the murder, just minutes before it happened...'

The prosecutor looked at the jury, looking almost gleeful.

'... were you, or were you not, at the very same premises where the body of Mr Walker was found?'

'Yes,' Ned said softly, his head bowed. He was starting to

feel a sense of inevitability. Tears of frustration started to flow.

'I beg your pardon,' the prosecutor said, his voice rising. 'I don't believe the jury could hear you properly. Were you at the pub just before Tony Walker was murdered?'

'I was, but I–'

'A "yes" or "no" will suffice,' snapped the barrister. 'Mr Chandler, we also have a witness who states that on the night in question, he saw you make a threatening gesture to the victim shortly before his body was found. Come now, with all of this compelling evidence, you surely can't expect the jury to believe anything other than that you murdered Tony Walker?'

47

PRESENT DAY

After uniformed officers had taken Amy away, Harry checked on PC John Stephens.

After being jabbed in the hand by the syringe, he had been looked over immediately by a doctor. He had Rohypnol in his system, but only a small amount. Amy hadn't had enough time to fully depress the plunger.

Harry wondered if she had intended to take Stephens' unconscious body to another location and finish the job by strangling him. She could easily have transported the body out of the hospital using a wheelchair or a trolley.

Harry thanked his team and the hospital staff and drove back to his office.

It was a big result, but it wasn't over yet. Harry was assuming that Amy and Sam were one and the same, but he wasn't one hundred percent sure how many others were involved in this Circle of Hera. He needed hard evidence, and his only key was Amy Peters.

He was still shocked at how things were turning out. He had met three different versions of the same woman – the bright, flirty, confident go-getter on the plane, the defensive, guarded person at the Moon pub with her apparent punter, and this version, who was obviously clever, devious, and resourceful.

'Are you okay?' Alex had entered the office holding a bag. 'I bought you lunch, you must be starving.'

Harry looked on as she laid out a variety of Chinese take-away dishes, his mouth watering.

'You shouldn't have... But I'm glad you did.'

Some twenty minutes later, Harry sat back in his chair. 'I needed that. Thanks, Alex. I'm ready for a snooze now.'

'You do what you like,' she laughed, and then her face turned serious. 'So you and this Amy – do you have a history with her?'

'No, at least not in the way that you mean. We met on the plane when I came back from America. We sat next to each other and got along. And then she sort of disappeared.'

'Disappeared?'

'Yes. We had arranged to have coffee together, but she blew me out.'

Alex arched an eyebrow. 'Some men pay good money for that!'

Harry laughed at her quick wit. 'It's funny you should say that. I saw her recently in a pub and she gave me the impression that she was on the game.'

'Really? How?'

'Just something that she said – and the fact that she was with some low-life, who might have been a punter.'

'Ouch. Are you still angry with her?'

'Absolutely not. Well... maybe a bit. She has certainly fooled me a couple of times. What I feel is curiosity. What will she be like when we interview her tomorrow? Will she be acting a part? Or will we see the real Amy Peters?'

The next day brought the first onslaught of winter. Freezing rain and howling gales vied with each other to see which could create the most discomfort. Harry watched through the window at Farrow Road, at the pained expressions on the faces of passers-by, as they battled against the elements.

He turned back to the comparative warmth and comfort of the interview room. Next to him sat Sandy Sanders, together with Amy Peters and her solicitor, Robert McGuire.

Amy was staring across the table at Harry, wearing a half-smile, which he found mildly disconcerting.

After going through the formalities, Harry began. His plan was to start at the end and then work his way back to the beginning.

'When we caught you yesterday, you were about to administer a drug to PC Stephens. Can you tell us what the drug was and why you were going to use it?'

Harry heard Amy's solicitor tell her that she didn't have to answer the question.

'But she does, Mr McGuire,' Harry said. 'If she wants us to know the truth about everything. We have more than enough evidence to make a case, so if you like, we'll fill in what we know – and can prove – and we'll send Amy back to her cell to await her fate. It's entirely up to you.'

Amy turned to her solicitor. 'I want to tell them everything.'

'Are you sure about this?' McGuire looked deeply concerned. 'You must understand that by doing that, you could inadvertently be–'

'Don't worry, I know what I'm doing.'

'This is contrary to my advice,' McGuire said sternly.

She nodded. 'I know.'

She faced the officers.

'I committed the murders.'

Her solicitor looked aghast. 'Miss Peters, you are going too far–'

'All of them. I plead guilty to all charges.'

Harry and Sandy looked at each other. A full confession – this early?

'Miss Peters, it doesn't work that way. We have to establish the facts.'

'But I'm confessing. Nothing more needs to be said. I'm guilty – put me in prison and save the taxpayers' money. I did the murders.'

'With whom?' asked Harry.

'Nobody else. Just me.'

Harry shook his head. 'No, no, no. Okay, Miss Peters. Let's try again, starting from the beginning.'

Amy Peters' plea that she was the only person involved in the murders was quickly dispatched by Harry. Over the next couple of hours, he questioned her thoroughly, his questions jumping from the murder of Kevin Stock to that of Greening and Hamilton and then back to Stock again. This technique kept Amy Peters unsettled, giving her no time to think. When he got to Phillip Greening's body being found in the hotel room, he asked to see Amy's arms.

Despite her solicitor's protestations, Amy pushed up her sleeves to reveal her slender arms.

'Now, your solicitor, Mr McGuire, will appreciate that in a court of law, no jury is going to believe that you, a slip of a woman, held a sixteen-stone man up against a bathroom door with one arm, threw the rope over the door, and then knotted it around the door handle on the other side.'

Harry paused and looked at her pointedly.

'Miss Peters, if you're expecting to get away with taking the blame for the other people you have been working with, then I'm sorry to tell you that it just isn't going to work. Surely you can see that?'

She folded her arms. 'I stand by what I said. I did everything on my own. You've got me. You haven't got anything else, have you?'

She shot him an almost triumphant look. Harry ignored her and concentrated on the paperwork in front of him.

He eventually looked up across at Amy, his eyes boring into hers. 'You really have no idea, Miss Peters.' He held the look before adding, 'It's no use you trying to protect your sister. I believe she is as guilty as you – probably guiltier.'

For a second, the light dimmed in her eyes. 'You've got nothing on her.'

'We know that you and your sister had a tough childhood before your father left home. We know that he was replaced by your mother's boyfriend, Tony Walker, who was a bit of a player, shall we say, and that he was murdered. Who by? Perhaps we'll never know for sure. Maybe it was you or your sister. Or both of you.'

'I really must protest,' said McGuire. 'You are more than straying beyond the boundaries of evidence.'

'If I am, then I apologise for the inference,' Harry said. 'Ned Chandler was found guilty of Tony Walker's murder. Ned is still in prison. He's looking well, by the way, and looking forward to getting out soon.' He stared at Amy Peters, who was looking agitated for the first time. 'But how soon he gets out will be up to you.'

Once more, McGuire cut in, 'Really! I've never encountered such an interview in my entire career. You have absolutely no foundation for these wild accusations. I wish to terminate this now and consult with my client.'

'As you wish,' Harry said. 'Interview terminated at eleven seventeen.'

He switched off the digital recorder.

'You should advise your client in the strongest possible terms,' Harry said to McGuire, looking directly at Peters, 'that we *will* find her sister, with or without her help, but if she helps us, it could go in her favour.'

As Amy Peters was led away, Harry stood up and looked back out of the window. The sky had darkened and there were far fewer people around. *They're going home to their cosy lives*, Harry thought, feeling a twinge of something. Jealousy perhaps?

An hour later, he was in his office. He had briefed the team and was now surveying the faces before him. 'Any thoughts?'

'How did you know about the sister?' Sandy asked. 'And about the man in prison, Ned Chandler?'

'Everything linked together. I just googled it. First, I found out what school Amy Peters attended, and then I went there to see if any teachers remembered her. I spoke to a Mr Forester, who not only knew Amy and her sister Mary, but he also remembered that their mother had died. I then spoke to the vicar who had taken the funeral. He remembered the service because there were so few mourners, it was one of the smallest gatherings he had experienced. He remembered Tony Walker and the two girls being there. As a musician, Tony was well known in the area.'

'But what about Ned Chandler?' Dawn asked.

'Tony Walker's death is a matter of public record. I just followed it up, read the reports, and then visited Chandler in prison.'

'You actually went to see him?'

Harry nodded.

'He's in Wormwood Scrubs, so it wasn't far to travel. He is a very bitter man, and if he was telling me the truth, understandably so. He swears he is innocent – of course he would, wouldn't he? But I believe him.'

'So, we are thinking the two sisters had something to do with Tony Walker's death,' Sandy said.

Harry nodded. 'Yes. There's motive, means, and opportunity. The sisters have a motive because Tony was having an affair with Ned's wife. This was discovered by Amy – she apparently had a crush on Tony. Consequently, her sister and mother got to know about Tony's affair with Linda, which led to the mother committing suicide. I suppose that's two motives.'

'What about opportunity and means?' Alex asked.

'The "means" was a house brick, which was used to knock Tony out. He was then strangled with a rope – similar to our recent murders. It might be a little harder to prove that the girls had the opportunity, because so did Ned, who was in the vicinity that night.'

'Theoretically, what would happen if we just let her plead guilty as she wishes?' Dawn Koorus asked.

'She'd get off scot-free,' Harry said. 'Her solicitor would trot out the same argument that we've already made. How can an eight-stone woman lift a heavy man like Phillip Greening? It would be case dismissed.'

'Yes, of course,' Dawn said.

'And apart from anything else, it would obviously be immoral to know about someone else's involvement in a crime and not investigate it.'

'In that case,' Dawn said, 'we have to find Mary Peters.'

48

Alex and Dawn arrived at Amy Peters' house. The police and the forensic team had already been through the property. The officers were looking for anything that would indicate Mary Peters' whereabouts.

It was an old, semi-detached building with large, bay windows. Upstairs, it was clear that the sisters had a bedroom each, and there was a smaller room that was being used as an office.

Alex picked up a photo frame that held a picture of two young girls and a woman. 'That must have been their mother.'

'She'd be turning in her grave if she could see how her daughters turned out,' Dawn said.

'We don't know that both of the daughters committed the murders though,' Alex said. 'We believe that Amy must have had an accomplice, but that's as far as it goes. Her sister might be innocent.'

'Talking of which...' Dawn was holding aloft another photo. It was Mary Peters. She had shoulder-length, fair hair, grey eyes, and was staring unsmilingly into the camera lens.

'My God, she has cold eyes.'

'You wouldn't want to cross her, would you?' Dawn replied.

Alex went into the office. In the corner was an old bureau. It was beautifully carved and had a highly polished finish. As Alex was admiring it, she found herself trailing the letter "H" into the fine layer of dust that covered the surface. Quickly, she smudged it out.

'Have you found something?' Dawn asked.

'No,' Alex said quickly, her face starting to burn. As she stood back, she noticed something white peeping out from under one of the bureau legs. She bent down and pulled at it. It was a sheet of paper that had been folded multiple times and then put under the bureau to stop it wobbling. It was a letter dated a couple of months prior, marked "Very Private and Confidential" and headed "St Anne's Wellbeing Centre."

'I think we might have a lead on Mary Peters' whereabouts,' Alex said, waving the page at Dawn.

'What is it?'

'It's a recent letter from a care home. It's from the manager to Amy Peters, inviting her to an open day. It says, "Family only."' Alex tapped her finger on the paper. 'Mary could be a patient at this wellbeing centre. Why else would Amy have the letter? I think we should pay a visit.'

Alex phoned Harry to update him.

'What are your thoughts?' he asked. 'Would Mary be allowed to come and go from the institution whenever she liked? That would enable her to help her sister commit the murders. Or is she a full-time patient and is totally innocent in all of this?'

'I don't know, Harry, but it's a lead, and we don't have anything else at the moment.'

There was a sigh at the other end of the phone. 'I suppose you're right. I'll meet you there.'

After a quick bite to eat, Alex and Dawn drove to St Anne's Wellbeing Centre. It was at the end of a long drive, lined by wire fencing. Grazing animals in the adjoining fields looked up at them as they passed. They pulled up at a barrier where a security guard stood with a gloved hand raised.

'For what purpose are you visiting?' he asked, peering into the driver's window.

Alex showed her warrant card. 'We're here to see the nursing manager.'

'Park over there,' he said, picking up his walkie-talkie.

They were shown into an opulent office that featured a leather-topped pedestal desk, behind which sat a prim looking lady with short, fair hair and glasses.

'I'm Mrs Burnett, but please call me Trudy. How may I be of assistance?' she said, motioning at the two chairs in front of her.

The officers sat and introduced themselves.

'We are hoping that you have an inmate–'

'Not inmate. Patient,' rebuked Burnett with a slight smile.

'Sorry, patient, by the name of Mary Peters.'

'Mary Peters. Yes, we do have someone by that name. What do you need her for?'

'She's wanted for questioning about a series of murders,' Alex said.

'Murders... Mary... really? Good gracious, I should hardly think so.' Burnett sat back in her seat, her hand to her mouth, looking shaken. 'I'm terribly sorry but I find that difficult to believe.'

'I'm afraid it's true. Can we see her?'

Burnett stood up. 'I'm sorry, but you may have had a wasted journey. She's not here at the moment. I understand that she's gone to see her sister.'

'Do you mean Amy Peters?'

'Yes, that's right. Why? Do you know her?'

'Oh yes, we certainly do,' Dawn said. 'We're holding her for murder too.'

'Really?' exclaimed Burnett, sitting down again. 'Are you sure we're talking about the same women? I've known both ladies for years, and they are the–'

'Is it possible to see Mary's room, Mrs Burnett?' Alex cut in.

'Of course, forgive me. If you'd like to follow me, I'll take you there.'

They went through a series of electronic doors, each one opened by a card on a lanyard around Mrs Burnett's neck, until they finally came to a hefty looking door with a reinforced glass panel.

Burnett produced a large key from a bunch, unlocked the door, and opened it wide.

'There you are,' she said. 'Please have a good look around. You'll need to sign for anything that you want to take away.'

The officers went into the room. There were a couple of easy chairs and a shelving unit, on which there were books, a variety of folders, and some framed photos. There was a door which Alex assumed would lead to Mary's bedroom and bathroom. She pushed at the door, but found that it was just a stationery cupboard. There were no other doors apart from the one leading into the room that they were in.

In the meantime, Dawn was perusing the photos. 'That's funny,' she said.

'What is?' asked Alex

'These photos are all standard stock photos that you can find on the internet. There are no personal ones, or any that appear to be family. In fact...' She opened a drawer, which was empty, as was the next one she tried. 'There's nothing else here.'

The officers looked at each other.

There had been something niggling at the back of Alex's

mind since they'd arrived at the wellbeing centre, and suddenly it hit home. It was Burnett's eyes. Take away those glasses and...

The door slammed behind them.

Alex flung herself across the room, shouting, 'Stop!'

But the big key had already turned in the lock. Burnett's face appeared in the glass window above it, smiling.

'Trudy... Mary Peters, let us out now!' Alex shouted.

But she was gone.

'Shit, shit, shit,' Alex said, pulling out her phone.

She filled Harry in on everything that had happened.

'I'm so sorry, Harry, I should have sussed it. I knew there was something wrong.'

'I'm just about to turn into the drive that leads up to the centre now,' Harry said. 'How long ago did this happen?'

'Just a couple of minutes. I phoned you straightaway.'

'If she tries to escape by car, there's only room for one of us on this lane so there's no way out, unless there's another exit somewhere.'

'I can see her!' Dawn shouted from the window. 'She's driving a red car, I think it's a Corsa.'

'Got that,' said Harry, looking up the drive. 'I can see her.'

He disconnected the call and watched the car come down the track. She seemed to be getting faster. *She's surely not going to plough into me*, he thought.

He braked sharply as the Corsa hurtled straight towards him. Then, at the last minute, it veered off the road, snapping the wire fencing and skidding into the muddy field.

Harry drove his Saab through the newly made gap in the fence and took off after her, both cars bouncing and slithering around the uneven field. Cows languidly looked up from their grazing, still chewing, as the two vehicles slewed around. Harry watched as the red Corsa skidded in a semi-circle, He could see the occupant looking straight back at him. Even at that distance, Harry could see her resemblance to Amy. Then she sped off again, haring across the field to a five-bar gate that was being opened by a farmer.

Harry was only about fifty yards behind her, but it was difficult going. He vowed that his next car would be a 4x4. He could feel the car chassis striking the protruding stones of the field underneath. The Corsa was having difficulties too, but she steered through the gate just before the first cows came through it from the adjoining field.

The farmer had watched the Corsa come into his field, a disbelieving look on his face, and then had looked back at Harry who had had to stop so he didn't hit the animals.

Shaking his head, the farmer got back to his task and whistled for his dog.

Harry groaned and sat behind the wheel. He could do nothing else but wait for the cows to take their time to plod into the field.

In the distance, he could see his quarry. She was still slithering from side to side, but well ahead of him.

Then he had a thought. A lane ran parallel to the field he was in. There surely had to be an entrance to the field to allow tractors in and out. He'd be able to go a lot faster on the lane and would stand a better chance of catching her. He drove towards the perimeter of the field. To his relief, there was an opening that led out over a cattle grid onto the lane.

Now Harry could really put his foot down. The Saab's engine screamed as he tore along the country lane. He swerved around a corner, nearly running into a group of cyclists. He sped up again, ignoring the abusive shouts behind him.

He could now see the field where he'd last seen the Corsa. There was no sign of her. He reasoned that she would probably try to hide the car rather than go onto the major roads. She may even ditch the car and go on foot. He slowed down.

He took a turn to his left, which he reckoned would cut her off, and drove along slowly, his eyes carefully scanning the surrounding fields and woodland.

Then he saw a flash of red through the trees. He reversed the Saab to get a better look. He could see a barn in the distance and the Corsa, the driver's door wide open. If the car hadn't been such a bright colour, he was sure he would have missed it altogether.

He drove towards the barn and pulled into a shingle drive in front of the Corsa, blocking it in. He checked the interior to ensure it was empty, and then moved cautiously towards the barn, knowing full well that Peters would have heard his car draw up and would either be running to hide in the nearby woods or would be in the barn.

He didn't know what he was dealing with. Was Mary Peters a mass murderer, a patient in a psychiatric ward, or something else?

He pushed open the door to the barn and peered into the gloom. The barn contained a rusty, old tractor and some bales of hay. *Seems familiar*, he thought. Except that the last time he was in a barn, he'd had a gun pointing at him. The thought concentrated his mind. *Perhaps she is lying in wait?*

As his eyes adjusted to the dim interior, he could see a wooden landing high up on his right. There was a ladder attached. He put his foot on the bottom rung and waited, hardly daring to breathe.

He heard a rustling sound above him. It was either some rodent, or it was Peters. If it *was* her, then there was nowhere else she could go.

Quietly, he climbed up the ladder, unwilling to look down, and hauled himself onto the vast, wooden platform. There he stopped and listened, crouching, attempting to get his bearings. He peered around, cursing the lack of light but unwilling to turn on the torch on his phone and give away his position.

He stood up, trying to hear beyond the silence.

There was that faint rustling again. He moved towards the sound and then stopped once more to listen.

Suddenly, he was being strangled.

A rope had been thrown around his neck from behind and he was being pulled backwards, the cord squeezing into his throat, cutting off the air to his lungs. There was a pounding in his head as his hands tried to grab the rope. He was seeing darkness and shapes, and felt helpless. He was being choked to death.

It was as though a hefty man was behind him, such was the strength and force around his neck. He stayed on his feet and wrenched his body around, which allowed him to draw some breath. It also gave him a glimpse of his attacker.

Mary Peters was before him, her face a screaming mass of hatred as she tightened the rope that was ending his life. Harry let his body go limp and slumped towards the floor. She lessened her grip slightly, which enabled him to pivot around. He drove his knee hard into her stomach. She gasped and doubled up, presenting Harry with a clear target. He had never hit a woman before, but she was a multiple murderer – and she was trying to kill him.

He punched her hard in the neck. She staggered and fell backwards, disappearing into the gloom.

Harry swiftly took off the rope around his neck and breathed in deeply. He didn't care about the farmyard smell; it was the sweetest air he'd ever tasted.

He peered around to see where she'd landed. He knew he'd hit her with some force, so he thought she might be lying unconscious, but he wasn't sure. She had been as strong as an ox. He waited, bracing himself against another onslaught from her, but there was just an unnerving silence.

He pulled out his phone, switched it to torch, and shone the light around cautiously.

Several coils of rope sat next to the edge of the platform. Carefully, Harry stepped over them and shone the beam down onto the floor below. In the dim light, he could see a figure, upside down, buried into the seat of the old tractor. There was little doubt that Mary Peters was dead. She must have caught her feet on the coils of rope, and fallen headfirst onto the tractor.

The reality of the situation hit Harry. Not only had he never hit a woman, but he hadn't killed one either. While it wasn't deliberate, he had caused her death. The thought made him feel sick.

He clambered back down the ladder and left the barn, squinting in the harsh daylight. He radioed Control, then sat on the ground waiting for his colleagues to arrive.

49

For the next few days, the barn was a hive of activity, with the forensic team taking over.

Because Mary Peters' death had involved a police officer, Harry was immediately suspended pending enquiries. This was standard procedure. The powers that be had to investigate, to see if Harry had a case to answer.

He had been taken to the hospital to be checked out. He had severe bruising around his neck, and the bandages around his head needed to be changed. His tussle with Mary Peters had left him looking like an unravelled Egyptian mummy.

The two officers had eventually been freed from the room at the wellbeing centre, with Alex desperate for a wee and Dawn complaining about being hungry. Alex was still angry at herself for falling for what she considered to be the oldest trick in the book. She went to visit Harry at his flat. Perhaps to apologise, she didn't know. But she wanted to see him anyway.

He opened the door to her, unshaven and dishevelled. The red weal from the rope stood out on his neck. The nurse had put a dressing on it, which Harry had promptly removed, along with the bandages around his head. He was a mess. His newly bald head looked scarred; red and pink blotches dotted his skull with tiny tufts of baby hair.

'I know,' Harry said, seeing her reaction. 'I look like Freddy Krueger. You don't have to be kind to me.'

'That looks nasty,' she said.

'You should see the other guy. Come on in. Excuse the mess.'

Alex wandered through Harry's flat, finding herself thinking about how she would rearrange it. *None of your business, Alex*, a voice in her head chided. *Nothing's going to happen between you.*

'Coffee?'

Harry's voice broke into her thoughts.

'Yes, please.'

Harry's lounge gave conflicting statements, Alex thought, as she looked around. There was an old-fashioned, framed photo on his windowsill of a much younger Harry with a woman, possibly his mother, and there was another of the same woman on his mantelpiece. *There was clearly a big love for this woman*, she thought.

Two speakers dominated the room. An abundance of sound equipment was stacked on a shelf beside a collection of CDs, mostly rock and jazz. She recognised the music that was playing softly in the background as Mendelssohn. Here was a man with extreme tastes – a complex man. Although she had already sensed that.

'Your mother?' Alex asked, nodding at the photos, as Harry came into the lounge with a tray bearing matching cups and a coffee pot.

'Yes. Sadly, she's in a home now,' he said, setting the tray on the coffee table. 'She has Alzheimer's.'

'I'm very sorry.'

'That's okay, she's had an amazing life, and she still tries to keep mentally active now, despite her condition.'

'Do you get to see her much?'

'Not as often as I should, but now that I have some enforced time off, I'll go down and see her.'

'If you'd like me to go with you...'

'I'll bear that in mind, thanks. Milk, sugar?'

They chit-chatted the morning away. Harry was happy to have Alex's company.

'So where did the name Harry come from?' Alex asked. 'Wasn't it an unusual name for your generation?'

'It wasn't so bad. My name came from my grandfather, who was a Harold. As I grew up, Prince Harry was born, so some people thought it was cool.'

The phone rang. It was Mainwaring.

'How are you feeling, Harry?'

'Fine thanks, ma'am.'

'Good. I need you back here as soon as possible. Amy Peters says that, in the light of her sister's death, she wants to make a full confession, hopefully the honest version. However, she says that she'll only speak to you, and no one else.'

'Really? But what about my suspension?'

'I've already spoken to IOPC. Because of the circumstances, they're quite happy for this to go ahead, particularly given that the outcome, as far as you are concerned, will be pretty much cut and dried. They don't see that you could have a case to answer. So they are seeing this as what they call a "professional interruption to your suspension." It's amazing what you can do with words when you have to.'

'Indeed. How did Amy take her sister's death?'

'I'm told that she's devastated and hasn't stopped crying. When can you come in?'

'Just let me shower and I'll be there.'

Harry and Alex arrived at the station to find activity and chaos. The newspapers had got hold of the story about the Circle of Hera, the revenge angle, and the death of Mary Peters, so journalists were all over the steps at Farrow Road station.

A microphone was shoved into Harry's face as he pushed past. 'What do you know about the killings and the Circle of Hera?'

'No comment,' Harry said, thankful for the fact that the journalists didn't yet know how involved he had been in the case.

Mainwaring was standing in the lobby of the station, preparing to make a statement. She was looking at the crowd outside the doors and glanced at Harry's head in mild surprise as he passed. 'Thank you for coming in, Harry. Are you sure you're okay?'

'I'm fine,' he said, still wondering how her personality had changed so radically. Less than a month ago, she wouldn't have given him the time of day.

The interview room was already set up; cameras were ready, as was the digital sound recorder. Amy Peters was led into the room. She was white-faced and her cheeks were streaked with dry tears. She was clutching a box of tissues and looked withered and vulnerable. A very different Amy from the one he had interviewed earlier.

By the end of the afternoon, Harry had a complete picture of all that had happened. His brain was reeling from everything he had heard.

Amy admitted assisting Mary to kill Tony Walker. Amy said that Chandler being in the frame for the murder let them off the hook and gave them the confidence to do it again.

It appeared that Hera's Circle was international. The sisters had flitted back and forth to the States, and Harry now knew that the American police were investigating the murders of several males who had been executed in the same manner.

Harry made a mental note to email his contacts in the NYPD. Perhaps he might find himself over there, helping out again? He shrugged off the pleasant thought and forced his mind back to the present.

'Miss Peters, I am only interested in the murders that you and your sister are responsible for in the UK. Anything else will be dealt with as a separate investigation. Do you understand?'

'Yes,' she replied, in little more than a whisper.

'We know that you were contacted by Laura Hamilton, Lisa Stock, and Sarah Greening prior to their husbands' deaths, but who contacted you prior to Jeremy Baxter being murdered?'

'Who's Jeremy Baxter?' Amy Peters looked at Harry with what seemed like genuine bewilderment.

'Jeremy Baxter was your last victim. He was killed in the same way as the others. Don't tell me, Miss Peters, that you and your sister have committed so many murders that you've forgotten who you've killed.'

Amy shook her head. Her solicitor Robert McGuire rose to his feet. 'Are you going to attempt to pin all of your unsolved crimes on my client? You have zero evidence and I strongly–'

'All right, Mr McGuire, I will take that accusation off the table – for now.' Harry didn't want to muddy the waters until he had more evidence. 'Miss Peters, you've told us that these murders were committed by your sister Mary and assisted by you. But how do we know that Mary was guilty of these murders? It could just as easily have been you.'

'Yes, it could,' replied Amy, 'but I think *you* know the truth. I don't care what sentence the courts give me.'

Harry didn't get the feeling that he was being played in any way. Her manner seemed very resigned. Distant, even.

Amy and her sister had got the idea for Hera's Circle after watching a documentary about how the Olympic games had originated. The program suggested that the original games had been started in honour of Zeus, the husband of Hera.

Amy had gone on to read how Zeus had famously cheated many times on Hera, and how she'd got her own back. Hera's capacity for revenge had inspired them.

'Then you and your sister decided that you would spend the rest of your lives punishing men by offering this service to cheated wives?'

She nodded. 'After Tony, I suppose it got easier and easier.'

'Jesus. You must really hate us men,' Harry said.

'Not all men,' she said softly. 'You were different. I liked you.'

'You had a strange way of showing it.'

'I'm sorry about the airport, and that time in that pub when I had company.'

'I remember it well. Talking of which, what about this other profession of yours?'

'What other profession?'

'When I saw you and that guy in the pub, you told me that your job involved men, which gave me the impression you were some kind of sex worker.'

Amy's face crinkled into a smile. 'Me, a sex worker? Ah, when I said that the job involved men, I was talking about Hera's Circle.'

'Then who was that man?' Then Harry suddenly understood. 'Don't tell me he was being lined up for Hera's revenge.'

She nodded. 'You effectively saved his life by coming over

to talk to me. We obviously couldn't go ahead with him after that.'

Harry wondered if the man would ever know what a lucky escape he'd had. 'Why couldn't you have just led an ordinary life with a husband and kids?'

'I could never have a proper relationship with any man.'

'Why?'

'Because of various events in our childhood,' Amy said. 'Our father was a bully who Mum eventually threw out. Then there was Tony, who was a cheating bastard. We blamed him for our mum committing suicide. After that, we both had other bad experiences with men. Then Mary and I had a pact where neither of us would get involved with any man ever again. When you and I met, I was tempted to break that pact, but I couldn't. When you invited me for coffee, there was a small part of me that really wanted to meet up with you, honestly.'

'But why did you sit next to me in the first place?'

'Because there was a spare seat next to you.'

'Was that the only reason?'

'Oh, don't worry. I wasn't sizing you up to be the next victim or anything.'

Harry hadn't considered that. The thought shocked him. 'Is that how it worked? Did you size up innocent men to be your victims?'

'No. It was all done through the website. Unhappy women contacted us to say that their husband or partner was cheating, and we would deal with it.'

'When you say "deal with it," you mean "kill them."'

There was a long pause. Amy looked down at her hands. She looked up into Harry's eyes, and whispered, 'It wasn't meant to be like that. Our original idea was to honey-trap the cheating husband by coming on to him. If he responded, we would embarrass him by tying him up and leaving him somewhere with a message telling the world that he was a cheating bastard.'

'So why did you murder them instead?'

'That wasn't my idea. After Mary killed Tony, I think she got a taste for it, and when we eventually had our first client, she went all the way.'

'So, to be clear, you're still trying to make me believe that you personally didn't murder anyone?'

'That's right. My role was to entice the husband somewhere, such as an empty house.'

'Or hotel room.'

'Yes, and drug them. My sister would then arrive and finish them off.'

'You mean she would arrive and murder them?'

'Yes.'

'Who was Sam?' Harry asked.

'That was me. The name Sam came by accident when I was a kid. One Christmas, I left a note for Mary saying, "Go to bed early, Santa is coming 5am." She misread the note and woke me up to ask who "Sam" was. And it stuck. Sam became an alter ego. One of a few, as it turned out.'

Harry found it difficult to believe that this seemingly sensitive, intelligent woman in front of him could be party to such atrocities. It seemed almost unthinkable. When they had met on the plane, he had felt that he knew her, connected with her even. Seeing her for that second time at the pub had still given him no clue what she was capable of.

'I know what you're thinking,' she said, as if reading his mind, 'but you must understand that after Tony, there was no going back. It was all about me and Mary sticking together.'

'You realise that an innocent man has been in prison for many years, thanks to you?'

'Yes, and I regret that. But my priority is – or was – to look after my little sister, no matter what.' Her face clouded over.

'No matter what,' Harry repeated.

'Yes,' she said, tears again streaming down her face. 'Of course, I wanted it to stop. I even left clues for the police to find.'

'What clues?'

'Who do you think left the rope message?'

'Hera, of course. That was you?'

'Yes, and I left the message written in blood on the hotel room wall.'

'You wrote "Her," instead of "Hera."'

'I did. Mary was getting worse. It was all getting out of hand, but I didn't know what to do. It was a kind of cry for help, I suppose. I know I should have told someone, but...' She shrugged.

'Talking about the murder in the hotel room, why did you stray away from your normal methods?'

'How do you mean?'

'When we found Phillip Greening, he was strung up over a door, and he had been hit over the head.'

'Yes. He really deserved to die. He attacked me in the hotel room. Mary had been waiting outside. She heard me shout and let herself in. She hit him with an ornament and knocked him out.' Amy looked away into the distance as if reliving the entire episode. 'She was so upset that I'd been attacked – it was as if she was trying to make a statement to tell the world that he was even worse than the others, so we propped him up against the door.'

'How did you manage, just the two of you?'

'Mary was exceptionally strong.'

That's true enough, Harry thought, lightly stroking the weal on his neck. 'So why did you drug the victims before strangling them?'

'Practicality. It was just so much easier to get the rope around them while they were unconscious.'

'About your sister, what exactly was her role at the St Anne's Wellbeing Centre?'

'She was really the nursing manager.'

Harry looked at her in amazement. 'Good God.' He looked down at his notes. 'She was using a different name – Trudy Burnett.'

'Yes, Mary loved being other people. In another life, she would have made a great actress.'

'As would you,' Harry said pointedly. 'What a waste of a talent for both of you.'

'What's going to happen to me now?'

'In light of your confession, you'll be charged and held. Ultimately, you'll go to prison.'

'I always knew it would come to this,' Amy said, looking down at the floor, 'but I thought it would be me and Mary together forever.'

When Harry returned to his office, there was a carrier bag on his desk. Inside was an envelope and a bottle of single malt.

Harry smiled appreciatively and opened the envelope. 'Bloody hell!' he exclaimed. Inside was a card. It read, "Congratulations on a great result. – Liz Mainwaring (aka The Führer)."

Harry wasn't sure if he was more surprised at the gift or the way his boss had signed the card.

There was a tap on the door. Alex entered. 'Good work, Harry. I see someone else feels the same way,' she said, eyeing the bottle.

'Yes, but this is from Mainwaring. Amazing, isn't it? A short while ago, she wouldn't have pissed on me if I was on fire.'

'People can change their minds about people.'

'I know, but I wonder what gave her such a bad opinion of me in the first place?'

Alex shook her head and took a seat opposite Harry. 'Harry, I'm so sorry I screwed up at the psychiatric facility. I should have seen through Trudy Burnett. If you hadn't arrived when you did, we might still be searching for Mary Peters now.'

'Maybe, maybe not. The fact remains that the pair of them are off the streets. There's no point beating yourself up about it, Alex. It could have happened to anyone. There's no harm done. Forget it and have a drink.' Harry reached for the bottle.

'I won't, thanks, and neither should you – at least not yet. There's a bit of a celebratory drink-up in the War Room this evening – some wine and nibbles laid on by the Führer herself.'

'No longer a Führer, it would seem,' said Harry. 'What's the occasion?'

'What's the occasion?' Alex asked, disbelief across her face. 'You're the occasion!'

When they later entered the War Room, a spontaneous round of applause and a cheer erupted from the assembled officers.

'For goodness' sake,' Harry said, reddening.

'Just enjoy it,' Alex whispered in his ear.

So he did.

Even Mainwaring herself joined in the celebrations. There had been such pressure on the department and the officers to get a result. This was like a collective sigh of relief. The newspapers hadn't helped with their analysis of what the police should and shouldn't do, which had fuelled pressure from the public sector.

However, the news about Amy Peters' involvement in the murders hadn't reached any editor's desk yet. They would make a public statement the following morning. It was known that Mainwaring was already rubbing her hands at the prospect of being able to announce the good news.

A dozen or so bottles of wine later, the War Room had thinned out, leaving just a few members of the team. Mainwaring was one of them. Her face was glowing, and she was swaying slightly.

'How are you, ma'am?' asked Harry.

'Please call me Liz – it's a social event.'

'How are you, Liz?'

'Thank you, I'm fabulous. I feel like an enormous weight has been lifted off.' She leaned forward and planted a kiss on Harry's cheek, then stood back, looking shocked at herself. 'I think I'd better go now,' she said, holding onto the table.

'I'll give you a hand,' said Alex.

They lurched toward Mainwaring's office, holding onto each other, Mainwaring thanking everyone she passed, including a bemused office cleaner.

'I think I'll call it a night,' said Harry, yawning and knocking back the last of his wine. 'I'll hang on for Alex. We can share a taxi.'

'I think I'll make tracks too,' said Sandy. 'Can I ask you something, Harry?'

'Fire away.'

'It's slightly personal.' Sandy hesitated.

'Get on with it, lad, we haven't got all night.'

'Do you fancy Alex? You'd make a lovely couple.'

'For God's sake, don't talk daft,' said Harry gruffly. 'Anyway, even if I did, you lot would be the last to know. Private life should be kept away from work. You should know that, of all people.'

'What do you mean?' Sandy asked.

'You and Dawn – you two are the ones who should be getting together officially. Even the Führer knows about you two.'

'The Führer, guv?'

Harry looked embarrassed, then a smile crept over his face. 'Yes, I meant DI Mainwaring, of course. Touché.'

They looked at each other and laughed.

Harry woke up early the next morning with a start. A burst of clarity had seared through his throbbing head. He went to the bathroom, threw cold water onto his face, and then picked up his phone.

50

The War Room had been converted from a celebration party zone back to its true purpose. Harry surveyed the tired faces of the surrounding people.

'Hope you all enjoyed last night's celebration and thank you for attending this meeting at such short notice. As you know, we have Amy Peters in custody, who has admitted assisting her sister Mary in the murders of Hamilton, Stock, and Greening.'

'What about Baxter?' Dawn asked.

'Now, there's a question. What about Baxter? Amy Peters was quick to admit being involved in the three murders, and also to the murder of Tony Walker, which will allow Ned Chandler out of prison. This made me curious about why she was so insistent that she had nothing to do with Jeremy Baxter's death.'

Harry sipped some water. He was still feeling dehydrated from the previous night's celebrations.

'I believe that this latest killing is absolutely nothing to do with the Circle of Hera.'

A murmur went around the table.

'What are your thoughts, guv?' Sandy asked.

'I think this is a standalone murder that has been committed by someone who wants us to believe that The Circle of Hera is responsible.'

'Is there any evidence to support this, guv?' asked Dawn.

'There is a bit of circumstantial evidence that shows that the rope used to strangle Jeremy Baxter was different to the rope used on all the other victims.'

'They might have just run out of the rope they used before,' observed Carl Copeland, an up-and-coming sergeant.

'That's a possibility,' conceded Harry. 'However, whoever killed Jeremy Baxter wasn't aware of the reasons behind why the Peters sisters killed those men.'

'How can you be so sure?' Carl asked.

'Because the victim of the latest murder was a Mr Jeremy Baxter, and according to his social media account, he was homosexual.'

'Now I understand where you're coming from, guv,' Dawn said

'Perhaps there is a gay version of Circle of Hera,' Sandy said.

'No, that would be the *Ring* of Hera!' Carl Copeland said, laughing at his own wit.

Harry scowled. 'Grow up.'

'Have you got a suspect in mind?' Dawn asked.

She's shrewd, thought Harry.

'Maybe. But before I go full pelt on this, I need to establish a couple of connections. One is the relationship between my suspect and the victim, and the other is to discover the reason the victim, Jeremy Baxter, was murdered. That, my wonderful circle of hungover detectives, is why we are around this table right now. Ideas, anyone? If not, I have the beginnings of a plan.'

'We don't have to dress up as doctors and nurses again, do we?' Carl asked with a smirk.

'You can dress up how you wish. There's a long, blonde wig in the evidence room you can wear,' Harry said, standing up and turning over a page of the flip chart. 'Okay, guys, shall we get to work?'

Jeremy Baxter had lived in a small bedsit in a terraced Victorian house in a leafy part of Harrow. Harry pushed open the curtains of the flat as wide as possible, as if to shine a light on any concealed evidence.

'Search every drawer thoroughly. I'm going to knock on the bedsit next door.'

'Of course,' Dawn said in a patient tone.

They had already found a revealing photo beside Baxter's bed, which Harry had photographed, labelled, and bagged. Rosko and his team had already gone through the premises, so there was no danger of compromising any evidence.

A thin, gaunt man opened the door. He towered over Harry. 'Can I help you?'

'I'm DI Black. I'm investigating the death of Jeremy Baxter.'

The door opened wider to reveal a bedsit almost identical to Baxter's. 'I'm Lennie. Please come in. I am so sorry that Jerry is dead. He was a lovely, decent man.'

'Did you know him well?'

'Did I know him well?' Lennie laughed. 'Let's put it this way, I could almost write his biography. Every time he had a new boyfriend, there were dramas.'

'In what way?' Harry asked. He took the offered chair while Lennie perched on the bed.

'At least twice a week, Jerry would invite me in for tea and tell me everything that was happening in his private life. Some things he told me, you could put into a film. It didn't matter who the boyfriend was, there was always a situation of some sort.'

'Really?' Harry said. 'Tell me more.'

'Gladly,' Lennie said. 'Would you like a cup of tea?'

By the time they left, Harry felt that he had a more complete picture of Jeremy Baxter.

When they got back to Farrow Road, Alex was putting her coat on. 'Fancy a farewell drink, you two?'

'Farewell drink?' Harry asked. 'Are you off somewhere?'

'Yes, you didn't think I'd be here forever, did you?'

Harry hadn't considered the prospect of Alex leaving. The thought took the varnish off recent events.

'When do you go?' he asked, trying to mask his disappointment.

'I'm back to Galashiels in a couple of days, but I thought we could have a farewell drink this evening, and another one tomorrow.'

Harry laughed. 'Sounds like a plan.'

'Not tonight for me, if you don't mind,' Dawn said. 'However, I can make tomorrow's farewell drink. I'll get Sandy along for a couple.'

An hour later, Alex and Harry were jammed in a crowded bar.

'I hate Friday nights,' Harry said. 'The pubs around here are so packed you can't have a decent conversation.' He was, however, enjoying the closeness of Alex and her subtle perfume, which was tickling his senses.

'You're showing your age,' she responded playfully. 'Although we could go somewhere quieter, if you like.'

'Good idea. We'll drink these and move on. What are you going to do about your job when you go back to Scotland?' Harry asked, his mouth closer than necessary to her ear.

'You mean, what am I going to do about working with my ex? I don't know. I'll have to make a decision sooner rather than later. Being down here has helped put things into perspective.'

'You could always get a transfer,' Harry said. 'Don't let all that experience go to waste. You could come down here.'

'I don't know if you can just transfer between the two countries. I think you have to make a cold application.'

'It wouldn't be that cold, I'd put in a good word for you.'

She looked at him coyly. 'And what word might that be?'

'Well, I would...' He stopped to pull out his phone which was vibrating in his pocket. Harry spoke for a minute and then disconnected.

'Who was that?' Alex asked.

'It was the voice of common sense.'

'Pardon?'

Harry grinned. 'That was Mainwaring. We are game on for tomorrow, and we'll need our wits about us. So, I'm afraid it's goodbye to our farewell drink and off for an early night.'

51

Alberto's restaurant was busy – busier than its owner had known it for some time. There was a hen party in, for which the restaurant had allocated an area just off the main part of the restaurant, so the other diners wouldn't be affected. There was a family party going on at the top end, and the rest of the tables were taken up with other bookings.

Alberto left his restaurant and walked up the road, peering in at the windows of the other establishments. None of them was nearly as busy as his. He walked back to his own restaurant, looking very pleased.

'No walk-ins tonight,' he instructed his head waiter. 'Put out the "house full" sign.'

'But we're not quite full up yet.'

'I know, but if we put out the sign, then people will talk about it, and then other people will be even more inclined to want to eat here. Don't you see?'

It didn't matter if the waiter understood, or not. Whatever the boss wanted, the boss got. He collected the sign and carried it through the restaurant, passing the table where the family celebration was taking place. It was a birthday that was being celebrated, judging by the cards and presents that were on the table.

'Excuse me, waiter. When you have a moment, would you mind bringing us another bottle of champagne? In fact, you'd better make it two.'

'Of course, sir. Whose birthday occasion is it?'

'My lovely wife's.'

'Many happy returns, madam.'

'Thank you,' she said warmly, her eyes sparkling with delight. 'All of my family and friends are here to help us celebrate.' She swept her hand in an arc to indicate the other diners at the table who were beaming at him.

He placed the "house full" sign outside and went to collect two bottles of Bollinger from the fridge. As he was leaving the kitchen, a man blocked his way. 'Are you taking that champagne to the birthday party at the back of the restaurant?'

'Yes, why? What's wrong?'

'Nothing for you to worry about,' said the man, showing the waiter his identification. The man looked him up and down. 'Can I borrow your waiter's jacket for a few minutes?'

The restaurant owner was still by the front door, turning people away and proudly pointing to the newly placed "house full" sign. He closed the door.

'That's it,' he said to his head waiter. 'All of our pre-bookings have turned up, there's no more to come.' He turned around to survey his packed restaurant – and frowned. 'Who the bloody hell is that?' he asked the waiter. 'I haven't seen him before, and he's carrying that tray of champagne all wrong.'

'I don't know. He is in Carlo's section, but there's no sign of Carlo.'

The owner swiftly moved towards the table. He could see

a group of smiling faces surrounding a couple. She was middle-aged and had black, curly hair. Next to her was a man with the most beautiful head of silver-grey hair Alberto had ever seen. As he drew closer, he saw the waiter put his hand on the man's shoulder.

'Mr Donald Fox, I am arresting you for the murder of Jeremy Baxter.'

There was a gasp around the table. Two guests tittered, thinking it was a comedic set-up. The restaurant owner stopped in his tracks, his mouth hanging open.

Few people have watched someone else being arrested for murder, and the people who were eating in Alberto's restaurant that night literally dined out on the events they had witnessed. The story grew, of course. Much later on, one of the hen party swore that she had seen the man frogmarched out of the restaurant. Another said that there was a gun involved. But, in actual fact, it was a quiet arrest.

After Harry and his officers had taken Fox away, his family and friends had sat in silent, embarrassed shock before getting their coats and going their separate ways with muttered words of support for Fox's wife.

52

Fox sat in the interview room, his silver-grey hair ruffled. Harry was surprised that he hadn't asked for a mirror.

'What the hell am I doing here? You've embarrassed me in front of my family and friends.'

'You have been arrested for murder, plain and simple. If I thought for a second that you were innocent, you wouldn't be here.'

'So how am I supposed to have committed this murder?' Fox asked.

His solicitor spoke into his ear, and Fox's mouth closed like a Venus flytrap.

'That's excellent advice your solicitor is giving you. Shut up and listen. You can answer the questions as and when they arrive.'

Fox's face was a strange mixture of grey and purple. He looked as if he might implode, but his mouth stayed shut.

Harry looked up from his notes. 'You were having an affair with Jeremy Baxter. It was quite an intense affair, and I would say that he fell in love with you. However, to the outside world, you were straight, married, and had a family, and you didn't want to sacrifice that.'

'This is absolute rubbish! I'm not gay.' Fox's face had turned more grey than purple.

'Your sexuality is not the issue. The fact is you had a relationship with Jeremy Baxter that got out of hand. I believe that he gave you an ultimatum. You had to choose between him and your wife, which put you under pressure. Or perhaps he blackmailed you by suggesting that he would tell your wife about your affair.'

Harry put a picture up on a large, back-lit screen. It showed the framed photo of Jeremy Baxter and Don Fox that he had found at Jeremy Baxter's apartment. Their cheeks were together, and they were smiling directly into the camera.

'That's just a photo. It proves nothing,' Fox's solicitor said.

'True,' Harry said. 'But it proves a connection between Fox and Baxter. If you add to that the repeated visits your client made to Baxter's apartment, and the numerous rows they had, which were overheard by the neighbours, then the jury will get an idea of the state of the relationship, and they will draw their own conclusions.'

Harry paused and looked at the pair facing him across the table. 'There is one neighbour in particular, a friend of Baxter's, who is more than happy to testify that he heard arguments and shouting on the days leading up to Mr Baxter's murder.'

'That doesn't mean I murdered him.'

'But you did,' Harry said. 'In fact, it could only have been you.'

'What do you mean?' Fox asked, looking uncomfortable.

Harry paused. 'This next part may be a bit confusing to you both, but stick with it.'

Fox and his solicitor sat, their faces a study of concentration.

Harry cleared his throat. 'When I visited you at your estate agency, just after you discovered the body of Paul Hamilton, we were all under the impression that the rope that was used to strangle the victims was arranged to form the word Herg. We even talked about what Herg could mean, do you remember?'

'Yes, I remember. The rope around his neck spelt Herg. What of it?' Fox asked, looking confused.

'You were the only person outside of the police who knew about Herg. Later on, we became aware that it was actually Hera, but you weren't to know that. So after you murdered Baxter, you arranged the rope to clearly spell out Herg, not Hera. That, with all the other evidence, puts you squarely in the frame for his murder.'

'But why would I kill him?'

'You tell us... But my guess is that Jeremy Baxter fell in love with you and wanted you for himself. He possibly threatened to make your relationship public, on social media or whatever, to make you leave your wife for him. This probably put so much pressure on you that you decided to kill him, so that your family wouldn't find out about that side of your life.'

Don Fox's face was now just plain grey.

Harry continued. 'Mr Fox, you tried to make the murder of Jeremy Baxter look like the revenge murders, but you didn't do your homework. Apart from the Herg issue, you used the wrong type of rope. The rope used in the revenge murders was jute, but you used a cheaper rope which was identical to rope we found in the garage at your home.'

'This is ridiculous,' Fox exclaimed, looking to the man at his side for assistance. His solicitor seemed to ignore him and was staring down at his paperwork.

'In addition,' Harry went on, 'in the revenge murders, the victim was given a knock-out drug and then executed. You didn't give Baxter a knock-out drug, you actually poisoned him. Toxicology reports show evidence of paraquat in Mr Baxter's system, some of which was also found at your address. You then arranged the rope around his neck to make it look like another revenge murder.'

Fox started to protest, then stopped, his eyes holding a look of defeat.

'Mr Fox, is there anything you'd like to add?'

'He was going to tell my wife about us – on her birthday. I had to stop him. I had no choice.'

53

Mainwaring sat with her elbows on her desk, fingertips together.

'So that's definitely it, then? No more surprises?'

'No more surprises,' answered Harry with a smile. 'Unless there's yet another copy-cat murderer we don't know about.'

'The papers are full of it. They're making more of the Fox murder than the two sisters at the moment.'

'Maybe it's a more dramatic storyline: "Family man murders gay lover."'

Mainwaring laughed. 'Perhaps.'

It was strange but wonderful to see the positive change in Mainwaring, who now seemed so much calmer and more content. When she laughed, her normally serious eyes shone with good humour.

Harry stood up. 'I'm off to the hospital. They're going to see if it's possible to make my scalp look better than it does now.'

'Good luck with that. By the way, Alex is travelling back to Scotland today.'

'I know,' Harry said. 'I'm giving her a lift to the station.'

54

They stood on the platform, Alex looking up at Harry. 'No rain for a change. Christ, it's been worse down here than back home.'

'What will you do now?' Harry asked.

'When I get back, I'll have a good look at my options, but I will probably return to work and make the best of it. One benefit of having helped out down here is that I now understand what it is like to have a busy workload. What are you going to do?'

'Business as usual, I suppose. Plenty to get on with and lots of loose ends to tie up. It's been an eventful time.'

'It certainly has. I won't forget you and the team, Harry.'

Harry nodded distantly. He was going to miss her, but didn't really know what to say.

The train pulled up, and they gave each other a long, meaningful hug.

'You'd better go before you miss it,' Harry said.

'There's just one more thing,' Alex said softly.

She put her hands on either side of Harry's face and put her lips on his. He responded immediately and enthusiastically. The two entwined themselves in a long, passionate embrace, oblivious to the world around them, and the train that was now pulling out the station.

~

HE FLICKED the butt of his cigarette. The red tip arced before landing, sending a fountain of sparks into the air. He watched it die until it was grey ash, and decided that it was the last time he'd smoke.

He straightened up and adjusted his tie again. He never wore a collar, but he knew that he'd have to get used to it. He walked up the steps into the grey building ahead of him, smoothing down his jacket.

He arrived at a desk with a sign that indicated, "New Recruit Police Interviews."

The desk sergeant looked at him expectantly. His face showed experience and warmth. 'What's the name, son?'

'James Grafton,' he said.

~

Harry Black will return in
'Who is the Tigerman.'

NOTE FROM THE AUTHOR

I sincerely hope you enjoyed my first novel.
Authors depend on what people say about their books, so I would be so grateful if you could spare a minute to leave an Amazon review.

Read on for details of the next book
in the Harry Black Thriller series.

WHO IS THE TIGERMAN?

Having suffered a huge personal loss, Harry must quickly put his grief to one side to discover who hired the hitman. His investigation leads him into a quagmire of political intrigue; a party-leader's wife, who has been offering sexual favours to other politicians behind her husband's back, blackmail and corruption at the highest levels. In the meantime, some spice is added to Harry's love life which gives him a dilemma.

The story culminates with a face to face encounter, but with whom? And of course, there are twists in the tale...

Who is The Tigerman? will take you on a breathless journey and keep you gripped until the very end!

Would you like a sneak preview?
Then read on!

55

WHO IS THE TIGERMAN?

The man in the cream suit walked across the lobby of The Grand Hotel, conscious of the interested looks of two women. One was wearing an alluring, black dress; the other had on a smart, beige trouser suit.

He went into the cloakroom to freshen up. The humidity of Kuala Lumpur was at its seasonal worst. When he returned to the lobby, the lady in the black dress had gone. The other was leaning against one of the pillars, examining her nails. She pulled a clip from the back of her head allowing her hair to fall to her shoulders. The movement drew his attention.

Their eyes locked, and she beckoned for him to follow her. He followed her in silence as they walked through the marbled corridors.

She led the way through an exit door. The intensity of the sun was like the hot waft of a baking oven being opened.

Outside was a newly concreted area containing various construction vehicles that were resting for the weekend.

The other woman stood waiting for them, her black dress fluttering in the warm breeze.

He eyed them both with curiosity. 'Can I be of help?' he enquired politely.

He was used to unusual approaches, it went with his line of work.

He was disappointed when the one wearing the trouser suit undid a couple of buttons on her blouse. 'Perhaps you'd like to spend some time with us. One of us or both, you have the choice.'

The man looked around. Everything was Sunday-quiet, and no windows overlooked them from the hotel.

'You don't have to worry,' Black Dress said. 'Just tell us your room number and we'll come and relax you.' She spoke with a soft Spanish accent.

'There's been a mistake,' said the man politely. 'I actually thought you were, well, someone else. I'm sorry for wasting your time.'

As he turned to go, instinct made him glance at Trouser-Suit, and too late, he saw the flash of metal lunge towards him. Feeling the full force of the knife sink into his leg, he grunted with pain as the metal tip hit his thigh bone.

As her hand released the knife he grabbed it and twisted it whilst smashing his elbow into Black Dress's face. She staggered back, clutching her nose, blood spurting. He twisted Trouser-Suit's hand even more. He could feel bones break. Amid her screams, he applied further pressure. 'What do you want with me, who sent you?' he demanded.

Black Dress was fumbling in her handbag. She produced a gun and levelled it at him, her expression one of professional indifference.

He yanked Trouser-Suit in front of him while pulling out the Glock from the shoulder holster under his jacket, and firing. The force of the bullet blasted Black-Dress against the wall of the hotel. She slid down slowly, already dead, the blood from the wound in her forehead merging with that from her nose, making her face look like a grotesque mask.

Trouser-Suit's screams intensified, as she stared with horror at her colleague.

'I'll ask once more, who sent you?'

Minutes later, the man in the cream suit was again crossing the hotel lobby, this time casually holding his jacket by his side, covering the widening patch of blood that was spreading down his leg.

56

WHO IS THE TIGERMAN?

The leader of the opposition was clapped to his feet. Charles Brandon was a formidable character and a popular figure within his own party.

He hooked a thumb into the pocket of his waistcoat and made a theatrical gesture toward the Prime Minister. 'You are a disgrace to your position and are not fit to run your party, let alone the country.'

The Speaker of the House half stood from his throne-like seat: 'I'm sure that the honourable gentleman is aware, but may I remind him he cannot address the Prime Minister directly.'

'I'm sorry, Mr Speaker. I only meant to say that the Prime Minister is a disgrace to his position, and a liability to this country and an embarrassment to his own family.'

From his position on the Tory back benches, Peter Finch, the MP for Middlington, stared at the leader of the opposition with a grin of appreciation, his hand rubbing at a missed piece of unshaved bristle on his chin.

Prime Minister's Questions was a weekly event much looked forward to, by all parties.

A few hours later at the Garrick Club, Covent Garden, Finch lounged in a leather chair regarding the man opposite. 'I have to say that you did an admirable job today. Our leader would certainly have felt those stinging attacks of yours. It's a great pity you're not on our side.'

Charles Brandon took a gulp of brandy and set the crystal glass on the polished table next to him. 'Thank you, Peter, but I sometimes wonder whether I give him too hard a time.'

'Why wouldn't you? It's your job.'

'True, but these days, politically, there is negligible difference between the two parties. The Tories have always favoured the capitalists, but now they also champion the workers and poorly paid, which was always Labour policy. But the voters don't seem to care either way, these days. Politics has become all about populism.'

Finch grinned. 'God, Charles, you're talking like a Tory. If the PM heard you speaking like this, he'd be pulling you over to our side of the commons and offering you a job in the Cabinet.'

'Not a chance. I enjoy the charade too much. Anyway, what about you? Isn't it time that the PM offered you a position, instead of you hiding in safety on the back benches?'

Finch shook his head. 'Not me. I'm just happy to serve my constituency.'

Brandon held up his glass, marvelling at how the crystal caught the light, reflecting tiny blue and white beams. He cleared his throat. 'Peter, I need to say something to you.'

Finch waited, as Charles seemed to ponder on what to say next.

'Despite being on opposite sides of the house, we've been close friends a long time, and what I am about to say to you, must not be repeated.' He looked hard at Finch. 'To anyone. Agreed?'

Finch nodded and sat forward, his expression curious.

Brandon took another gulp of brandy and cleared his throat.

'I'm being blackmailed.'

'You're what!'

'You heard.'

'Do you mean metaphorically, as in the political sense?'

'No. Someone is actually trying to blackmail me, and I'm not sure what to do next.'

Finch looked searchingly at Brandon's face. 'You're actually being serious. So what is it they've got on you, have you been a naughty boy? Have you been watching porn, cheating on your wife, fiddling your expenses... what?'

'I'm probably guilty of at least one of those things, Peter, but it's not me that has strayed from the straight and narrow. It's my wife.'

'Petra? What's she been up to?'

'She has been having an affair,' Brandon said. 'Or to be more precise, affairs.'

'Are you certain about that?'

'Look Peter, I'm sixty-four. Petra is still in her forties. When we married, I was so proud of the fact I had such a young, attractive wife and...'

'She's still attractive,' Finch said.

'Exactly. The problem is... well...' he paused and fiddled with his watch. 'The problem is that I can't keep her happy in every sense, if you see what I mean.'

Finch nodded. 'I understand, but that's no reason for her to be cheating on you.'

'Peter, I really don't care. When we're together, she makes me laugh, and she's great to look at. I see other men tripping over themselves to ingratiate themselves to her. When we go out to dinner or parties, she turns heads. If that makes her happy, then I'm happy.'

'So how does this blackmail situation involve her?'

'I'm about to come to that. Before we met, Petra worked as an escort girl.'

'What, like a prostitute?'

'No, no... I mean, she was a proper escort. Men would book her through an agency, and then take her to dinner, functions, that sort of thing.'

'And then sleep with her?'

'Well, I suppose...'

Finch looked amazed. He leaned forward, 'So tell me exactly how you are being blackmailed.'

Charles Brandon pulled out and envelope from his inside pocket and passed it across.

Finch turned it over. 'It's House of Commons stationery, how did you receive it?'

'It was in my post-tray. To be honest, anyone could have put it there.'

Finch took the letter from the envelope and paused. The potential enormity of the situation seemed to hit him. 'Charles, shouldn't you be going to the police with this?'

'I can't, and I won't, there's too much at stake. Read it.'

Finch pulled out the letter and unfolded it. At the top of the letter was the House of Commons crowned portcullis, above which was printed 'Charles Brandon.'

'They've used your own letterhead.'

'Yes, I know. Cheeky bastards.'

The printed message read:

'FAO Charles Brandon. You are to step down as Leader of the Labour Party, otherwise the world will discover that your wife hasn't always been the perfect lady.'

Finch handed the sheet back and put his fingertips together. He looked at Brandon. 'This could be a shit storm. Who would do this to you?'

Brandon shrugged. 'I don't know. I haven't any enemies apart from most of the Tory party.' He smiled humourlessly.

'This person obviously knows your wife was an escort, or maybe was an ex-lover. What are you going to do?'

'I'm afraid I'm going to have to think about stepping down. don't see that I have much choice. I don't want our children to know about their mother's past, and I certainly don't want it all over the front pages of our beloved national press.'

'And you definitely don't want the police involved?'

'Absolutely not. Apart from anything else, the Home Secretary would inevitably find out, and that would defeat the object. I don't see that I have any alternative other than to resign my position.'

'It seems a shame,' Finch said, signalling to a passing waiter for a refill. 'This could just be someone chancing their arm, with no proof, hoping that you'll be stupid enough to believe their threat.'

'No such luck,' Charles said, slipping a hand into his other inside pocket. He pulled out a small bundle of photographs. 'These were in the same envelope.'

He placed them on the coffee table between them and pointed to the one on the top. It was an older photo of Petra, half naked on top of a man, facing back towards the camera, smiling.

'Oh my God, Charles, this must be awful for you.'

Charles gave a thin smile. 'It gets worse, carry on.'

Peter put the photo face down next to the pile and picked up the next, which looked as though someone had cut it from a magazine and was of Petra posing with another man. She was wearing a maid's outfit and had a stockinged leg outstretched across his lap.

Finch picked up the next. Petra was wearing a short black dress and was with a fellow MP, Gavin Smart. The photo showed them leaving a hotel in Knightsbridge hand in hand clearly enjoying each other's company, and oblivious to the photographer.

'These are just photos of your wife from years ago. They could have been snapped at a fancy-dress party or even a themed charity event. The one with Gavin Smart might raise a few eyebrows, but it's no big deal to hold someone's hand.'

'Look at the next one,' Brandon said.

The next photo was far more explicit. Someone had clearly pushed the lens of the camera through curtains to get a picture of Petra naked on her knees, getting rear attention from another of Peter's colleagues, Nigel Kendall.

'Good grief, I thought he was gay,' remarked Finch.

Brandon smiled, 'It just shows you can't judge anyone.'

The server appeared, and Finch quickly concealed the photos as the drinks were placed on the table.

'You'll find the final picture interesting,' Brandon said as the server left.

As Finch turned it over, his stomach did a somersault and his face whitened. 'Oh God Charles, I am so sorry, I...'

Charles sat back in his chair.

'There's not a great deal that you can say, is there, Peter? That is you with my wife, isn't it?'

57

WHO IS THE TIGERMAN?

Resting the rifle against the scaffolding, he waited. He was unconcerned about being observed by any of the tourists or locals, as far as they were concerned, he was just another construction worker doing his job. Besides, he was far too high up, for them to notice him.

Thick plastic weather drapes protected the construction site, through which protruded the ends of the scaffolding. *One more metal tube poking out was unlikely to be spotted*, he thought.

Putting the scope to his eye, he squinted through the lens, adjusting to the sudden vividness of the imagery, and moved the device slowly along Garrick Street until he could see the entrance to the club.

He had it on good authority that his target would leave shortly after eight. He glanced at his watch. *Five minutes to go.*

He put the scope down and took another careful look around the construction site, listening intently for anything untoward.

Although the workers had long gone for the day, he felt a

sense of unease. He'd been experiencing this feeling since the attack by the two women in Kuala Lumpur a few days ago.

He involuntarily put his hand down to the side of his leg and winced. He still felt the pain where the blade had hit bone.

The attack made him wonder who would want him dead, and how they'd traced him. Very few knew his true identity, let alone his movements, and yet the two women at the hotel had known he was going to be there.

He breathed in slowly and deeply, and then focussed his whole attention on the entrance of the Garrick club.

Who Is The Tigerman will be available in September 2021
Further details at gordonwarden.com

Printed in Great Britain
by Amazon

72841949R00180